Grandmothers

SALLEY VICKERS

PENGUIN BOOKS

PENGUIN BOOKS

UK | USA | Canada | Ireland | Australia
India | New Zealand | South Africa

Penguin Books is part of the Penguin Random House group of companies
whose addresses can be found at global.penguinrandomhouse.com.

First published by Viking 2019
Published in Penguin Books 2020
001

Copyright © Salley Vickers, 2019

The moral right of the author has been asserted

Typeset by Jouve (UK), Milton Keynes
Printed and bound in Great Britain by Clays Ltd, Elcograf S.p.A.

A CIP catalogue record for this book is available from the British Library

ISBN: 978-0-241-37143-5

www.greenpenguin.co.uk

In memory of my much-loved grandmothers,
who gave me their time.

And for Rowan, Sam and Martha,
who shall have as much of mine as they want.

Nan Appleby, waiting for the kettle to boil in the kitchen of her fifth-floor flat, observed the signs of weather. The sky was a Turner palette of brooding colour. A storm looked to be brewing. Nan liked storms. She liked it that so far – but who could say for how long? – the weather still eluded the creeping control of humankind. Outside, the tops of the trees, which were at a level with her window, lifted and fell and then lifted again, heralding the storm. In the oiled-wool fisherman's socks she wore for slippers Nan carried her mug of tea back to bed and opened her laptop.

Peace of Mind Funeral Planning, she read with a sense of pleasant expectation. *Act Now to Spare Your Loved Ones the Anguish of Rising Funeral Costs.*

Nan was engaged in her favourite occupation: research-ing her own funeral. Only the other day she had come across a tempting possibility, a firm offering a cut-price casket of Norfolk reed – a material that usually commanded a price that was high even in the exorbitant market of funeral services – and she was about to scroll through her search history to recover the details.

On that same morning at a later hour Blanche Carrington woke in her comfortable mansion flat to an unlocatable sense of despair. The day, she divined, without bothering to go to the window, was an accomplice to this mood. The bedroom felt chilly – the boiler had given out and the man had not called to see to it as he had promised. Behind the heavy curtains she heard the thin wail of a wind get up and – memory broke rudely in – all this only went to emphasise the misery induced by the dreadful row she had had with her son. Her only son, Dominic, the light of her life, as she had once held him.

The faint whining sound outside seemed to bind her to these dark thoughts. Unwilling to leave the insulation of the down-filled duvet, Blanche turned on the bedside radio.

Storm Christina, she heard, was moving south and motorists were recommended not to undertake needless journeys. Well, she wasn't going to make any journey if she could help it. She would quite happily stay where she was in bed for the rest of the year, for the rest of her life if it came to that.

Minna Dyer woke to the sound of rain making a rousing kettledrum of the roof of the shepherd's hut that stood in Frank Fairbody's smallholding and sighed contentedly. She especially liked it when it rained. The hut was cosy with her newly installed stove and she had banked up the coals so they would smoulder overnight. The wilder the weather outside, the more she enjoyed her snug cocoon. She leant down from her bunk bed to fish up the book she had set aside the night before. A long read but, she had been assured by the nice volunteer at her local library, a worthwhile one. She would finish the chapter she had started last night and then get cracking on the doll's dress.

Summer Term

I

It was Nan's day for collecting her grandson, Billy, from school. The storm had swept in splendidly while she was checking out the details of a willow coffin advertised as fashioned to fit around the living form.

Many of our satisfied clients the blurb ran *take home our lovely caskets and decorate them in their own unique and personal style so family and friends can become acquainted with their loved one's chosen end-of-life journey.*

There were photos of caskets stuffed with flowers – artificial ones, Nan judged: detergent-white lilies, electric-blue delphiniums and egg-yolk daffodils all mixed together without regard to season in shades that cheated nature's own. One of the featured pictures had a casket's intended content lying in an imitation of repose with a smug would-be-seraphic smile.

Now in raincoat and wellingtons, Nan waited with the assorted mothers, fathers, grandparents, the odd nanny, for the children of St Monica's Primary to come out.

They were let loose according to a system intended to allow one lot of chattering children to disperse before the onset of another wave. Billy didn't appear with the rest of Year 5, who straggled out swapping sweets and jokes or cheerfully shoving each other, apparently oblivious to the rain.

Nan enquired of a boy with a plump rosy face, 'Laurence, have you seen Billy?'

'He's been kept in.'

'What for?'

'For swearing at Josie Smith.'

Oh Lord, Nan thought. 'What did he say, do you know, Laurence?'

The boy looked at her, sizing up her resilience. 'He called her an effing little shit – only,' he added tactfully, 'it wasn't "effing" he said.'

'Oh Lord,' Nan said, aloud this time. 'I suppose I'd best go and brave Miss Green.'

Laurence looked sympathetic. 'She's in a cross mood.'

'Who can blame her? Thank you, Laurence, wish me luck.'

Nan met Miss Green with Billy in the corridor.

'Mrs Appleby, I'm afraid I am having to take Billy to Miss Rainwright's office again.'

'I'm so sorry, Miss Green. What is it this time?' Nan shot a glance at her grandson, who, mulish, was examining the floor.

Miss Green frowned. Her healthy young face was creased with fatigue. It must be hell, Nan thought, coping with a class of nine- to ten-year-olds with all the cuts to the budget and no assistant. 'I'm afraid Billy used language.'

Billy's mule expression turned to blaze. 'Josie Smith said I was on the spectrum.'

Nan looked enquiringly at Miss Green, who looked embarrassed and said, 'Josie has also been reprimanded. And I've asked to speak to her parents.'

'Well, now' – Nan sensed that the teacher was keen to be

free of this nuisance – 'Billy shouldn't swear of course but perhaps with the provocation . . .? I'll give him a telling-off worse than Miss Rainwright's, I can promise you that.'

Miss Green had a hair appointment and was anxious to be off. 'Billy, if it happens again then you will not be coming on the field trip. Is that quite clear?'

Billy examined his shoes. 'Yes, Miss Green.'

'Well, run along with your nan.'

'She's not my nan,' Billy said. 'She's just "Nan",' but his teacher, relieved of the burden of imposing discipline, had already hurried out of earshot.

Nan looked at her grandson, who said, 'Anyway, I don't want to go on a stupid field trip.'

'That's as may be but right now you can have a quick slap and then come back to mine and no more said or we can go back to yours and you can write a letter of apology to that girl.'

'Smacking's illegal,' Billy said. 'You could go to prison.'

'Ah, but who's to tell?' Nan asked. It was not that she was in favour of corporal punishment but she heartily disliked the modern habit of subjecting children to prolonged reproach or dismal lectures. 'It'd be your word against mine.'

This was a well-rehearsed dispute and both were familiar with the terms.

Billy considered. 'Is there cake at yours?'

'Mr Kipling and some Battenberg.'

'I don't like Battenberg.'

'Suit yourself,' Nan said. 'Back at yours it'll be oatcakes and almond butter. What's that little girl's name again?'

Billy settled for a token slap on the back of his calves.

They walked briskly back to Nan's flat, past 'Geraldine's' the corner shop, still valiantly holding its own against the vastly superior, in terms of stock, supermarkets. Although she generally shopped from the market in the Portobello, Nan made a point of buying the odd thing she needed from the struggling local shops. Now she bought a loaf of sliced white and a tin of baked beans and agreed with Geraldine that outside it was perishing. One of her reasons for patronising the local shops was that there, as with the market-stall holders, one could hold a genuine conversation.

After chatting with Geraldine Nan offered to buy Billy a traffic-light lolly. 'That's a reward for making up your own mind, not for the slap,' she explained. 'All ways of life have a cost,' she added. She was aware that for the present this wisdom would mean little but she hoped it might lie dormant in her grandson's mind. It was a useful observation. One she had learned from her own grandmother.

Back at Nan's flat Billy inspected the weather house which hung in Nan's hall. For as long as he could remember the inhabitants had been out of sync with the weather. True to form, the lady with her red sunhat was out, which by rights should indicate sunny weather. Outside, rain like a hail of knives had joined forces with the wind howling round the flats. 'Your weather house still isn't working,' he called to Nan, who was opening the tin of beans in the kitchen.

'Don't go fiddling with it, you'll upset their balance – you know they're used to it that way.'

Billy went to the bedroom and opened his grandmother's laptop. He took an interest in her search for the perfect send-off and was keen to discover the latest candidates for her funeral. He had once mentioned his grandmother's preoccupation to his mother but she had warned him off the subject, saying that it was 'morbid' and that he must not think about his grandmother's death, which would be a long time off. This was in spite of an awareness of her son's unusual interest in naked truths. His mother, terrorised by any threat to her vision of life, attempted to curtail this trait much as she attempted to discourage his taste for unwholesome foods.

Nan came through to the bedroom and found Billy absorbed in the details of the 'take-home, tailored-to-fit all-natural willow casket'.

'This one's cool,' he decided.

'I was thinking of going to take a look next Saturday. Your beans are ready. Milk or tea? I've just brewed a pot.'

Billy said he'd have tea and could he go with her to view the casket.

'If your mother says you can. I'd be glad of your opinion.'

They ate beans on toast at the gate-leg mahogany table in Nan's snug sitting room. Billy ladled three spoons of sugar into his tea.

'Are you doing that to spite your mother or because you really like it?'

Billy considered. 'Don't know.'

'You should think about it. If you like it, all well and good. If it's to get at your mum, you're doing yourself more harm than you're doing her. There's rebelling and there's revolting.'

'Revolting? Like fish pie?'

9

'Different meaning, or it's come to have. You can turn against things for the sake of it, that's rebellion, or because you see them as wrong, that's revolt.' *The two conditions look alike*, she reminded herself but said, 'It looks the same but it's all the difference in the world.'

'How?' he asked, truly interested and sure of a real reply, for his grandmother understood his urgent need to get to the bottom of things.

Nan thought, then said, 'One's reaction, the other's action. You taking all that sugar because your mother doesn't like you to is reaction; it takes no account of what you like or don't like yourself.'

Billy sipped his tea. 'Would I like it without sugar?' he enquired.

His small white triangular face with the peat-dark eyes looked so ardent, so utterly honest and trusting, that she leant across and kissed his forehead. 'You won't know till you've tried, pet.'

Her heart ablaze with love for him, she watched as he went to the kitchen and fetched a mug and poured himself fresh tea. Adding only milk, he sipped it cautiously. 'I think I do prefer it with sugar.' But he put in a single spoonful, stirring it extra to extract all the sweetness. 'Can we look through the funerals?' he asked when he had eaten his beans.

'No Mr Kipling?'

He looked a mite anxious and she said, 'Listen, I'm not saying liking sweet things is wrong. Just be sure why you are choosing them.'

'Then I'll have one.'

She got up to fetch the tin from the kitchen. 'A little of

what you fancy does you good. Now once you've eaten that and helped with the dishes we can check out the coffins. There's another's caught my eye that comes in parts they say'll double up to use as a bookcase beforehand, which could come in handy.'

2

Blanche was summoned from the padded security of her bed by the persistent ringing of her landline. She stumbled to it, praying that it was her son calling to apologise. No such luck. Only her cleaner, Marissa, ringing to say she was not able to come tomorrow as she was 'bleeding'.

'Oh dear. What sort of "bleeding", Marissa?'

'I think maybe a miscarriage. My boyfriend will take me to the hospital.'

'I'm so sorry, Marissa. I didn't realise you were pregnant.'

'I did not realise either. But it happens.'

Although Blanche did not especially like her cleaner this felt like a further dereliction. Not only would there be no company tomorrow but the solicitous boyfriend – and the pregnancy, miscarried or otherwise – emphasised her own isolation. Her closest friend, Maggie, was away on one of her singles cruises, hunting, as Blanche put it, more or less humorously, for a man.

'Not any man!' Maggie had objected, but Blanche's guess was that for Maggie any man was better than none. She herself, she liked to think, had better taste. Or was more fearful, as Maggie had hinted. Certainly, since the death of Dominic's father she had been out only once on what might be described as a date.

The date had been with a former colleague of her dead

husband's – a seemingly decent man who had also recently lost his spouse. She had dressed carefully, with some excitement, for the dinner he had proposed at a well-reviewed Italian restaurant. The dinner had seemed to pass off well – he had been courteous and amiable and had asked just enough questions to register a lively interest in her and not too many to seem to presume. Neither of them had drunk more than a couple of glasses of wine. What then, had prompted him to make that sudden and crude pass as he dropped her in his car outside her flat? A quite disgusting pass which involved grabbing her hand and laying it – no, clamping it, rather – on his bulging flies.

She had not liked to tell even Maggie about it. Maggie would laugh or suggest that she should have hit the bastard hard where it hurt. She had been too appalled at the time to do more than disentangle her hand and flee from the car with all speed. He had sent her a nasty text too, implying she had led him on. The experience had so disturbed her that she was loath to risk any further assignations and had determined henceforth to settle all her love and devotion on Kitty and Harry, her grandchildren. Especially on Kitty, her most beloved.

At the thought of the children her eyes filled again with tears.

'You shan't be seeing them again,' Dominic had said, his voice colder than an Arctic floe. Terrible words. Terrible Dominic. Terrible *terrible* Tina, for surely it was Tina, her daughter-in-law, who was behind all this.

Still trembling with rage and misery, Blanche began to dress. She dressed with none of her usual care, pulling out drawers savagely, throwing on the first dress to hand from the wardrobe, and without any chosen purpose decided to go out. There were things she needed, in so far as she needed anything other than the recovered certainty of seeing her grandchildren. But she could at least stock up on alcohol. Wine and possibly gin or brandy or both. Whisky, even. She disliked whisky but believed it might be palatable with ginger. If her son was going to accuse her of being a drunk, well then, she would become a drunk. The idea was a boost to her spirits, if a temporary one. That was it – she would become a drunk. Then they would see what bad behaviour was really like.

In the High Street, almost bowled over by the onslaught of a viciously rain-charged wind, she passed Boots and thought to buy paracetamol. If she was going to get drunk she would need it.

The entrance to Boots in Kensington High Street is given over to the various cosmetic houses and their latest eye-catching products. As Blanche wandered through the store her eye was caught by a colourful display of lipsticks. She stopped to examine these, pulling out some testers to try out on her wrist. Without premeditation, she found that rather than returning them to their places in the stand she had slipped them into her pocket. She looked round furtively. No assistant was in sight. A selection of eye shadows in the same range was also displayed. Artfully, she pocketed a couple, moving seamlessly on towards the pharmacy at the back of the store.

Heart pounding, for never in her life before had she stolen more than a hotel pencil, she bought paracetamol and made to hurry out of the shop. But even as she sped she passed the stand of another cosmetic house, attended by no assistant, where expensive-looking gold-capped tubes of cream were displayed. Before she had consciously registered what she was doing two tubes had slid into her other pocket and she was outside on the pavement breathing hard.

She patted her pockets. The coat was long and the pockets capacious. There appeared to be no betraying signs. Nevertheless, she took herself off to the Ladies' in nearby Marks and Spencer to examine the spoils: two lipstick testers, Geranium and Black Hibiscus; two eye shadows, Lichen and Birch Bark; and two tubes of a night cream costing – here she felt a little dizzy – £75 apiece. She could feel sweat began to drip down her back as she deposited the eye shadows and the night creams in her handbag, wrapped the lipstick testers in a paper towel and thrust them deep in the waste bin.

Downstairs in the M&S food hall she collected in her trolley two bottles of red wine, two of white, a large bottle of gin and one of White Horse whisky. To this she added a pack of tonics, some dry ginger and two giant bags of popcorn. Passing the shelves of nuts, she slid a packet of smoked almonds and another of salted pistachios into her pocket. More aware this time of the risk she was taking, she still felt powerless to stop. The coat pockets seemed to have taken on an imperative all their own.

Blanche hurried home sweating badly despite the freezing wind, her hands cut by the plastic bags bearing the weight of her supplies. Back in her flat she didn't wait to take off her coat before opening the gin and pouring a hefty slug into a glass. As she attempted to open the tonic tin the pull came away in her hand. Swearing loudly, she dashed the unopened tin to the floor and knocked back the neat gin. With that down her she poured herself another slug, hacked a hole with a knife in the stubborn tonic tin, walked back to the bedroom, shaking off her shoes and dropping her coat on the floor, then stripping off her tights and dress, retreated back to bed with her drink, the popcorn and her laptop.

She opened the laptop to find an email from some health guru. *Right now, your body is like an apple, sliced open and sitting in the open air about to deteriorate.*

'Oh great!' Blanche said aloud. 'Bloody bloody great!' Violently, she shoved the laptop aside, wriggled down and pulled the duvet tight around her.

3

Before rising that morning Minna Dyer had read the opening pages of *Swann's Way*. She had just embarked on a course of reading French literature. For the last three and a half years she had been doing the Russians: Tolstoy, Dostoyevsky, Pushkin, Pasternak, Turgenev and Chekhov. She was no judge, but Tolstoy she reckoned could do with some editing. Dostoyevsky struck her as gloomy and she preferred the film of *Dr Zhivago* to Pasternak's rather heavy-handed story. Turgenev was the one she liked best. Chekhov too. She was captivated by his stories.

But Proust – there was a challenge. Even longer than *War and Peace*, which with all the battles and the Russian names she had found tough enough going. So far Proust had kept her attention with the scenes of his childhood. It reminded her of her own childhood and how she had waited, forcing herself to stay awake, for her mother, with her scent of sweet violets and softly powdered face, to steal in and kiss her goodnight. Her trusting mother had supposed her fast asleep on these occasions. She wasn't a deceitful child, quite the reverse, but she had been good at acting sleep.

Minna climbed out of her bunk and pulled on tracksuit trousers under her long shirt, which doubled as a day shirt. Over this she pulled a seaman's jersey and knotted round her neck, for a bit of colour, a red scarf. She made tea and boiled herself a duck egg, gift of Frank, in whose grounds her shepherd's hut stood free of rent. She and Frank went way back. They traded assets: she cleaned for him and he helped with any maintenance job and gave her eggs if his ducks or hens were laying. Above all they gave each other mutual support.

Over breakfast Minna did the previous day's *Guardian* crossword. She got the crossword online at the library, where she also printed it out. There was one clue that escaped her: something to do with a French winter. Maybe Proust would help.

Her breakfast finished and the crossword still incomplete, Minna set it aside and reached for the little frock she was sewing for Patsy Doll, cut from the material of an outgrown school uniform. Minna planned to give the doll a smart blue blazer too so she would be a miniature version of a schoolgirl. Minna put on her glasses, threaded the needle, turned on the radio and began to sew.

She had finished the frock, taken her daily walk and her mind was on the tip of solving the elusive crossword clue when there was a faint rap at the hut door and a girl with her hair in plaits and a freckled face came in.

'Rosie darling – squash or milk?'

'Milk, please. Is Patsy's dress ready?'

'All done and dusted. Look.' Minna presented the doll for inspection.

Rose examined her. 'She hasn't got pants.'

'I'll see to those. No one but you'll know.'

'She'll know.'

'True enough, but we shan't take her out till she's modest.'

'I'll make her some for now. Can I use your scissors, please, Minna?'

Once Patsy had been made modest Rose drank her milk and ate a Rich Tea biscuit while Minna completed the crossword.

'It's "hierarchy". Of course. Silly me.'

'What's "*hier*thingy"?'

'Like at school where Year 5 is higher than Year 4, and Year 4 is higher than Year 3.'

Rose nodded, not really understanding. She knew Minna's crossword mattered to her and had asked out of a sense of good manners. 'Can we play Gin Rummy?'

'Of course. I'll get the cards.'

Gin Rummy was a game that the more sophisticated toys joined them in. Some of them cheated. The small pink unicorn was especially bad that way.

'Rainbow's cheating,' one of the elderly rabbits complained.

'Rainbow! I'll put you in the drawer if you cheat,' Rose reproved.

Several of the toys were accomplished card players and indeed altogether they were a skilled and lively crew. They put on plays, sang, danced and went in for various sports and hobbies. When Minna and Rose had been first told about the film *Toy Story* they had been surprised that the idea of toys with an inner life was considered original and amusing.

'My toys are always like that, only they're like it when I'm there,' Rose had explained to a kindly relative.

'She's fanciful,' her mother had said. 'Always had a fertile imagination, haven't you, Rosie?'

Over the years, Rose had gradually transported the most cherished of her toys to Minna's hut. This was to deal with the clearings. Her mother sporadically instituted a clearing out of what she considered an overpopulation of toys and these raids sometimes took place behind Rose's back.

Minna was not Rose's grandmother. She was in fact no relation to her at all. Minna had no children of her own but got on with children more easily than those who, through having them, might have been expected to understand them better. It sometimes seemed to Minna that the act of conceiving and bearing children in some mysterious way lobotomised the recollection of the state of being a child and implanted instead a whole new set of behaviours. Over the years Minna had acquired the trust and friendship of many children. But no attachment went as deep as hers to Rose.

It was not that she had not known other loves. She had loved her gentle, talcum-powder-smelling mother with a depth of feeling that she recognised in Marcel Proust. She had loved her brother, Miles, who had died before he reached his teens. And she had loved, loved still, and with a whole heart, John Carpenter. Without question she loved Rose. But it was not the love that made her feeling for Rose unique; it was the simple certainty without effort or strain or any need to think of knowing and being known. She *knew* Rose: without being told, she felt how Rose was feeling, what she did or did not mind, how her mind and her heart worked, were working.

Rose and Minna met when Minna was a teaching assistant at Rose's school. Before Minna retired she had started an after-school book club and it was through this that she had really got to know Rose. The book club had dwindled finally to the two of them, when Minna chose *The Princess and the Goblin* as the next story to read. All in the club but Rose had voted with their feet but Rose had wonderfully, in just the way Minna had, grasped the story's beauty – although 'grasped' was perhaps not what you did with a story which revealed with such quiet tact the deep and mysterious other world which lies for those with eyes to see within our own. It seemed to Minna a story as fine and supple and strong as the spider's web the grand-mother with the silver hair spins for the princess to keep by her in order to find her way through the dark terrors of the goblin terrain. And she was overjoyed to find in Rose someone who shared her vision.

It was after this that Rose had got in the way of visiting Minna, whose shepherd's hut, on Frank Fairbody's small-holding, stood across the field by her house.

As a child, Minna had not been especially interested in reading. She wasn't what was then bluntly referred to as 'backward'. She could grasp the meaning of words and follow a storyline. The verdict on her reading had been 'average' and 'average' was the general assessment of her throughout her school years. It was not an era in which many children went on to university and it would never have occurred to Minna that she might.

She left school at sixteen and having grown up loving her mother's sweet-scented aura took a job serving at a local chemist's. Thereafter she took a number of jobs, all fairly dull but none so dull that she was tempted to pass any free time in reading. And that was the straightforward unre-markable progress of her life until she met John Carpenter.

It was not that John was any great reader either. He had read more than Minna but such books as he read tended to be political and non-fiction. So it wasn't John's influence on her tastes that brought about this seismic shift in her life. Rather it was the fact of his removal.

For after having made the monumental effort of leaving his wife to set out on a brave new life with Minna, John had resiled. And after some desperate shilly-shallying he had returned to his wife's triumphant embrace and swiftly fathered two children so there could be no backsliding.

The effect on Minna was as if she had been in a near-fatal accident. Not only her heart – which as everyone knows is liable to a physical pain in sympathy with the emotional kind – but her head, back, limbs, fingers, toes all screamed in agony for her loss.

She had not been bitter. It had cut too deep for that. She had not at first even been suicidal (that would come later). She was what people, ignorant of the real implications of the word, will lightly claim to be – shattered. Her heart, her mind, her very soul seemed to have been smashed into tiny, irreparable fragments.

It took years for her to recover. (It is possible that she never did quite.) And it was not for trying remedies: alcohol, drugs, magic charms, sex, diets, meditation and in a last-ditch effort even Anglicanism. Nothing worked. She was like a woman gone overboard in a wide and dangerous sea, who, finally hopeless of rescue and fatally resigning herself to unconsciousness, awakes to find she has been washed ashore on a richly fertile island, undiscovered and full of new promise.

Because in the nick of time Minna found reading.

4

Nan called round to her daughter-in-law's to collect Billy to take him with her to inspect the latest candidate for her coffin. She had advised him not to tell his mother the purpose of the trip.

Nan was on a mission to teach Billy how to lie. 'It's not that I want you to deceive,' she had explained. 'It's for self-protection. Sometimes you have to say or do things to look after yourself. And remember, you are the only person truly entrusted to care for yourself. Others will tell you otherwise but in the end it's all down to you.'

Billy had listened without comment to this and to connected advice: 'The important thing, Bill, is to know you're doing it. Most people lie to themselves more than anything. That's the royal road to ruin' and 'If you're going to lie the first rule is don't be found out.'

The young Nan had early recognised that much of what passes for human relationship is really a form of blackmail. Her Scottish grandmother, who had never lapsed into the frailty of old age, had been an example to her. All but bald, certainly toothless but with her marbles almost shockingly intact, she had commanded her life right up to the point of leaving it, which she had done with exemplary timing on the cusp of a new year, in the middle of 'Auld Lang Syne'. Her grandmother had brought up her three children single-handed after her young husband was drowned while helping to save a craft in trouble off the coast near St Abbs. Resisting all offers of help in her widowhood, she had relied on her own shrewd cunning, an invincible charm – even in great old age – the stark realism of the Scottish border ballads and the certitude of the sterner Old Testament prophets, whose moral terms she interpreted liberally.

Nan had inherited her grandmother's strength of character, her capacity for endurance and keen ear for cant. But her grandmother's most practical legacy had been this pearl: 'Muddle them, Annie. Muddle them is what I do.'

For much of her adult life Nan had followed this sage advice. She had divined that to be free from human interference some form of disguise is necessary. In her view, her grandson was one of those born with a skin too few and this, along with his intractable honesty, meant that he was badly in need of camouflage.

'Lovely morning, Ginnie,' she greeted her daughter-in-law with maddening chirpiness. 'How are you?'

'I've a splitting headache,' Virginia said. She did indeed look peaky, though in Nan's view this was more likely the result of her daughter-in-law's health-food diet.

'You need iron, dear. A nice spot of pig's liver.' She was perfectly aware from Billy that her daughter-in-law was contemplating going vegan.

Virginia ignored this and asked if her mother-in-law would like tea.

'Only if it's builder's, please. D'you need a codeine? I keep one in my purse.'

Virginia grimaced and said, 'You know I try not to take drugs.'

'Quite right,' Nan said, suddenly changing tack. 'My grandmother swore by Spike Lavender.'

Virginia, who was rightly suspicious of claims made by her mother-in-law's dead relative, called up the stairs, 'Billy, love, your grandmother's here.'

'I thought I'd take him into Richmond,' Nan said. Richmond was where the weaver of bespoke coffins worked. 'With the weather like this we can walk in the park.'

'What about lunch?' Billy's mother asked, sounding nervous. She and her mother-in-law waged a silent war over food. 'I can pack some sandwiches.'

'That would be very nice, dear. Don't bother about anything for me, though.' Nan and Billy usually disposed of these lunches to obliging waterfowl.

The sandwiches, composed of a rough indigestible bread and a pallid salt-free nut butter, were now in Nan's bag. An overripe blackening banana had already been disposed of. Billy and Nan had taken the tube to Hammersmith, where they changed on to the District line for Richmond. Now they were walking to Richmond Green, where the willow weaver lived, apparently in some style.

'They cost a fortune, those houses,' Nan said. 'There must be good money in death.'

The weaver turned out to be the daughter of the owner of one of the houses. She introduced herself as Charmian. She was of the build, Nan noted, commonly termed 'willowy'. Perhaps it was this that had put the idea of the willow coffins into her head in the first place.

Charmian took them through to her studio in the garden, where bundles of willow lay strewn about.

'What took you into this line of work?' Nan asked.

Charmian explained she had recently completed a degree in Art History, her dissertation had been on folk craft and she was 'fascinated' by rituals to do with death.

'Why?' Billy asked.

Charmian, who had so far ignored him, turned her eyes, the dangerous baby-blue that incomprehensibly entraps the male sex, on her questioner.

'Are you interested in rituals?'

'I'm interested in death.'

Charmian giggled. 'How sweet.'

'We're here to look at your coffins,' Nan said sternly.

'Surely not for you, Mrs Appleby?'

'Well, we've not come for Billy here.' She hoped the girl was not going to be skittish.

Charmian tittered again and indicated a pale oatmeal sofa covered in Indian shawls where they could sit.

'Can I get you tea or, Billy, what would you like?'

'Is it PG Tips?' Billy asked – on her behalf, Nan guessed, and was touched.

Charmian looked puzzled. 'It's Twining's.'

'Twining's is fine,' Nan said. 'And we both take milk and sugar.'

Charmian went behind a screen to put on a kettle. She re-emerged with a tray on which were three unmatching bone-china teacups, clearly antique, a blue enamel teapot of the kind taken on camping trips and milk in a Pyrex measuring jug. Very contrived, Nan thought.

'So' – Charmian raised her voice to a sales-talk pitch – 'my caskets.'

'We've read the puff about the coffins online,' Nan said, 'so there's no need to go into that again. What we're here for is for you to measure me and give us an idea of cost. I don't want anything too bulky.'

Under the skittishness Charmian had a hard head. She promptly got out a tape measure, measured Nan's body, went over to her laptop and came back with it. 'This is how it would look – there's some variation in the colours of the willow but this gives you an idea.'

Nan and Billy examined the image on the screen of a plain willow basket, human size. No flowers.

'It's not too bulky, as you see, Mrs Appleby. You're so petite.'

Billy frowned and Nan, sensing that he feared 'petite' was some sort of insult, asked, 'What d'you think, Bill?'

'Where'd you put it?'

'In the bedroom, I was thinking.'

Billy frowned again, considering. 'You could put it in the sitting room and fill it with cushions. If you put enough in it would make a kind of sofa.'

'I see your grandson's artistic,' Charmian put in.

This was a habit of which Nan strongly disapproved: talking about children as if they were not there in plain sight to be addressed directly. Deliberately, she said nothing and Billy, apparently answering this suggestion, said, 'I might be dyslexic. They're going to test me.'

From what Nan had seen Billy could read perfectly well; it was simply that he didn't choose to read the milk-and-water stories imposed on him at school. But she was interested in observing how he was trying out this idea.

'Many artists are or were dyslexic,' Charmian assured. 'I am too, as it happens.'

To Nan's mind, she rather spoiled the effect of this by adding that what didn't kill you made you stronger. 'How much is the coffin?' she asked.

Charmian appeared to consult her laptop. 'One thousand two hundred and fifty pounds, free delivery if you're within the Greater London postcode. And next year I'll be having to charge VAT so . . .' She shrugged, smiling, above spelling out any financial vulgarities.

Nan had more than that sum ready and waiting in her specially designated savings account. 'How soon could you get it done?'

This time Charmian made no pretence with her laptop. 'I've enough of the willow coming in so I could get it to you by the beginning of next month.'

'We'll think it over and get back to you,' Nan said. As she was being shown out of the door of the six-million-pound house she said, 'By the way, the Pyrex jug is over the top.'

They decided to give Richmond Park a miss and visit Kew Gardens instead. It was an old stamping ground of theirs and Nan had invested in an annual pass. They took a bus, which dropped them by the Victoria Gate. On their way to the Palm House they stopped to feed the geese with Billy's sandwiches.

'I do like it here,' Nan said as they entered the great Victorian jelly-mould of glass and the warm air hit her in the face like a lover's amorous smack. 'It's free treatment for my blessed rheumatism.'

Billy pointed out that it wasn't 'free' since she paid a large sum for her pass. He liked it there too. He liked the humid planty smell and the respectful hush that the extravagantly green growth seemed to encourage in visitors.

A wrought-iron spiral staircase led up to a gallery on which to patrol the upper part of the Palm House.

'Can I go up?'

'I'll stay below if you don't mind.'

'If I leave my phone can you take a picture?'

Billy raced up the staircase and moments later called down at her from the walkway above.

'I can hardly see your face,' Nan said, squinting through the phone. 'You look like a little monkey up there grinning through the banana palm.'

He made his way round the gallery and down the far steps and came running back, stopping at the top of the stairs to the basement. 'Do you think the ballan wrasse is all right?'

Billy had been very taken by the large spotted fish that had swum, solemn and solitary, in a tank in the aquarium that had once occupied the Palm House basement. The aquarium had been closed down and he fretted about the fate of the fish. Nan who as a girl had swum with a ballan wrasse in its native waters said, as she had before, 'I only hope they took the poor creature back to where it belongs in the sea. It looked miserable in that tank.'

They strolled round the lake, past ducks and geese noisily canvassing for more sandwiches, and up a broad avenue bordered in bright spring flowers. In the Orangery café Billy chose a sausage roll and a strawberry smoothie and Nan a Chelsea bun. Billy, a Chelsea supporter, was approving.

'You don't see Chelseas much these days,' Nan said. 'I

had a yen for them when I was pregnant with your father. I like to have one now and again to remind me.'

Nan had been surprised when her son had told her he was marrying so late in life. She had concluded that, like his father, he was gay – at least sexually ambiguous. She was even more surprised at his choice of wife. Virginia had struck her as a feeble sort of girl. Maybe, though, it was that Alec had liked in her: the fact, as Nan could hardly help observing, of Virginia being so very unlike herself.

Her husband, Terence, Alec's father, marrying she could understand; he had come of age at a time when homosexuality in a man was still a crime. Even so, she had inevitably felt some resentment when quite late in their marriage, during a row over something quite other, he had confessed his real sexual preferences.

'Did you never like it then with me?' she had asked, wounded but at the same time wildly curious.

'Oh, I did, Nan. It was fine with you – better than "fine",' he had added quickly, seeing the cloud pass over her face. 'But that was because it was you, you see?'

She could half 'see', with that corner-of-her-eye understanding which had drawn him to her in the first place. And they had stayed good friends after their parting. Nan was too sensible and had lived too long in the world to jettison an old friend out of pique.

What, once she had got over the knock to her pride, she had minded most was her own failure to recognise her husband's nature. She had married him, after a long spell alone, because he was clever; by this point in her life it was men's minds she was attracted to. And it had been a loss she had felt personally, as well as on Billy's behalf, when, with his new partner, Terry finally sold up and retired to Spain.

Alec, their son, had grown up apparently ignorant of his father's sexuality – though inevitably he must have picked up hints. But Alec had left home and was leading his own life by the time his father came out. Unlike his gregarious father their son had always seemed to Nan a natural loner so why he had persisted in the affair with Virginia she couldn't fathom. Maybe to have a child; but it wasn't as if he engaged much with his son. It was a puzzlement.

She worried that it was hard on Billy, though he showed no signs of embarrassment. It was more obviously hard on poor Virginia. Nan in truth was impatient of Virginia's refusal to get over the slight – as she, after all, herself had done – but for this very reason Nan was sorry for her.

Now in the arcadia of Kew Gardens Nan and Billy sat outside the Orangery enjoying the late-April sunlight. They ate in the contented silence of those who have nothing to fear from the other and have no need to keep intimacy at bay through a barrier of conversation. Nan finished her bun idly wondering, as she had done before, how they got the sugar to crystallise in that clever way. 'What do you think about the coffin, Bill?'

Her grandson chased flakes of pastry round his plate with his finger. 'It'd fit in at your flat.'

'You can have another sausage roll if you're still hungry,' Nan offered, but Billy said he just liked licking up the crumbs and that he thought she should go for it.

'Will I ring Charmian then and clinch the deal?'

'We could decorate it,' Billy said, looking at a cluster of narcissi and daffodils. 'It'd look nice all decorated.' He envisaged the coffin with flowers and maybe some of his less important Chelsea regalia.

'Right then.' Nan took a decision. 'No point in hanging about. Can you get me her number on your phone, pet?'

'I'll pay half now and half on delivery,' she said to Charmian. 'And if I've gone already by then I'll see to it that Bill knows where to find the balance. Does that sound fair?'

'Can we go and see the pagoda now?' Billy asked.

Kew's most eye-catching ornamental building, the pagoda, had been having a major facelift and had just been reopened for the summer to the public. They made their way there past the Queen's Beasts, the line of heraldic statues that stand guard along the Palm House. Billy was on good terms with them all but his favourite was the Yale. 'You could write about him,' Nan suggested. 'Next time you're asked to write about "What I did at the weekend" for English.'

'Maybe,' he said, and she kissed the top of his head, for this was the response she had advised him to use on occasions when he had had no time to make up his own mind.

They strolled down the tree-lined avenue towards the refurbished folly, where dragon effigies painted a gleaming green and gold glared at them from the several ascending roofs.

'Did anyone ever live in there?' Billy asked.

'No one of flesh and blood,' Nan told him. She had been drawn to the pagoda ever since her first visit to Kew over forty years ago. In her mind's eye she had always envisaged it peopled by shadowy antique presences. She imagined them now, as Billy began to count the dragons, calmly observing the human scene from an invisible vantage point on the topmost roof. *Their eyes mid many wrinkles, their eyes*, she thought. *Their ancient, glittering eyes, are gay.*

5

The morning after her shoplifting escapade Blanche, unwilling to face the day and suffering the after-effects of her drinking bout, heard keys in her door. She sprang out of bed, grabbing her dressing gown.

It was her cleaner, Marissa. She was standing in the hall looking at the trail of clothes Blanche had discarded the day before.

'Marissa? I thought you were in the hospital.'

'The bleeding is my period only. No baby. So I came here. You want me to stay?' Marissa had progressed into the sitting room and was staring at the bottle of gin, almost empty on the coffee table.

'I wasn't expecting you,' Blanche said. 'I –'

Her dressing gown swung open, revealing a flimsy pair of black lace knickers, bought long ago on a whim. She must have pulled them blindly from her drawer the previous morning. Marissa, who had only encountered her employer's everyday serviceable cotton knickers, was visibly struck. Out of the blue, inspiration alighted on Blanche. Barely missing a beat, she completed the sentence which had been hanging in the air: 'I have company, you see, Marissa.' She fixed her cleaner with a think-what-you-like gaze.

Marissa's eyes, which habitually looked at her with a veiled contempt, became respectful. 'You want me to go?'

'Please. I'll pay you, of course.'

'Thank you, Mrs Carrington. I come Friday, as usual?'

'May I let you know, Marissa? Maybe a little later in the morning?'

Blanche ushered her cleaner out with a novel feeling of triumph. Before returning to bed, and her mythical lover, she made herself a pot of coffee, extra strong.

By the following Saturday Blanche had grown rather frightened. That is, when she wasn't also feeling strangely elated. She found on her shopping expeditions it was almost impossible not to slip a little something or other into her pocket or bag. It was not that she was in need of these items; indeed, some were almost ostentatiously surplus to requirements: a candle shaped like a small green lamb, a pair of pink angora gloves – these were hardly needed and had they been she had ample means to pay for them. Her husband, Ken, had left her what he would have called 'comfortably off'. The council tax, the service charges (high even for Kensington), her phone and broadband bills and TV licence were all easily met by the substantial pension and life insurance that came to her when Ken died. And she had a portfolio of her own, built up over the years with the help of her accountant. She was able to buy clothes, not too many but of good quality, have her hair cut well and coloured discreetly at a top-class salon, dine out, go to the theatre, take regular holidays and there was still enough over for her to liberally treat her grandchildren. But this was a thought that Blanche had not to allow; the grandchildren were no longer available to her.

Her son had not phoned. She had sat, hand trembling, finger poised over the telephone dial, and had not dared to phone him. In the evenings she had drunk until she collapsed and crawled stupidly off to bed. Once, she didn't make it to the bedroom and awoke on the floor at 3 a.m., with sandpapered eyes, a taste like black tar in her mouth, a fierce crick in her shoulder and doom in her heart.

Fired by a conviction that nothing could bring her any lower, she picked up the phone, dialled Dominic's number and let loose a stream of violent obscenities, the precise nature of which, in the dismayed aftermath of a cruel grey-skied morning, she was unable to accurately recall.

More than once she contemplated killing herself; a suicide accompanied by the dignified last letter of unstated reproach that Dominic would find. But then Kitty and Harry would if not find it get to hear of it. And there was Mary, her blameless daughter, far away, it was true, but a distance that was purely physical and not of an unkind and deliberate making.

And Tina . . . Tina, for all she would act the part of sorrowing relative, Tina would secretly in her heart of hearts – if she had a heart – rejoice. She would be glad to be rid of her mother-in-law; would probably cook up an act of regretful forgiveness for unspeakable misdemeanours with which she would then taint Kitty and Harry's memory of their grandmother. One of Tina's methods, Blanche had discerned, was to subtly alter the children's recollections with what in the past Blanche had overlooked as embroidery. But it was not embroidery, it was not even embellishment. It was rank manipulation – tinkering with the children's recollections, informing them how they had felt and behaved in a past of which they themselves had no formed impressions to judge by.

She was not going to take herself out of the picture to be turned into a false 'memory' of God knew what kind of character. Unreliable, certainly. Unhinged, probably. Obscene, very likely, given her recent phone tirade. No – Blanche had almost physically ground her teeth as this image rose to mind – she was buggered if she was going to afford her daughter-in-law the pleasure of removing her living presence, which could at least stand as a future counter to any propaganda. If anything, she would try her best to outlast her daughter-in-law.

Propelled by these and other rebellious thoughts, in the daylight hours Blanche went out stealing.

Marissa had come on Friday at a slightly later hour as requested. 'If you wouldn't mind,' Blanche had said in her message. 'It would be more convenient.'

It had always, in fact, been more convenient for her cleaner to come a little later in the day; but in the past Marissa had said that the timing with her next job would make this impossible. Unquestionably, her cleaner had been impressed by the turn of events and conversed with Blanche in a new woman-to-woman tone. Blanche had been careful to use two cups while drinking her breakfast coffee and leave them unwashed for Marissa to find. She had also inadvertently added to the myth of a lover by leaving a full ashtray in the sitting room, for in a further attempt to anaesthetise her broken heart she had taken up smoking.

'Your friend smoke?' Marissa had said. 'You let him,

yes?' She had smiled, indicating her understanding that this was the kind of indulgence a woman must allow a man. One of their few former points of contact had been an agreed dislike of smoking.

On Saturday Blanche shifted her district not so much through fear of detection but from a desire for a better class of loot. She headed towards Knightsbridge, first to Harrods – but here she hesitated. Her husband had allowed her an account at Harrods. It was closed now but to steal there seemed somehow disrespectful to the dead. However, in Harvey Nichols she discovered a sky-blue silk shirt without the usual security tag and in her size. Bundling it in with an armful of other garments, she ducked into the dressing cubicle, where she rolled it into a sausage and plunged it into her bag. This theft successfully accomplished, she went prospecting for other spoils.

By the end of the afternoon Blanche had bagged the silk blouse, a skirt considerably shorter than she was used to wearing and a bright red thong. The last item was a lucky break, left behind in another dressing cubicle and, like the shirt and skirt, without a security tag. She lifted it less with a mind to wearing it but more with the aim of impressing Marissa. Marissa, she felt, would rate a thong.

Blanche took the bus back to Kensington High Street and nipped into Boots, from where she came out with two lipsticks, some lash-extending mascara and a tube of body scrub. Now for a celebration, she exulted, almost cantering down the stairs to the M&S food hall to stock up with strong drink.

6

On the same Saturday Minna was helping Rose with her homework.

'I don't know why they give you so much,' she complained. 'We never had homework at the primary in my day.'

'It's because of SATS.' Rose sighed. 'We've got *another* test next week.'

Minna often helped Rose with her homework. Occasionally, if Rose was under pressure, she did the homework for her. But not maths. Or not any longer. There had been an occasion where she had done Rose's maths and the teacher had asked Rose to stay behind after class. 'You don't seem to have taken in a word I said, Rose Cooper,' she had reproved, and Rose had been given extra homework.

Minna had been mortified by this, not because she minded being found ignorant but because the ignorance had got Rose into trouble. But Rose thought it hilarious and after a time Minna saw that she done Rose a favour by being demonstrably worse at maths than her. Maths was Rose's bugbear.

'It doesn't matter,' Minna had tried to reassure. 'You'll get to your next school anyway.'

But Rose explained that it did matter because you were 'set' in your next school on your SATS results and once you were set it was very hard – impossible, in fact – to get moved.

'That makes no sense,' Minna said. 'You can't be placed aged eleven for the rest of your school career.'

But Rose was adamant that this was so.

They finished off the homework and assembled the toys to audition for the play they were writing. Easter had fallen late and the play was a reworking of the Easter story.

Rose attended a Church of England primary school where the Christian story, or a version of it, was much emphasised. Shocked by the heartless transition from baby Jesus in the crib to the cruelty of the cross, Rose had decided the story of the Son of Man was in need of radical updating. So far, she was proposing to have Pontius Pilate dismissing the pleas of the Jews to have Jesus crucified and electing to have Barabbas nailed up instead.

'You have to remember that Jesus was a Jew himself,' Minna said. 'People forget that.'

This fact had bypassed Rose too. 'Was he?'

'And all the disciples.'

'So why does it say in the Gospel that it's the Jews who want him crucified?'

'That's only in the Gospel of St John,' Minna said. Her reading life had in fact begun with a reading of the King James Bible. 'It was only a section of the Jews, the kind who believed in rules and regulations more than common human kindness, though from what I've read, the Pharisees weren't actually that bad.'

Rose was intrigued. 'Why do they say that they are bad then?'

'It's called propaganda,' Minna said. 'When you want to make someone think your way.'

'That's lying,' Rose said. 'The Bible wouldn't lie, would it?'

'The Bible was only written by people,' Minna said. 'People do lie. They may not mean to, but they do.'

They decided that if Pontius Pilate was going to pardon Jesus then there wasn't much of an Easter story to retell.

'We could do *The Wizard of Oz* instead,' Rose suggested. Musicals were another bond.

Rose's mother on the phone to her own mother said, 'Nick's had a promotion but it means moving to Glasgow. We've not broken it to the children yet. Justin's too young to take it in but Rosie might be upset.'

Her mother at the other end of the phone made encouraging remarks about the resilience of children and their known ability to make new friends.

'To be honest, it's more her having to leave Minna, that old woman she's so fond of, that's going to bother her. She's round there now. And Glasgow's too far away for her to see her once we move.'

Her mother had heard about this Minna and resented her. 'That may be for the best' was her view.

7

The bus from Kew took Nan and Billy down Kensington High Street, where they got out.

'Why we getting out here?' Billy asked.

'I want to go to that Boots. The Notting Hill one hasn't got Germolene.' The old-fashioned pink ointment that Nan swore by had become increasingly hard to find.

The Kensington Boots was as barren as the other branch. 'All these fancy creams and you can't get a blessed tube of Germolene,' Nan complained.

They made their way to the exit through crowds sampling cosmetics and scent sprays. One woman, a tall blonde dressed in a long cream-coloured coat, caught Nan's eye. Was she? Yes, she was shoplifting. Definitely, she had slipped a lipstick into her coat pocket. And now she was swiftly moving on.

Nan and Billy followed behind. The woman had stopped and was spraying herself with scent with one hand and with the other . . . there went another cosmetic. Nan moved closer to look. Some sort of fancy mascara this time.

Again, the woman moved on. Just before the exit her hand shot out and collared a tube of something placed on a low shelf and whipped it into her pocket.

Nan approached the stand and inspected an identical tube.

'What that?' Billy asked.

'*Nature's way of bringing your skin back to life,*' Nan read out. 'Bloody rubbish. Nature's way? Jesse Boot's way more like.'

'That lady took one,' Billy said. 'Shall we tell them?'

'I don't think so,' Nan said. 'The poor soul's probably not quite right in the head. We don't want to add to her woes.'

'Is she Jessie Boot?' Billy asked.

'It's not Jessica. Jesse Boot's a man, or was. He was the fellow who way back started Boots the Chemist. It was more a figure of speech.'

'What's a figure of speech?' Billy asked.

'Maybe I mean poetic licence.'

'What's that?'

'You can look it up when we get home.' He would too, Nan guessed. Hardly dyslexic then.

They caught another bus and got off near Nan's flat.

Nan had bought her flat when she and her husband parted. The modest-seeming house in Chiswick that they had acquired when they married had risen in value to an amount so improbable that Nan didn't like to think about it. Terence had offered to let her stay in the Chiswick house but Nan said that given she was embarking on a new life she would prefer a change. She had taken less than half the value of their home to buy the little flat off the Portobello Road and ever since her husband had been paying her the balance in monthly instalments. It was a deal that suited them both.

With Terry's instalments, her pension and money that came from another source, she lived quite contentedly.

'All this moaning about what you can't have,' she had once allowed herself to say to her daughter-in-law. 'We none of us had that stuff when I was growing up, rich or poor.'

The house which Alec and Virginia had bought when Billy was born was further down Ladbroke Grove in a less salubrious area. But it was close enough for Nan and Billy to walk to each other's homes. Walking to Billy's now, Nan said, 'What happened with that girl you swore at? Did she apologise?'

'She wrote me a letter.'

'What did she say?'

'Didn't read it. It'd only be stuff she was told to say.'

'You're probably right,' Nan agreed. 'Saying sorry's pointless if you don't mean it.'

'Anyway,' Billy said, reassured by this vote of confidence, 'I never said what she said I said.'

'*Didn't* say. You mean "a fucking shit"?'

'No. Yeah, I mean I didn't. I called her a cunt but she didn't want to say that word so she made the others up.'

'Billy, do you know what "cunt" means?'

Billy looked puzzled. 'Someone you don't like?'

'Not exactly,' Nan said, and explained. Billy said he'd never heard it called that and when they had their sex talk at school it was called something else.

'"Vagina", I dare say,' Nan said. 'Though they seem to be calling it "vulva" these days. But swearing's not a great idea, though we all do it. At your age it can get you into more trouble than it's worth. Much better put her down next time with words she'll not have heard of.'

'Like?'

44

Nan thought. 'Like "an unmitigated falsifier of veracity".'

Billy was impressed. 'What's it mean?'

'Roughly speaking, it means someone who lies breathing in and breathing out.'

'But you said lying was OK,' Billy pointed out.

'To save your own skin when you're being got at it is. Josie what's-her-name was saying something untrue to hurt you. That's different. But anyway, all you would have been doing calling her that is speaking the truth.'

'That what you said? An . . .?'

'Unmitigated falsifier of veracity. That's it. I wouldn't explain to her what "cunt" means, though,' she added.

The following Monday Nan received a call from Boots in Notting Hill.

'We've got Germolene in, Mrs Appleby, so I'm giving you a bell like you asked.'

Nan thanked the helpful chemist and later in the day walked up to Notting Hill. She had paid for the ointment and exchanged a few words with the chemist when her attention was caught by a cream coat.

It was the tall blonde she had seen with Billy in Kensington and instinct told Nan that the woman was again shoplifting. She watched her moving from one stand to another. And yes, there was the sleight of hand she had witnessed before. Little palettes of eye makeup were being slipped into the pockets of the cream coat.

The woman must have sensed her gaze because all of a sudden she began to move hurriedly towards the exit. Nan followed her and before the woman quite got to the door Nan touched her on the shoulder.

She had to reach up to do this because the woman was unusually tall and Nan was short.

'Excuse me,' Nan said.

The woman started and made to dash away but Nan took her arm. 'It's OK. Let's go outside.'

Still holding the woman's arm, once outside Nan steered her towards the next-door McDonald's. 'Can I buy you a tea? Coffee?'

The woman dumbly shook her head. Her face, Nan saw, had gone ashen.

'Listen,' Nan said. 'I'm not a store detective. I just wanted to say that I'd seen you and if I can then . . .' Seeing the pallor of the woman's face, she allowed the sentence to peter out. 'Come on,' she said, almost pushing the woman back through the door to McDonald's. 'I'm not about to hand you over to the authorities. Come and sit down. You're terribly pale.'

As if in a trance, the blonde woman sat down.

'What would you like?' Nan said. 'I'll have tea myself.'

The woman licked her lips. Finally, she spoke. 'Thank you. A coffee, please, if you don't mind.'

'Black, white, cappuccino, latte?'

'Just black, please,' the woman said. She was trembling.

Nan went to queue and returned with a tray. 'I got you a biscuit. You look as if you need sugar.'

'Oh no,' the woman began, 'I don't –'

'Just a bite,' Nan said. 'You've had a shock.'

The woman obediently nibbled. For all her height and elegant clothes, she looked like a little frightened animal. Nan stirred her tea, saying nothing. After a bit the woman said, 'I can take it back.'

46

'It?'

'Them.'

'Listen,' Nan said. 'There's no need for that. I reckon Boots can spare you a couple of eye shadows. I didn't stop you for that.'

'What then?' the woman asked. Her voice was stronger now and her colour beginning to return.

'You don't strike me as a thief,' Nan said, and regretted it when the woman flushed darkly. 'Look,' she said, 'the thing is, I saw you before in the Kensington Boots. And if you're in the habit of doing this it's only a matter of time before you're caught. I've spotted you twice already and I'm not a store detective. Ten to one you're already on some blessed CCTV whatnot.'

The woman looked freshly horrified.

'Good heavens, think about it,' Nan said. 'We're all spied on nowadays. But I shouldn't worry. If you are on camera they haven't picked you out yet and if they do spot you later they won't do anything unless you try it again. Unless you want to be caught,' she suddenly wondered. 'Perhaps you do and I'm just interfering.'

'Oh no,' the woman said.

'You might unconsciously want to be caught,' Nan said. 'That's not uncommon, I gather.'

'Oh no,' the woman said again. 'I don't think so. It's just that . . .' She began to weep and opened her bag to find a tissue. The bag, Nan could see, was crammed full of little packets of makeup. 'It's . . .' The woman tried to speak again. 'I can't explain,' she sobbed. 'It's just . . . I . . . no, I can't explain.'

Nan waited until she had finished crying. 'Well, you

wouldn't be able to explain. As I say, you don't seem like a thief. It's no odds to me but it's best not to be caught. I'm Nan, by the way.'

'I'm Blanche,' the woman said.

'Nan Appleby.'

'I'm Blanche Carrington,' the woman said. 'The Blanche is after my grandmother.' She said this as if she were apologising for her name.

One who's been bullied, Nan thought. Aloud, she said, 'I always wished I'd had my grandmother's name. She was called Nes, which means "gentle" in Gaelic, which she certainly wasn't. Mind you, I loved her, which was probably why I liked the name.'

'I loved my grandmother too,' Blanche said. 'She was French. I'm supposed to look like her.'

'She must have been tall, then. Mind you, you'll seem taller to me because I'm such a titch. Pint pot, my husband called me.'

By means of more steady conversation, Nan gradually calmed the other's agitation. When she saw that Blanche had somewhat recovered, she said, 'Might you fancy coming back to my flat for a bite? It's only ten minutes down the road.' Her new acquaintance had been drinking. She could smell it from across the table.

'Oh, I couldn't.'

'It's no bother – there's only me there. And it'd be company,' she added, aware that nothing is so helpful to those in distress as the thought that they are helping others.

Blanche consented to accompany Nan and as they walked down the Portobello Road she began visibly to relax. 'How lovely to live near all this,' she said, turning to Nan, smiling.

Good teeth, Nan noted. Probably bleached. Her own teeth were less than perfect. 'Everything you need on your doorstep: bread, cheese, fruit, veg, flowers, even toilet rolls and bleach and what-not you can get here, and the stall holders still call you "love" and "darling". That's probably illegal these days.'

Nan's flat, like Nan, was tiny and spick and span. Blanche went to look out of the window that ran across the sitting room and through to the cabin-size kitchen. 'What a view! You can see half London. Is that the Post Office Tower?'

'If you look a little more to the right you can see the Shard. There's sixteen churches you can see. My grandson likes to count them.'

'You've grandchildren?'

'Just the one. I'd have liked more. I say that, but maybe Bill and I wouldn't be so close if there were more of them,' Nan said, and was dismayed when Blanche collapsed, sobbing wildly.

8

Blanche was drinking her third cup of tea in Nan's sitting room. 'It's lovely tea,' she enthused. 'Much nicer than mine.'

'It's PG Tips,' Nan said, ready to stamp on any nonsense. 'My grandmother, who had a streak of Irish in her Gaelic, used to say tea had to be brewed strong enough to trot a mouse on.'

'My grandmother used to say, "C'est avec la première tasse de café du matin que pour moi la vie commence",' Blanche said, and then explained, 'For me life begins with the first cup of coffee.'

Nan, who spoke perfect French, said only, 'I like coffee but if you put a gun to my head it would have to be tea.' She had a mental flash of Blanche, her pale Gallic features taut with an unspecified rage, wielding a revolver. 'I have felt like killing myself,' she had confided to Nan and Nan, less tart than she might have been, had said 'I imagine that would be just dandy for your grandchildren,' and then when she saw Blanche showing signs of beginning to cry again, 'Much better kill your son's wife, if it's revenge you've a mind for.'

'So the long and the short of it,' she said now, 'is that in that household it's your daughter-in-law who wears the trousers.'

'I suppose so,' Blanche agreed doubtfully. She had kicked

off her heels and was sitting on the carpet, her back against the sofa, her long legs stretched out before her. She contemplated her toes, imagining them painted scarlet, or maybe green or blue as nowadays was more conventional.

'I've only the one son,' Nan said. 'His wife's not too keen on me either but he's flighty so she puts up with having me around.'

This was not a term Blanche associated with men. 'Flighty?' she enquired.

'He's gay, if he's anything. Not that I'm saying gay men are flighty. His father's gay and he's not flighty. Very solid in fact. But Alec is – always was.'

Blanche was astonished at the matter-of-fact way Nan divulged this. What she didn't perceive was that Nan was being kind. She was not at all inclined to personal disclosure but she could tell that Blanche was suffering from the common belief that she had been singled out for peculiar misfortune.

'Did you know that your husband . . .?' Blanche began to ask but Nan interrupted her. She didn't plan to pursue these revelations any further.

'They have you down as unsafe with the kids, is that it?'

'Yes. And I'm not,' Blanche said. She looked sulky.

'Because you'd been drinking?'

'Hardly at all. I had a couple of glasses of wine – well, maybe three or so – before driving them home. And Tina asked how much I'd drunk and I said . . .'

But Nan had heard all this already. 'You played it down and then they interrogated the kids. That's the bit that sticks in my craw.'

'The children didn't mean to give me away. My daughter-in-law asked them, "How much of the bottle of wine had Granny drunk?" and Harry said, "It was almost full." He didn't understand what he was saying.'

'It's parents feeling entitled to these inquisitions that's so wrong,' Nan said. It was Nazi, she felt. Children were in their parents' power – what choice did they have, when put to it like that, but to lie or betray? 'Mind you,' she went on, thinking of the drink she'd detected on Blanche's breath, 'you were rather walking into your daughter-in-law's trap, drinking if you were driving. Ten to one she was looking for an excuse and you gave her one.'

'I know,' Blanche looked mournful. 'I shouldn't have. It's silly but I feel scared when I go there. I love being with the children and they love being with me, I think, but the moment I step into that house I sort of freeze.'

'You fear attack,' Nan diagnosed. 'We're all animals when you come down to it. Animals can sense when they're in danger. They don't sound kind.' Kindness doesn't save you from sickness or death, or the humiliations of old age, she reflected, but it confers the saving grace of kinship.

'It's true,' Blanche said miserably. She said again, 'It's silly of me but I feel scared there and things come out all wrong. The drink is Dutch courage, I suppose.'

'It's partly because there isn't a man at your side,' Nan suggested. 'They'd be different if there was a man in the case.'

Blanche at once thought of Marissa. 'Funnily enough . . .' She told Nan about her mythical lover.

'There you are,' Nan said. 'I bet your daughter-in-law's

a feminist. I bet your son thinks he is too.' It had long been her view that causes made people callous. 'Like I said, we're all animals, going after the vulnerable, but with that sort because they have what they consider enlightened ideas they imagine they act enlightened. Their having a go at you is because they have you down as vulnerable.'

Blanche considered this. It was true that her sense of being under attack had grown since Ken's death. 'I sort of see what you mean.'

Some words came back to Nan. *'Had I been born crested, not cloven, you would not speak to me thus.'*

'What?'

'Something Queen Elizabeth's said to have said when she was feeling cock-pecked by her male advisers.' The first Elizabeth, who swore she had the heart and stomach of a king, had been an inspiration to schoolgirl Nan. 'She protected herself and kept everyone guessing with any number of possible candidates she might decide one day to marry. It's not my business but if I were you I'd peddle this mythic boyfriend. Has he got a name?'

Blanche looked out the window. From her position on the floor she could see none of the towers and spires. But across the expanse of sky a solitary bird flew, its wings a clear scimitar against the Delft blue. One swallow doesn't make a summer, she thought. She had been present at the arrival of the swallows one long balmy Easter holiday in the garden of her grandmother's house in France, to which she had been dispatched like a parcel while her parents tried and failed to sort out their bitter divorce.

There had been a young man called Albert who had helped with the rough work. He had worn the workman's *bleu de travail* and one unusually hot day, when she was trying to draw the garden as a thank-you for grand-maman, who loved her flowers, he had undone the top of the overalls in order to cool himself off under the garden tap. Blanche could summon to this day the fascination she had felt for the brown muscled back and the enticing musky smell of his armpits.

'Voici les hirondelles,' he had said to her, pointing out the swallows, 'elles amènent l'été,' and had smiled.

'Albert,' she said to Nan, giving the name the English pronunciation. 'He's called Albert.'

'Very good,' Nan approved. 'Albert's a solid-sounding name. Now you've named him he'll be real.'

She made lunch in the tiny kitchen and Blanche wandered about the sitting room inspecting its contents.

'You read a lot of poetry,' she called across to Nan, observing the neat rows of books along her shelves.

'Uh-huh,' Nan said. 'Gouda or Brie?'

'Either,' Blanche said. 'I like both.' She took down a paperback and inspected it. 'Gerald Manley Hopkins. I've never even heard of him.'

'It's Gerard,' Nan said, fighting irritation. She disliked anyone handling her books. 'There's toms and cuc and I've cream crackers or there's sliced white left over I can toast.'

Restored by lunch, Blanche walked back up the Portobello Road. She stopped to buy salad from a stall.

'That's five pound, darling,' the man said, his swollen

purple fingers twirling the brown paper bag to a neat close. 'Nice now that the rain's stopped.' He added the bag of little cucumbers to the plastic bag already full of chicory, celery and watercress.

'And four of the large oranges, please,' Blanche said. She could envisage their radiant colour in her blue-glazed Provençal bowl, like a painting she had once seen at an art fair and wanted to buy. Ken had considered it too expensive. 'Where would you hang it? You've so many pictures already,' he had said, amused. 'Our walls are full to bursting with your pictures.' She had wanted to say, But they are all reproductions – this is the real thing. But the remark would have had that slight edge of putting Ken down that she was aware he was sensitive to and tried to avoid. Ken's tastes were not hers but she would never willingly have hurt him.

Towards the top end of the street she came to a shop displaying in the window old-fashioned cotton night-gowns and went in and bought one. Albert, she was sure, would want her in white cotton. He's not a thong man, she decided, crossing at the lights at Notting Hill.

There was an afternoon film showing at the Gate cinema. *Jules et Jim*. Before she had met Ken she had been to see this film with a pimply young man whose name she couldn't recall. They had sat in the Hampstead Everyman and when he had tried to kiss her she had turned her head away. Poor young man, she thought. He must have felt rejected for his acne and all it was was that I didn't feel I was attractive enough to be kissed.

A mere handful of people had come to watch Jeanne

Moreau dazzle her two young men, driving them half-way round the bend with her capricious sexual allure. Blanche watched the film eating popcorn. Recollections of her erotically aroused twelve-year-old self in her grand-mother's garden mingled with regrets for the gauche young woman she had become. Was that because of her parents' parting, she speculated, as Jeanne Moreau, in fetching male disguise, now raced the two young men, cheating from the very start. She should have been allowed to stay on in the house as grand-maman had wished. Then she might have acquired some of that French self-assurance and elan. But her mother, remarried to her rich and possessive stepfather, had gone off to Dubai, relegating her daughter to the prissy Hampshire boarding school that was paid for by her father. Her father, alienated from his firstborn by the acrimony and expense of the divorce, had diverted all his devotion to his new wife and his new children. It must have been why she sent me there, Blanche had concluded. To make him pay, and through the nose.

The young Blanche had lingered in the emotionally damp environment, never making a fuss, getting by, neither popular nor unpopular, brainy nor stupid, her only talents being art, the subject for 'dim' pupils, conversational French and a natural sympathy for the homesick younger girls. Even at that she had failed. She had been cowed by catty suggestions of lesbianism and had dropped little Amanda Brown, who had looked at her thereafter with hurt, sleep-deprived eyes.

From this unpromising base she had moved on to a London secretarial college, where again she neither shone nor failed, and then, as if by some natural progression, to Ken.

She had met Ken at a tennis party where she had been partnering another, more dashing, young man whom she had shyly fancied. For a while she had nursed an excited conviction that the attraction was reciprocated and had, as her mother cruelly put it on one of her rare visits, thrown her cap at him. When it was obvious his desire went no further than an interest in a tennis partner whose height conferred a winning serve she accepted a date with Ken, really to allay the sense of humiliation. Ken, older, doing well in finance, already a little overweight and red-faced but admiring and pressing with his invitations, had been first a camouflage and then a solace. And it was a kind of rebuttal to her mother, who had conveyed a conviction that her daughter was unmarriageable.

Dear old Ken, she thought, as Jeanne Moreau prepared to drive the unsuspecting Jim to his death. Loyal, solid Ken had rescued her from her father's indifference and her mother's chronic undermining. Ken had given her safety, stability and material comfort. More importantly, he had given her Mary and Dominic; most especially Dominic. Too late, as the car, with Jeanne Moreau at the wheel, plunged into the water, drowning herself and her besotted passenger, the ragged nerve began to shriek again.

Her Dom. The tiny baby she had watched over, creeping into the premature unit where he lay in his glass box, his feeble heartbeat resounding through the monitor so that to this day she could hear its irregular thrum: dit – pause – dit, dit, dit – pause – dit, dit ditditdit – horrifying,

horrifying *please God, please let it go on beating* – pause. She, who had paid only lip service to the God of her schooldays, had prayed on her knees, day after day, night after night, embarrassing the nursing staff: God, if you save my baby boy, I shall never *ever* ask for anything more again.

Taking him home after many weeks, with Ken driving – Ken, who had been appalled into silence by her desperate unassuageable misery – her tiny precious baby rescued from the glass box, had stared up at her with wide all-comprehending eyes and the melting tones of Roberta Flack had suddenly issued from the car radio.

Always inclined to be superstitious, she had heard the song as a sign. And Dominic had been saved. But Dominic, for whom she would have willingly laid down her own life, did not love her.

He would claim he did, she bitterly told herself as, energised by the spirit of Jeanne Moreau, she emerged from the cinema into the late afternoon to stride down Kensington Church Street, impatiently skirting the stragglers in her way. Oh yes, he would assure her that 'of course' he loved her, 'it was only that . . .' And here she could only guess at the debits totted up against her by the hateful Tina. But much as she would like to, she couldn't put it all down to Tina.

Mary, her elder child, easy-going Mary, happily married to her engineer in Australia, harboured no such injuries. No doubt she occasionally irritated her daughter but not in this seemingly unpardonable way. She loved her elder child, of course she did. And yet if there were a God who had put out an immortal hand to pluck the newborn Dominic back from the brink of extinction and this God were to bear witness then He or She or whatever you wanted to call It would testify that of her two children it was Mary whom she could better spare.

Perhaps that was it, she speculated angrily, reaching her mansion block and bounding up the stairs to the second floor (because it was her habit to try to keep fit) – there was a price to be exacted by the inscrutable Being with whom on the Dettol-smelling floor of the premature unit she had made the bargain forty-odd years ago: she was being punished now for having loved her son the more.

9

'Glasgow?' Rose said. 'That's miles and *miles* away!'

'I know it seems that way now,' her mother had said, 'but Dad has had a promotion and we can afford a much bigger house and garden there. You'll make new friends in no time.' She was a little thrown by her daughter's passionate reaction to the news of the move.

'I'm afraid it's that Minna she's upset about leaving,' she confided later to her mother on the phone.

Her mother at the other end made the clicking knitting-needle sounds that generally heralded some negative pronouncement. 'I've wondered if I should say . . . you don't think, I mean she's round there an awful lot, there's maybe something, I don't know, *unhealthy* there . . .?'

'Oh, I don't think so,' Rose's mother had said, aghast – such a dismaying thought had never entered her head. 'She just pops in for her tea while I collect Justin from school.'

But it was true, when she thought about it. She had not quite noticed how Rose had got in the way of going over to the shepherd's hut more and more frequently. The idea once sown grew enough of a root that in bed that night she asked her husband, 'You don't think there's anything, you know, funny going on between Rose and that old woman?'

'Which old woman?' Her husband's mind was on other

things, such as how he was going to explain this move to his secretary, Emma. It was an affair that had started in the fuddled aftermath of an office party and had dragged on mainly because he was fearful of what she might say if he dumped her. Now he was kicking himself for not getting it over with sooner.

'That Minna who lives in the caravan.'

'It's a shepherd's hut, isn't it?' her husband said, employing the practised literal-mindedness that drove his wife mad.

'Whatever. Only Rosie's in a right spin over leaving her.'

'She's not that old, is she?' her husband said, deflecting again. He was wondering if Emma had kept any of the cards that had accompanied the inevitable gifts he had been obliged to fork out for at Christmas and birthdays. What for fuck's sake had he written on them?

'About Mum's age. Mum wondered if she was maybe, you know, gay. What do you think?'

'I thought old Frank what's-his-face was banging her? Doesn't he let her stay there for nothing?'

'Anyway, I think Mum is right,' his wife said, only partially reassured. 'I think maybe it's as well we're moving.'

'She'll get over it,' her husband said, digging about for some platitude. 'Kids are resilient. They do.' He was thinking wishfully of his secretary as he said this.

'But it's *miles* away, Glasgow,' Rose said for the third time. She had rushed tearfully round to Minna's on learning the news.

'We can write,' Minna said. 'And there's the phone.'

'You only have that old one.'

'I can get another,' Minna said, aware that that was the

least of the sacrifices she was willing to make to stay in touch with Rose.

'It's not the same. You know it's not. And what about the toys?'

Minna looked at the ranks of assorted toys, so loved, so invested with life, with whom she and Rose had enjoyed so many countless fertile imaginings. 'They'll survive,' she said. 'They're survivors, the toys, and you'll survive too. It's good to learn to survive.'

But will I? she thought. Will I survive?

'I'll hate it,' Rose said. 'It's all cold up there. I'll run away and come and live here with you.'

'You'd better not,' Minna said. 'You'd get us both into trouble. Listen, this is hard, I know, but we'll find a way. We're ace at that, you and me. A team.'

When Rose had gone Minna picked up her book. But for all her brave words she felt downcast and the effect of the news of the forthcoming move was to make her concentration lapse and she had to go back to pick up the thread. *In all weathers,* she read, *even when the rain was coming down in torrents and Françoise had rushed indoors with the precious wicker armchairs, so that they should not get soaked – you would see my grandmother pacing the deserted garden, lashed by the storm, pushing back her grey hair in disorder so that her brows might be more free to imbibe the life-giving draughts of wind and rain. She would say, 'At last one can breathe!' and would run up and down the soaking paths – too straight and symmetrical for her liking, owing to the want of any feeling for nature in the new gardener, whom my father had been asking all morning if the weather were going to improve – with her keen, jerky little step regulated by the various effects wrought upon her soul by the intoxication of the storm, the force of hygiene, the stupidity of my education and of symmetry in gardens, rather than by any anxiety (for that was quite unknown to her) to save her plum-coloured skirt from the spots of mud . . .*

Minna liked the grandmother and regarded her, especially her views on 'the stupidity' of her grandson's education, as a kindred spirit. But she had no heart for reading that day and felt the need for more tangible comradeship, so she walked across the yard to Frank's house.

Frank was outside mending a hen coop. 'The bloody fox got another last eve. I can't see how he got in.'

'The foxy-whiskered gentleman,' Minna said.

'Hardly "gentleman".'

'He's in Beatrix Potter,' Minna explained. 'He goes after Jemima Puddleduck.'

Frank, accustomed to not following Minna's lines of thought, suggested she put on the kettle while he finished with the coop. 'Unless you'd rather have a drop of the hard stuff?'

'I wouldn't mind, Frank, to be honest.'

'Well, you know where it is.'

Over their glasses of Jameson she conveyed Rose's news and, head on one side, his watery blue eyes full of concern, Frank listened, saying nothing while she unburdened. 'She'll get over it,' Minna concluded, trying to believe this. 'What I mustn't do is make her feel badly for getting over it.'

'I'm not so sure,' Frank said. 'People say that, "children are tough, they get over things", but I wonder if people only say that to cheer themselves up for the things they

63

didn't get over. There's things happened to me I didn't get over.'

'What, Frank?' Minna was alarmed.

'It doesn't matter what. I'm just saying. Folk say all sorts about kids and I reckon the kids grow up thinking that that's what they do feel, because it's what they've been told they feel, and then they repeat it unthinking to their own kids and so it goes on.'

Minna pondered this. She hadn't had anything serious to get over as a child. The odd hurt or upset at school, that was all. It was later, after John, she had had to summon all her courage to survive. 'I was lucky,' she said. 'As a child, I was. My mother was, well, I adored her.' She could almost physically summon up the smell of sweet violets.

'How old were you when you lost her?'

'Too young. For me, anyway.' Thirty-three, the day she got the phone call. And even recalling it brought back that deadly knocking of her heart as with every fibre of her being she urged on the taxi to the hospital. Too late, as it turned out. Only her poor father, dumb with grief, was there to meet her with the body of her mother, tantalisingly alive-seeming, her skin still imbued with the scent of the Coty's talc her father had brought to the hospital.

She had taken home the talc. She had the tin still, the gold a little patchy now from so many removals.

All that was before John. It was some time since she had first wondered if that was *why* John, to fill the black hole made by the death of her gentle mother.

'My mother was a right tartar,' Frank said. 'She tanned my backside till you could've made a cowboy's saddle of it. "Spare the rod and spoil the child" was her motto. And

64

years on, when I was grown and long left home, I asked her what she thought that meant and she said, "Don't ask me, Francis, I haven't a bloody clue."' He laughed in the way of those long practised at living with a chronic wound.

'No one ever beat me,' Minna said. Only emotionally, she thought. Only John.

'What you should do,' Frank said, pouring them both another tot of Jameson, 'is take her to things. Things she doesn't do with her parents.'

'Like what?'

'Well, you read books with her. Take her to one of those festivals you hear about. She'd like that, I reckon. You'd like it too.'

'She wants to take Rosie to some book festival, over the May half-term,' Rose's mother said into the phone. 'It's not that near but she says they can get there and back again in the one day.'

Her mother at the other end made considering noises.

'I don't see there's much harm in it,' her daughter suggested. 'Rosie does love her reading. Her teacher says she's way ahead of the rest of her class.'

To her husband in bed that night she announced, 'Rosie's going with that Minna to a book festival over the May bank holiday. I said she could.'

'Oh, right,' her husband said. His secretary had confronted him as he had tried to slip out through the fire exit to the car park.

'It's that author she's so keen on, Elizabeth Pattern.'

'Right.' Emma's eyes had had that glittering look which from the first had provoked anxiety in him. 'So, I hear you're off to Glasgow,' she had said, with the intonation that matched the glitter in her eyes. 'When did you get that exciting news, may one ask?'

Beside him Rose's mother, newly attractive for her lack of glitter, was saying, 'And it would mean we could do a quick trip to Glasgow and check out the property while she looks after Rose. Mum said she thought it would be OK. Of course she would love to take the children herself but she hasn't the time.'

'No, right,' her husband said. He was calculating how he could get into the locked drawer in Emma's desk without being found out.

'Mum would really love to do more with the children,' his wife said. 'But with the dogs being such a tie it's hard for her to get away.'

'Yes, right,' her husband said. He was of the view that his mother-in-law was an evil-minded old cow who bullied her daughter and disliked her daughter's family but in his present state there was a kind of comforting solidarity in joining with his wife in a lie.

Bank Holidays

IO

Nan was on the very edge of completing a poem when the phone rang. Usually when writing she turned off her phone. She thought of ignoring it but seeing it was Virginia she answered in case it was something to do with Billy.

'I'm not disturbing you or anything?' Virginia asked. 'Only I wondered if you could maybe have Billy for a sleepover this weekend. I know it's short notice, only it's the bank hol.'

'As you know, he's always welcome,' Nan said, who had forgotten that this was the first of the May bank holidays. She regarded holidays based on banks as a contradiction in terms.

'Oh thanks. Only my friend I just hooked up with again from uni has planned a get-together and –'

'It's fine,' Nan interrupted, wanting to be spared the ins and outs of her daughter-in-law's social life. 'Shall I collect him from school, then, on Friday?'

'If you wouldn't mind.'

'No.'

'Pardon?'

'No, I don't mind,' Nan said. She wondered if Virginia really didn't grasp that she was always happy to have Billy or if these protests were simply affectations. Probably a bit of both.

*

No living soul knew that Nan was a poet. She was brought up with her grandmother's border ballads in her ears and it was to her grandmother alone that she had shown the five-shilling postal-order prize that she had won in a poetry competition. Although she was just fourteen she had entered for the sixteen-and-over category. She could not have said at the time why she had done this but Nan knew now that it was because her chosen subject would have been considered too grim for a fourteen-year-old and that it had served her better in apparently coming from an older entrant.

She had written her winning poem, a broken lament from a shell-shocked veteran of the First World War, under the name of A. Nonne but at the advice of her grandmother had subsequently introduced a further initial.

'Some bright spark's bound to catch on it's Anon you are writing as,' her grandmother had said. 'Stick in another initial. Ten to one then they'll think you're a man.'

Not long after this Nan had come across 'A Valediction: Forbidding Mourning' and went on to explore the works of the seventeenth-century poet and divine who mourned the death of his beloved wife with the touching epitaph which played on the pronunciation of their name: *Anne Donne, John Donne, Undone.* Following the great poet's lead, but in reverse, she changed the spelling of her writing name to Nunne.

Her grandmother had been proved right. A. G. Nunne was now an admired if obsessively reclusive poet.

Not even his agent had ever been allowed to set eyes on the recluse, who was happily blessed with a devoted all-purpose typist-cum-secretary-cum PA who dealt with the poet's agent, his publisher at Faber, his tax affairs and all his correspondence. In times past the PA had communicated on an antiquated typewriter but these days she was expert with computer and email. The one advance she stuck at was a mobile phone. The prospect of being constantly on tap did not suit Nan.

The poem she had been trying to coax to its conclusion had evaporated. There was never anything to be done about this so she began to attend to Nunne's correspondence.

'Was Mr Nunne ever married?' some nosy parker wished to know.

Briskly, she typed back, 'A. G. Nunne never answers personal questions.'

The next was a request for an appearance at a literary festival. 'We know that Mr Nunne dislikes making any personal appearances but we live in hope that he might make an exception for us . . .'

They never learnt! She typed back that sadly Mr Nunne never made exceptions to this rule.

A schoolchild had sent a poem, prompted by her mother, who had suggested that there was an echo in it of Mr Nunne's work. This was trickier. Nan disliked hurting any child's feelings but this approach, she suspected, was more a mother's bid for celebrity rather than any real care for her daughter's creative talent.

Nan wrote back to the child saying that she was sure Mr Nunne would be glad to learn that she liked writing poetry and that his advice would be to keep at it.

Nunne's agent had emailed wondering about a seasonal poem for the *LRB* or even the *New Yorker*.

No dice, Nan thought, and wrote, 'Mr Nunne is engaged

in a cycle of poems about geological formations at the beginnings of time and feels that there isn't much scope there for a "seasonal angle".' That should settle his hash.

In point of fact, Nan had a soft spot for A.G.'s agent, who tried to butter her up in the hope of getting to his recalcitrant client. He habitually sent her flowers on her birthday (a date concocted by Nan which she had allowed him to wheedle out of her) and presents at Christmas, which she relabelled and redistributed among her less discriminating friends.

On Friday as arranged she met Billy from school.

He came out with the rest of his class in the company of a girl. There was a giggling exchange between the two before they parted and Billy yelled after the girl as she was getting into a car, 'See you, Jose.'

'Was that the girl that was rude about you?' Nan asked.

'Yep.' It was clear that Billy wished to say no more about his enemy turned ally so Nan didn't either. 'Can we get some sweets?' he asked as they passed Geraldine's.

'You can buy some now and eat them after your dinner. Deal?'

'Deal.' Billy chose two strawberry snakes and a packet of Love Hearts and Nan bought the *Radio Times* so they could choose what films to watch.

The following morning the intercom buzzer went and the voice on the speakerphone was Billy's father's.

'We were talking about you last night,' Nan said. 'Bill and I watched *North by Northwest*. I told him it was your favourite.'

'Did you like it?' Alec asked his son.

'Don't remember.' Billy, Nan was aware, worried that he was not brainy enough for his father and mistakenly took all his father's questions as a subtle test.

'Oh, come on! You must. It was only last evening.' Disastrously, Alec ruffled his son's hair.

'To what do we owe the pleasure of your company?' Nan interceded.

'I rang Ginnie and she said Bill was here.'

It transpired that Virginia had asked Alec to look after their son for the weekend before asking Nan. Alec had said that he could and then that he couldn't. Now, it seemed, his plans had changed again. 'And I've brought you a present,' he said to Nan. 'For your birthday.'

'Her birthday was last month,' Billy pointed out.

'Better late than never,' his father said, and Nan laughed and said she was very pleased to have a present any time.

The present was a neat digital camera which Billy took over at once and began showing her how to work.

'Did you really buy this for me?' Nan wanted to know.

'Oh, I thought you and Bill could have fun with it,' Alec said. 'It's good to try new things.'

'You think I am lacking in stimulants to keep my aged brain in good nick?' But in fact she was rather touched. She didn't often get presents from Alec.

Alec turned his smile on his son. 'So, what would you like to do, William?'

Nan knew that Billy hated to be called William and that his father was doing so with a mistaken idea that it would be received as an affectionate pleasantry.

'Bill,' she said. 'You can go with Dad now, if you want.'

'Or stay here with Nan,' Alec said, confusing things. 'Up to you, old son.'

'I don't mind,' Billy said. He put the camera down.

This was Billy's default position with his father. Nan decided to take over. 'How about we all three do something together? Then you can decide if you want to go back to Dad's or stay over at mine. Either's fine by us, isn't it?'

'Sure,' her son said. He was not, she could tell, bothered either way, which made her both fond of him and want to smack him. Billy, in her view, could do with more of his father minding.

The three of them went by bus to the Natural History Museum. This had been a favourite haunt of Alec's as a child and on the way he and Billy discussed the blue whale versus the diplodocus, who had until recently occupied the privileged position in the museum's entrance hall.

'It was stuffed elephants in my day,' Nan remembered. She had been taken there once as a child by a distant relative who had escaped from Scotland to Canada; but neither her son nor her grandson was interested in the long-gone elephants of her past.

She left them inspecting the whale and made her way through to the part of the museum which had once had its own esteemed establishment and had now shrunk in the public's interests to become a mere offshoot of the more popular museum.

Nan had known it as the Geological Museum, one of the oldest science museums in the world, and she still regretted that it had been shoved in, disrespectfully she considered, with the more ostentatiously appealing exhibits from the natural world. She had often taken Alec there as a small boy to show him the strange rocks and fossils.

She found the others at lunchtime in the crowded café. They had reached, Nan was pleased to see, a comfortable plane of communication so that after lunch it was easy to say, 'Bill, if you'd like to go along with Dad after all . . .?' and for Billy to agree without fear of making a wrong choice. He was not, she was glad to see, worried about offending her.

The truth was that Nan was glad to be free to get back to her poem. The Geological Museum had done its work and yielded up a spectral form and she was at her desk when the buzzer for the door went again.

'I was just passing,' a voice she could not at first place said. 'I hope you don't mind.'

II

Blanche had never been an imaginative child. At school her efforts at writing had been limited by a conventional notion of what 'imaginative' meant. For the same reason, she was a poor liar: her few attempts had been so easily seen through that she had taken flight into what passes in the world for honesty. Her one foray into faithlessness with Ken was with a German colleague of his who had come over to discuss some joint marketing enterprise and had taken an interest in her over a dinner held by Ken's firm. The German's tone had been warm and complimentary and she had felt a tingle of excitement at the invitation to a drink at the bar of the hotel where he was staying. She had gone, nervous already, to the assignation and had fled from it once she perceived that the invitation had been issued with a view to her possibly moving on from the bar to his room. It had occasioned no untruthfulness with her husband, who had only remarked when she got in, supposedly from meeting an old schoolfriend, 'You're back early. I was just about to settle down with the football.' She had pleaded signs of a cold coming on and gone upstairs for a bath. More like cold feet, she thought later.

But with the arrival of Albert she began to feel that she had escaped from some inner confinement into new realms of possibility.

Her best friend – her only really close friend – Maggie, back from her cruise, noticed the change in her.

'You've been on a diet,' she accused, and when Blanche denied this said, 'OK, but something's different. Have you met someone?'

'No,' Blanche said, warned off by Maggie's tone. 'I thought I needed to smarten myself up a bit, that's all.'

'You've done that all right. I've never seen you in eyeliner before.'

Blanche's reformation had brought out a side of Maggie that a more experienced woman than Blanche would have recognised.

'Where d'you buy that?' she enquired when Blanche tried out the skirt she had stolen from Harvey Nicks, adding, 'It certainly shows off your legs.' Maggie's ankles were not her strong point and she preferred to wear trousers.

It was this tone of Maggie's that somehow contributed to Blanche's keeping her in ignorance of the row with Dominic and by extension her acquaintance with Nan. She could not exactly call Nan a friend; but she was someone in whom Blanche had confided.

So it was to Nan's she went on receiving the letter from the Dean's School, where Kitty was due to start in the new school year.

'I'm sorry,' Blanche said, entering Nan's flat for the second time. 'I couldn't think who else to ask.' Then noticing Billy's hoodie on the sofa, 'Oh, but you have visitors?'

'That's all right,' Nan said. 'My grandson was here but he's off with his father. It's just me for now.'

'I'm sorry,' Blanche said again. She observed the open laptop. 'Oh, were you watching something?'

Not choosing to answer, Nan went over to her laptop and closed it down. She had rescued Blanche and there is a terrible responsibility attached to helping anyone which she knew it is useless to try to escape. 'Tea?' she asked.

'Yes, please. I love your tea.'

'As I said, it's only PG Tips.' Nan disapproved of this middle-class enthusiasm for perfectly ordinary culinary tastes.

'Does your grandson like being with his father?' Blanche felt she should ask as Nan presented her with a mug of tea and a plate of biscuits.

'I expect so,' Nan said.

'I was terrified of mine.'

'Ah well,' Nan, who didn't much care, said. 'That's a shame.'

'Did you like your father?'

'I didn't have a father,' Nan said shortly. 'Or not one you could speak to. What's up?'

Blanche explained about the Dean's School and the fees.

'What's wrong with the local comprehensive?'

'I don't know,' Blanche said. 'I don't know anything about the local comprehensive. It's never come up as a possibility.'

Nan bit into a ginger biscuit and chewed. 'Where do they live?'

Blanche said they lived in Teddington and Nan went over to her computer.

'There's two comprehensives in their area. Both got Ofsted excellent at the last report – not that that means much. Might do her good to go there. It'd certainly do her parents good.'

'You mean . . .?' Blanche felt a little frightened.

'I mean why not say you find you can't manage the fees, or whatever gloss you want to put on it.'

'But that's punishing them.'

'Yes,' Nan said. 'In a way. But it's also teaching them that things they do and things they say have consequences. It's amazing how few people see that. Bet you gave them money to buy their house.'

Blanche found she was blushing. 'It was Ken's money, really.'

'Well, I don't know about your husband,' Nan said, 'but Terry and I shared what we had. One pot between us. No question as to who earned it.'

'Oh, no,' Blanche said. 'I mean, yes. Ken would never have thought of it as only his money.' She wondered as she said this if that were quite true.

'Anyway,' Nan said. 'I bet one of the things your daughter-in-law has against you is your helping them out with their house. It takes a generous spirit to receive generosity graciously.' She went on scrolling down the information on the laptop. 'The university entrance for one of their local comps is in the top fifteen per cent in the country. I doubt the whatsit school is up there, is it?'

'The Dean's,' Blanche said. 'But it's Kitty. I would never ever want to hurt Kitty.'

'Who's to say you'll be hurting her?' Nan asked.

'She'd be going to the Dean's School with all her friends. At least I think so.' Tina had made much of this.

'She'll make new friends,' Nan said. 'And we're all on our own in the end. What's she like?'

79

Blanche considered her granddaughter. 'She's a sweetie. Very kind. Very giving and quite funny, actually.'

'Funny as in making folk laugh?'

'Yes. She makes me laugh anyway.'

'Oh well, then,' Nan said. 'If she makes folk laugh, she'll do fine at the comp if they can get her in. Kids like other kids who make them laugh.'

'But would she get in?' Blanche wondered. She was both frightened and excited at the boldness of Nan's proposal. 'It's terribly late. All the school places are settled.'

'Well,' Nan said, 'it's not my problem but if it were me I'd write and say I was wondering whether I wanted to cough up for the fees after all so maybe they should research the local comprehensives. When they've done that you can make a decision.'

'But Kitty,' Blanche almost wailed. 'I don't want her to think I'm punishing her.'

'And you think they'll make her think that?'

'Yes,' Blanche said. 'And I would be, wouldn't I?'

'If it were me,' Nan said again, 'I'd go and meet Kitty and explain. If the lass is all you say she is she'll understand. Children understand better than people give them credit for. I know I did.'

12

Blanche had dressed carefully in her stolen blue silk shirt to meet Kitty after school. She had chosen a day when she knew Kitty would not be met by anyone else. Sometimes when she worked from home her mother came to meet her to take her swimming with Harry. But today was Harry's violin lesson and Kitty either walked home alone or went back to a schoolfriend's.

'Granny!' Kitty called rapturously. She ran and buried her face in the silk shirt. 'Granny!' she said again. 'I've *missed* you.'

'I've missed you too, darling,' Blanche said. She was crying but that didn't seem to matter.

'Where've you been? Mummy and Daddy said you were "busy". You smell lovely.'

'I'll explain,' Blanche said. 'Look, I've got the car here. When are you expected home?'

Kitty said she'd been going round to her friend Faith's but Faith was off sick so she was planning to walk home and let herself in.

'OK,' Blanche said. 'How about we have tea somewhere and then I drive you home?'

'Can I have hot chocolate?'

'Of course,' Blanche said, ready to give her granddaughter the Taj Mahal if she took a fancy to that.

They had tea at Caffè Nero. Kitty's favourite. 'They do the best hot choc,' she declared.

'Darling girl, you have a chocolate moustache. This tea isn't nearly so nice as the tea I have at my friend Nan's.'

Blanche had decided to tell Kitty about Nan. Nan had also counselled her to tell Kitty about the row with her parents. 'She'll have picked it up anyway,' Nan said. 'They do. They don't say necessarily but they take it all in.'

Nan, it appeared, was right. 'I knew something had happened because I heard Mummy and Daddy talking about it,' Kitty said. 'I wasn't snooping.'

'I don't care if you were,' Blanche said, on whom a tinge of Nan's philosophy had begun to rub off. 'It's quite normal to want to know what your parents are saying. Especially when it concerns you.'

This prompted further confidences from Kitty. 'I heard them say they didn't want us coming to you because you drink. But you don't drink, do you, Granny?'

'I do sometimes, darling, when I'm nervous. But I shouldn't when I'm driving you and Harry.'

'But you weren't drunk with us. Harry didn't mean to say . . .'

'I know he didn't, sweetheart. It's . . .' She floundered a little, wondering what Nan would say. 'It's complicated,' she rather feebly finished. Nan would never resort to that kind of fluff.

Kitty ran her finger round the mug, catching up traces of cream. 'Aren't we going to have sleepovers at yours any more?'

'Maybe not for a while.'

Kitty looked at her with earnest grey eyes. 'They're silly,' she said. 'Don't cry, Granny. They're just silly. I told Faith. She says so. She likes you.'

'She doesn't know me!' Blanche laughed.

'I tell her about you.'

'Thank you, darling,' Blanche said. 'I'm flattered. But listen, there's something, it's complicated, but I want to tell you.'

Kitty listened attentively as Blanche tried to explain her predicament. 'Tell it to her straight,' Nan had advised and if not quite 'straight' in a Nan kind of way nevertheless Blanche was more candid than she was used to being.

'You mean you don't want to pay for me to go to the Dean's?' Kitty asked when her grandmother had finished.

'It's not exactly that I don't "want"–' Blanche was beginning but was interrupted by a Kitty with wide pleading eyes.

'That's *great*, Granny. I don't want to go either. Faith's going to St Anselm's and I'm *desperate* to go too.'

'St Anselm's?' This was not one of the schools Nan had found on her laptop.

'It's the Catholic comprehensive but they take non-Catholics. Faith isn't a Catholic either but her mum says, well, it's her mum's boyfriend, really, and he knows because his daughter went there. He says it's quieter than the other comprehensives and there's a good atmosphere, he says, and they're quite strict. And I don't want to be posh. Faith doesn't either. Oh please, Granny, say you won't give them the money for the Dean's. Please *please* . . .'

'It's outrageous,' Tina Carrington was saying to her husband. 'She can't just pull the plug like that. It isn't fair.'

'Well, she can and she has,' her husband countered. He had privately sent his mother a text with an expletive which he was now regretting – although he excused himself that it was after all a reasonable response given the string of expletives he had received from her on his answerphone.

'It's your father's money. Ken would be livid.'

'It's hers now. And she says . . .' Blanche's son read again the letter his mother had written. She had eschewed email and written it in by hand in ink so that it would seem more definitive to her son and daughter-in-law but more crucially to herself. He had hardly been able to believe what he read the first time round. 'She says here, "As it is my money, I think I can do as I like with it and for the time being I do not think I like the idea of the Dean's School. I'm sorry if this is an inconvenience."' Blanche had ripped up three efforts at writing this letter and had had to stiffen her nerve to cut out an apologetic 'terrible' 'horrible' and 'dreadful' with regard to 'inconvenience'.

'"Inconvenience"!' Tina was beside herself. 'It's vindictive. It's obviously revenge for what we said about her not seeing the children. And it's taking it out on Kitty, who's supposed to be her "darling".'

'It's not like her,' Blanche's son reflected. 'I wonder what's got into her?' He had not told his wife about his mother's abusive late-night call and had tried – almost successfully until now – to erase it from his mind.

'Have you tackled her?'

Her husband looked uneasy. 'I sent her a text.'

'And . . .?'

'She texted back that she was, well, that was her decision.'

He had in fact had a cool response containing no kiss.

'It's pure aggression,' his wife decided. 'I always knew your mother was fantastically aggressive. It was just hidden under that ever-so-polite "I'm such a terribly *nice* person" manner.'

Dominic offered no audible response to this. He was feeling that he had been wise not to report his mother's violent call, which had included some vicious analysis of his wife's fondness for money. It had frightened him and left him wondering how he and his mother were ever going to patch things up or find each other again.

Half-term

13

The book festival that Minna and Rose planned to attend was held in Oxford, which was a coach ride away. Elizabeth Pattern, much-loved author and former Children's Laureate, attracted large audiences and to be sure of getting good seats Minna had suggested an early start. She was dressed and ready when Rose arrived.

'Mum gave me five pounds to buy books with,' she said, arranging the toys. There were old alliances and factions among them which required a degree of apartheid in Rose's absence. 'But I should think Elizabeth Pattern's new book's more than that.'

'I dare say we can find the balance somewhere,' Minna said, pleased to be able to contribute to the sum of Rose's happiness.

'Her new book's called *The Lilac House*. Like the Lilac Fairy.'

(In the past, they had discussed this fairy and Minna had told Rose that she was also called the Mauve Fairy.

'What's "mauve"?' Rose had asked.

'An old-fashioned name for lilac.'

'Lilac sounds nicer,' Rose had judged.)

On the coach they ate the peanut-butter sandwiches Rose's mother had packed for lunch. 'We aren't allowed them at school,' Rose said, 'cos of nut allergies. They're my favourite.'

'It doesn't matter if we eat them all now,' Minna said, happy to see Rose wolfing them down. 'We can buy more there or we can go out to eat. There'll be plenty of places in Oxford.'

Elizabeth Pattern was due to speak in the Sheldonian, the building with the soap-bubble dome that stands shoulder to shoulder with the ancient and imposing Bodleian Library. Rose and Minna felt shy standing in the queue to be let in.

'Is that really a library?' Rose asked of the Bodleian. 'It's not very like our one.'

Rose and Minna's local library was now housed in a poky cabin with plastic windows and its opening hours had been reduced to one day a week.

'It's very old,' Minna said, feeling daunted by all this grandeur.

But the talk wasn't at all daunting. Elizabeth Pattern was as sympathetic in person as her books. A slight woman in jeans and trainers, she charmed the audience with her warm and funny talk. She explained how she had only become a writer because of a librarian who had recommended books to her – there had been no books, she told them, at home. 'When people ask me how I became a writer, I tell them by reading. Reading is really all you need to learn anything – anything in the world.'

'I'm going to be a writer,' Rose decided as they waited in the queue to buy *The Lilac House* and have it signed.

Elizabeth Pattern's fans were loyal, the queue stretched down a corridor and it was more than twenty-five minutes before they were even close to the table where the author sat, pen at hand, waiting to sign her books for her excited readers. Finally, there was only one girl and her mother ahead of Minna and Rose and there were still three copies left.

'Look,' Minna nudged Rose. 'One for the little girl in front, one for you and one for the girl behind. The Lilac Fairy has arranged it all for us.'

But the Lilac Fairy had not bargained for the girl ahead in the queue. 'I want all three copies,' she announced in a clear confident tone.

The bookseller looked awkward and glanced over at Rose and the girl behind her.

'Maybe just get one, Octavia,' the girl's mother said. 'We can get other copies when it's out.'

'No, I need three,' the girl announced. 'I've got the money.' She opened a bag, got out a leather wallet and extracted three ten-pound notes. She pushed them towards the bookseller. 'There.' Ignoring the change, she moved across to the table where Elizabeth Pattern was sitting.

'I'm –'

'Yes, I heard your name,' the author said. She poured water from a jug into a glass. 'Octavia. Are you named for a Roman emperor's wife?'

The girl looked blank. 'I don't think so. Can you put "To Octavia, who will one day be a writer"?'

'Please,' the girl's mother added.

'Please,' the girl repeated. She waited smiling.

'Well, I don't think I can write that,' Elizabeth Pattern said. 'Perhaps you will be a writer, who knows. But you see I can only write what I know; and I don't know that.' She smiled back at the girl and Rose, who had been trying not to cry, saw that the smile was not an encouraging one.

Unused to opposition, Octavia pressed on. 'Can you sign your name in all the books?'

The famous author again smiled the ambiguous smile. 'I think maybe one's enough. I'll sign my name in this one.' She did so and turned her face, effectively dismissing Octavia. 'I'm so sorry the books ran out,' she called over to Rose. 'It's very annoying when they do and however much I warn them to get in enough copies they never listen. But if you give me your address, I'll send you a signed copy. How's that?'

'Oh,' Rose said. 'I'll give you the money.' She hurried forward with the five-pound note that her mother had given her and its fellow from Minna.

'No,' Elizabeth Pattern said. 'You've had a disappointment, so this is on me. You too,' she said to the girl behind Rose, who had been sobbing noisily. 'You give me your address too and I shall see you get a signed book. Now tell me, both of you, your names.'

'She's a lady, your Elizabeth Pattern,' Minna said.

They had found their way to the Ashmolean and were eating orange and almond cake in the cafe. Museums had the best cake, they decided.

'D'you think she *will* send the book?' Rose asked. It seemed to her incredible that so celebrated an author could possibly remember her.

'I'm sure she will.' Minna was confident. She had caught Elizabeth Pattern's eye during the drama of the dwindling book pile and had been rewarded by a sense that her own opinion of Octavia was shared by the famous author. 'She knew how you were feeling. That's what makes her a good writer.'

14

'For God's sake, Alec!' Nan said. 'This is bloody irresponsible.'

Her son knew to agree with this. 'Uh-huh,' he offered, and waited for the rebuke.

'You did this the last bank holiday, in case you've forgotten. Do you feel it's OK to let your son down whenever your own plans change?'

'I didn't. I came to find him at yours, if you remember?' Long before he read law Alec had been schooled at home in hard dispute. 'It's a key witness who I can only see today because he's only in the UK for twenty-four hours. It's a huge case. Two Lithuanian business moguls, both rich as Croesus, both claiming the same strip of totally worthless tribal territory.'

Nan had heard this line too often. 'I suppose you want me to have him instead.'

'If you don't mind. Only Gin has something already fixed with her yoga pals.'

'You know I never "mind".' Nan, who found this jocular shortening of Virginia's name annoying because it conveyed a false notion of Alec's intimacy with his former wife, was now properly irritated. 'It's Billy who might. He needs his dad.'

'He loves being with you. You know that.'

Nan did know it. But she was disappointed in her son.

In the past she had talked this disappointment over with his father. 'How did he grow up so damn thoughtless, Terry? What did we do wrong?' But Terry had gone and it was not the kind of conversation she cared to conduct on Skype.

'Dad said we could go to Oxford to see the shrunken heads,' Billy told her when she rang to arrange their Saturday.

'What shrunken heads?'

'In the Pitt Rivers Museum, Dad said. He said we could get the tube there.'

About to expostulate that his dad needed his head examining, Nan realised that this was the Oxford Tube – the coach that usefully runs between London and Oxford.

'That might be all right,' she conceded. 'Tell your mum I'll be round nine o'clock sharp to pick you up.' And 'Make sure you bring a coat,' she added. Billy had the child's common oblivion to cold.

The Pitt Rivers was holding a half-term children's event so that when Nan and Billy entered the place was jam-packed. Numerous stalls were offering insights into the environment: the uses of bats' hearing in aeronautics, patterns of swallow migration and ice flow, the potential energy sources of tidal rivers and recycled sewerage – 'Let's hope not together!' Nan observed – were all being demonstrated to children brought by their socially minded parents to have their consciousnesses raised.

Billy ignored the clarion calls to aid the environment. 'I want to see the shrunken heads,' he insisted. He and Nan battled through the crowd to a lower part of the museum which was closely packed with cases crammed with exotic exhibits from far-flung regions of the world.

'The heads'll be here,' Billy said, pleased.

They wandered about examining the contents of glass cabinets containing weirdly painted masks, necklaces made of seeds and worrying-looking teeth, tired-looking grass skirts, shields, bows and arrows, funeral urns and countless amulets to help the passing soul into a later life – but no shrunken heads. Nan, suspecting that the heads were an invention of Alec's, began to feel anxious and annoyed.

Billy was becoming agitated so she applied for help from a friendly-looking couple. 'The heads are over in the middle there, by the drums,' the man said. 'But I think that they are really the skulls of monkeys.' He winked at Nan.

That was Nan's view too when they at last located the cabinet with the pathetic-looking dried-leather-skin death masks taut over fragile skulls.

Luckily, Billy was quite satisfied. 'They magicked them,' he explained, taking custodial possession of the grisly specimens. 'They killed their enemies and magicked them like that, so all their strength went into their own selves.'

The woman of the couple, who was interested to see how the heads went down, smiled at Nan. She felt some pity for the little old lady landed with her rather uncouth grandson.

'Can we take a picture?' Billy asked.

Nan handed him the camera and he took a dozen photos of the heads from different angles.

'Would you like me to take one of the two of you?' the helpful woman asked.

'No, thanks,' Nan said. She moved abruptly aside.

'She doesn't like them,' Billy explained. 'She thinks it takes your soul away.'

With the orange and almond cake inside them Minna and Rose felt ready for the Ashmolean's trove of treasures. There was too much to take in on one visit – a dozen would hardly do it – so they settled on exploring the ground floor. They meandered through the ancient Greeks and Romans and came to the Chinese gallery.

'Look at that,' Minna said. She pointed out an exhibit resembling a deposit of melted wax from some massive burnt-out candle.

'*A Yellow Scholar's Rock*,' Rose read. 'What is it?'

Minna read the notice aloud. '*A scholar's rock is a naturally formed stone. Such stones were used to adorn a scholar's desk and represented mountains, while acting as indoor versions of the magnificent natural stones installed in the gardens and palaces.* It's the Tang dynasty,' she went on. 'AD 618–907. What was happening here then, I wonder?'

Rose said she didn't know and could they go and look at the Egyptian mummies because at school they'd learnt that the Egyptians mummified cats so they could take them with them into the afterlife and Gemma White, who had seen some in the British Museum, said they looked cute.

'*In the Tang dynasty (AD 618–907) a set of four principal qualities for scholar's stones were developed,*' Nan read out. '*Thinness, openness, perforations and wrinkling.*'

'What's "perforations"?' Billy asked. They too had eaten

at the café in the Ashmolean and were feeling restored after the Pitt Rivers scrum.

'Try to work it out. It doesn't do to expect answers from other people for all your questions.' Nan had also stopped by the scholar's rock and she had been taken by its qualities of thinness, openness, perforation and wrinkling. She dug out Alec's camera and took some pictures.

'It's useful, this,' she said to Billy. 'I'd never have thought of getting one for myself. Remind me to tell your dad.'

Billy was staring at the yellow convolutions resting on the carved-wood stand. It looked to him like a waxwork of someone's intestines. There were twists and turns, waterfalls and tunnels. 'Does "perforations" mean holes?'

'Well done,' Nan said. 'See, you know more than you think.'

'That's the trouble with schooling,' she suggested later. They were on the coach home and Billy was looking through the book she had bought at the museum shop about the Tang dynasty. 'School teaches you to rely on what other people tell you. The trouble is they're either liable to tell you all wrong or stop you from finding out for yourself.'

'But I have to go to school,' Billy said. It didn't seem to him fair to have to hear this and still go to be taught all wrong.

'I know,' Nan said. 'It's hard. But there are other things you learn there.'

'Like?'

'Like getting along with other people.'

Or learning how to lie, she thought but did not say,

looking at her 'dyslexic' grandson, who appeared now to be engrossed in the other book she had bought about the Silk Road.

There was a picture of a glazed pottery figurine of a horse. Billy liked horses. And he was liking the thought of them bearing saddlebags of precious silks, their hooves pounding the dusty trail, their turbaned riders, daggers at the ready, on the lookout for brigands and thieves.

15

Wrung out by the excitement of meeting her favourite author and the exhaustion that is brought on by any visit to a museum, Rose slept on the coach all the way back from Oxford. Minna tenderly observed her charge's blooming young face relaxed in sleep, her mouth slightly open making a whisper of a snore. From time to time an overwhelming pressure of love obliged Minna to gently stroke the girl's gleaming hair or wipe the thread of saliva from the corner of her mouth.

Frank had suggested that if it meant so much to her Minna should move up to Glasgow too. But Minna knew this wouldn't work. It was too great a move on her part for a child who was not a blood connection, she reflected. It would look odd and 'odd' easily turned to something more sinister in the world's eyes. 'Odd' would in time make Rose uncomfortable. Better to suffer the pain of separation.

She and Rose walked home from the coach stop along the roadside, holding hands against the menace of passing cars. The cold start to the day had given way to a balmy warmth and the evening was still light. In the ditches beside them the massed cow-parsley umbels made traceries of ghostly lace against the dark hedgerows. One or two stars had made a faint but palely exquisite appearance in the blue-lilac sky. There will be other nights, Minna thought, but this particular night in all its beauty won't ever come again.

Her thoughts returned to the author Elizabeth Pattern and her kindness towards the disappointed girls. She had looked into the writer's eyes and seen sadness there. Was it sadness that made people kind – or was it that kind people were more liable to sadness?

The toys were just as Rose had left them when they reached Minna's hut. For all that, she knew they had been larking about.

'Hello, toys,' she said. 'Did you have fun?'

The toys said nothing, keeping their own counsel.

'We did,' Rose said. 'We met a famous author and she's going to send me her book herself. What shall we read tonight?' she asked Minna.

How about *The Children Who Lived in a Barn*? Minna suggested. This was an old book which an enterprising small press had republished. Minna was not quite aware that her reason for liking this story was that in it the parents go off and abandon their children, leaving them to cope alone.

Up in Glasgow Rose's mother was getting ready for bed. A medley of estate agents' property particulars was spread about the hotel room.

'I like the one with the big garden,' she advised her husband. 'But it needs a lot of work.'

Her husband was inwardly dealing with a particularly nasty text from Emma. 'Right.'

'But then there was the smaller one, you know, with the monkey puzzle and the little brick outhouse, near the

Botanical Gardens. We could build on to the footprint of the outhouse without planning permission, the agent said.'

'Mmm.'

'The agent said it's not a problem taking down the monkey puzzle. We'll certainly get a lot for our money up here.'

'Sure.'

'What did you think? The Botanical Gardens is better pollution-wise.'

'Mmm.'

'Are you listening to me?'

'I'm trying to deal with a problem at work.' Her husband allowed himself to vent what he felt was understandable irritation.

'It's a bank holiday. How can there be a problem at work?'

'No rest for the wicked,' her husband said with a certain pertinence. Emma was threatening to reveal their affair. This could easily affect his promotion and he was wondering if he should anticipate this and maybe drop a hint to his boss that she was a little unhinged.

'I think on balance the bigger house is better,' his wife decided. 'It's work but it'll be a better investment.' A thought struck. 'We could convert the basement as a granny flat for mum. What do you think?'

Her husband, who thought this idea frankly appalling, knew better than to say so. 'Will she want to be so far from her friends?'

'Oh. Mum is very flexible,' her daughter assured him.

'Right,' her husband said. If a lifetime of meeting her mother's self-centred intransigence had not persuaded her daughter of the falseness of this judgement, he wasn't going to argue about it now.

'And she can bring the dogs. What do you think?'

'How about the schools?' he hastily threw in: 'The one near the Botanical Gardens had better schools, I thought.'

His wife reviewed the agents' details again. 'You might be right,' she said, pleased that her husband was at last giving thought to the move. 'I wonder how Rosie is getting on. D'you think I should ring?'

'I wouldn't,' her husband advised. 'She'll probably be asleep. Least said soonest mended,' he added, unconsciously giving himself advice over what best to do about Emma.

'What *are* you talking about?' his wife asked. 'Least said soonest mended? What's that supposed to mean?'

'Let sleeping dogs lie, I meant.'

'That's not a very nice way to talk about your daughter.'

Bloody bitch, her husband was thinking. What a bloody idiot he was to get mixed up with a bitch like Emma Stratton. 'I was thinking more of the old what's-her-face.'

'Minna.'

'What kind of name's Minna anyway?' her husband asked.

'How would I know?' his wife said. 'What's got into you? Why are you in this mood?'

Rose was not asleep. She was cocooned in a sleeping bag on the upper bunk in the shepherd's hut. 'Tell me again how you came to be Minna,' she called down.

'You've heard that a hundred times.'

'I know. I like it.'

'Will I put out the light then or do you want to keep it on?'

Rose considered. At home she always slept with her light on beside her bed but with Minna so close it felt safe to be in the dark.

'I don't mind it being off because you're here.'

'You've your torch if you need it.'

Rose tested the torch that Minna had put by her pillow. She swept the beam around the hut on to the bank of toys. 'Night night, toys, sleep tight. Minna's going to tell us a true story.'

'It was like this . . .' Minna began.

Minna's uncle Willem had been a member of the Dutch resistance during the war. Her father had come to England in search of work but his younger brother had stayed behind. When Willem was shot by the Nazis his elder brother suffered the notorious guilt of the survivor, the more so as he felt he had not been sufficiently ardent in persuading his brother to come to England at the outbreak of war. He had planned to call their first child, if a boy, William, after his brother, but when a girl was born, he suggested Wilhelmina after the doughty Dutch queen who had abdicated that year and who had been a staunch ally of the Dutch resistance.

'"Wilhelmina"'s a bit of a mouthful,' his wife had said doubtfully, cradling her tiny baby close. 'And it sounds German,' she added. 'She might get called a Hun at school.'

'They shorten it there to Minna,' her husband had said.

'And so,' Minna concluded, 'that is how I got my name.'

'After a queen,' Rose said contentedly. Like most children she was a natural royalist. 'I wish I was called after a queen.'

'You're named after a flower,' Minna said. 'The flower of England. To be named for a flower is much better than for an old queen.'

16

Blanche awoke on the first morning of the half-term to a glaring prospect of nothingness. Before the row there had been plans for Kitty and Harry to stay. A blast of white blossom, May's parody of snow, shot past her bedroom window as she looked out. Cold. Unseasonably so. The mood of the day chimed depressingly with the state of her heart.

Her first impulse was to ring Nan. But she held back; there had been that slight irritation when she had called round unasked over the question of Kitty's school fees. There was Maggie – but Maggie's company had palled and her other friends all had families to be with. But then, savingly, there was Albert.

'I'd love to,' she found herself saying when Maggie rang later with a suggestion of a film. 'But I have something on.'

'What?'

'An old friend I said I'd meet.'

'Which old friend?' Maggie was familiar with all Blanche's so-called friends and was aware that the list was not long.

'Someone I knew years ago as a child in France,' Blanche said, surprising herself with the smoothness of her reply.

'Get you, with your mystery foreign lover.' Maggie waited,

expecting to be corrected, and when she wasn't an atmosphere of annoyance became almost palpable to Blanche at the other end of the line. 'Who is he? Go on, tell.'

'He's called Albert,' Blanche said and before Maggie could ask, 'He's a gardener.'

'You mean he does over people's gardens?' Maggie was prepared for indulgent scorn for this probable has-been whom Blanche had rashly acquired.

'He runs a garden centre,' Blanche said. 'Rather a successful one, actually, near Orléans.'

Orléans was where her grandmother had told her a supposed ancestor of theirs had once held court. She could see Albert's garden centre, housed in the stables of her ancestor's chateau. She conjured a picture of herself there, treading with bare feet paths of fragrant chamomile to a bower of briar roses where green-fingered Albert waited for her in his workman's *bleu de travail*.

She turned to consider the dress she would be wearing. A long green-and-white silk dress, she decided. More green than white, maybe, like the chamomile.

The dropping of the tradition of the children staying with their grandmother over the May half-term was proving something of a nuisance for Dominic and Tina. They had planned for themselves a little trip away. After some phoning around Harry had gone grumblingly to Tina's brother's ex, who had a boy Harry's age. Kitty, easier to place, was staying at her friend Faith's.

'It's not fair,' Kitty was saying. 'I'm the only one in our class who hasn't got a phone.'

'I've got two,' Faith said. 'You can have one of mine.'

'Really?'

'I've got the pay-as-you-go my dad gave me and my mum's boyfriend just gave me the new iPhone.'

'That's so unfair!'

'It's to get in with me. He thinks I can be bought.' Faith laughed a cynical laugh. 'Men are so dumb.'

Kitty wondered if she could be bought and suspected that she could be. 'Do you want any money for it?' she asked. She hoped the answer would be no. Faith's mum's boyfriend was generous and Faith was a practised beneficiary.

'You can lend me your angora jumper with the flamingos for it.'

Kitty said Faith could keep the jumper. 'It suits you better than me.'

'You're kind,' Faith said. 'I wish I was kind.'

'Oh but you are,' Kitty felt bound to protest; but she was aware her friend lived on an altogether superior plane.

Already alive to life's shortcomings, Faith's shrewd brown eyes looked out at life without illusion. 'I'm not,' she averred. 'I'm smart, me. Your family's different,' pity made her add. Poor Kitty was rationed severely as to TV and pocket money and bedtimes. 'I expect you were brought up kind,' she added generously.

'Yes,' Kitty said uncertainly. She wasn't sure how kind her mother was. Her grandmother, when she met her that time, had been in tears.

Though Blanche had weaned herself off excessive alcohol, the shoplifting had persisted. She was rather good at it, she found – you might call it an accomplishment. It was for Albert nowadays that she prowled the stores, her eyes peeled for pickings designed to impress and allure.

She was in Peter Jones when her phone blared out the tune that Kitty had selected for her. It was not one she liked but she kept it because it was a link with Kitty.

The phone was displaying an unfamiliar number. As a rule, she would have ignored an anonymous call but some instinct made her answer.

'Granny!'

'Kitten child. Whose phone is this?'

'Guess.'

'Not yours?'

'My friend gave it to me.'

'And what do your parents think?'

'They don't know. Granny, where are you? We thought we'd come and find you.'

'Who's we?'

'Me and Faith. She really wants to go shopping. But you and me could have lunch. Where are you?'

'I'm at Peter Jones in Sloane Square,' Blanche said. Excitement made her tremble.

There were sounds of a discussion at the other end and then Kitty came back on the phone. 'Faith says that's easy-peasy. We can get a train to Kew and the District line from there. We'll be there in about half an hour, forty minutes max, Faith says. I'll text when we're near.'

Blanche began to say 'How did you remember my number . . .?' but Kitty had rung off.

So far, the day's only contraband was a silk camisole. Blanche made her way to the ladies' cloakroom, where she took off her blouse. The vest she had been wearing looked grubby. She pulled it off, slid the camisole over her head and dropped the vest into the waste bin. There would be time before Kitty arrived to have her face made up in one of the complimentary makeovers offered by the competing cosmetic houses. Kitty would want her grand-mother to put on her best face for her friend.

'Is that her?' Faith asked as Kitty waved and shouted at a tall blonde woman standing outside Peter Jones.

Kitty, proud of her grandmother's elegant appearance, agreed that it was.

'Wow,' Faith said. 'She looks like she could've been a model.'

Faith continued to be impressed when Blanche asked if the girls would like lunch and made no demur when they chose all the things currently warned against as dangers to their health.

'Don't you mind what she eats?' she asked Blanche as Kitty went to the counter for a second chocolate short-bread.

Blanche looked vague. 'Well, for a treat . . .'

'She's cool,' Faith said approvingly when they were back on the tube. Blanche had bought both girls socks and T-shirts and had encouraged them to sample various cosmetics. Faith was still wearing Experimental, a lipstick by Chanel, and Kitty's cheeks were rosy with blusher.

Kitty felt relief. Faith was one of those natural arbiters of taste, born into the world to set standards among their peers, uncompromising in their verdicts, the terror of the doubtful and socially insecure. To be approved of by Faith, even at a remove, was to have arrived.

'Can I say you gave me this T-shirt?' she asked. 'Only my mum will ask how I got it.'

Faith nodded. She had long ago assessed the double-dyed hypocrisy of most adults and was protective of those children – the majority – who had yet to see through their elders and so-called betters. 'Why doesn't she like your grandma?'

Kitty shrugged. Her thoughts on this matter were complicated and even to herself she was not ready to expose them. 'Stuff.'

'It's because your grandma's got style,' Faith decided. 'Your mum's jealous. It'll be that.'

'Maybe,' Kitty said, unwilling to be disloyal to her mother. Privately, she suspected the jealousy was about something other than looks – something she hadn't yet words for.

17

Billy had spent the night at Nan's after their trip to Oxford. He slept, as always, on a mattress beside her bed in case of nightmares so that if need be he could slip in beside her and snuggle up. The nightmares were few but, in any case, he always climbed into her bed first thing.

They had their ritual tea and biscuits while they discussed plans.

'My coffin's being delivered today,' Nan told him.

'Good thing I'm here then.'

Owing to a mix-up made by the delivery company, there had been a delay with this. 'The lady who got yours instead of the one she'd ordered went nuclear,' Charmian, who had grown matey over this muddle, confided to Nan over the phone.

Nan, who was curious about this other customer's coffin, only remarked that death took people that way and there was no hurry.

They had washed up breakfast and Billy was constructing a cable car from a baked-bean can when the buzzer sounded.

Nan listened through the crackle to a man's voice. 'The coffin's here,' she informed Billy. 'Go down and give him a hand up the stairs, pet. He's complaining it won't fit in the lift.'

Billy disappeared and reappeared a little later backwards

through the front door. Issuing directions to his fellow bearer, he guided the more-than-life-size package through to Nan's sitting room.

The delivery man at the other end of this manoeuvre deposited his cargo with a soundless whistle. 'Glad I've finally got that to the right destination. Last port of call hit the roof.'

Billy was already undoing the bubble wrap.

'That a coffin?' the man asked. 'Looks more like an out-size laundry basket. Sorry, no offence meant,' he added, perhaps recollecting the casket's destined purpose.

'It's for her.' Billy nodded towards Nan. 'She's going to lie in it.'

'Trying it out?' the man said. He had the air of someone with time on his hands who might like to stay and watch the fun.

Nan gave him two pounds for his trouble and shooed him out. Together she and Billy examined the coffin.

'He's right,' Nan said. 'It does look like a laundry basket.' She stepped in and lay down.

'It fits OK,' Billy said. 'And there's room for pillows.' He wanted to be reassured that they hadn't made a bad choice.

'It fits a treat,' Nan assured him. 'It's quite cosy.' She lay there trying to imagine what it might be like to lie beneath the cold earth, eyes, ears, nostrils, all life's portals stopped with dank clay. Easier to imagine the willow basket as an adjunct to her sitting room. 'It'll look grand with cushions,' she decided. 'We did well, Bill.'

Billy had shown Nan how to print out photos from her camera and had gone home well pleased with his prints of the shrunken heads. The picture Nan had taken in the Ashmolean of the scholar's rock now stood on her desk, propped beside the only surviving image of her grandmother, a smudgy black-and-white crinkle-edged snapshot of her holding a baby Nan, bound like tiny white mummy, in the crook of her arm. The rock was not unlike her grandmother with its qualities of thinness, perforation and wrinkling. Perhaps not the openness, though.

The poem Blanche had interrupted was finished and Nan had settled down in solitary peace to make a new start. For some while she had had it in mind to write a long poem – an epic maybe. If everything that can happen will happen, she had concluded, then it was all a matter of Time.

She sat studying the scholar's rock and its strange folds. Quite suddenly, clear as day, she saw the figure of a man: a man in long robes, his face, old as time, yellow and wrinkled. A sage. A Chinese sage, his terrain the scholar's rock.

The man stood on one of the rock's plateaus looking out. He stared without visible emotion but it seemed to Nan that he had observed her and was dispassionately taking her in. After a while he sat down, limberly crossing his legs, lowered his gaze and appeared to retire within himself.

She blinked and he was gone. But he'll be back, she thought. It's his rock.

18

Blanche was so buoyed up by her visit from Kitty and her friend that she decided to walk home. She escorted the girls to Sloane Square tube and then set off round the back of Peter Jones towards South Ken.

After a while she was conscious of footsteps following her. At first she took them as no more than another pedestrian with a quick pace but the footsteps sounded to be gaining on her and she began to feel faintly oppressed. She slowed to allow whoever this was to overtake her but instead a hand fell on her shoulder.

'Excuse me,' a man's voice said.

Blanche turned, ready to run or hit him with her handbag, but he only tightened his grip.

'Excuse me,' he said again.

'I'm sorry . . .?' Blanche said questioningly.

'I think you have something in your bag, madam,' the man said. He stared at her with hard grey eyes.

This was certainly disturbing. Blanche felt she was going pale. 'I'm sorry . . .?' she said again, tentative this time.

'You took something from Peter Jones,' the man said. 'I saw you put it in your bag.'

Blanche, now thoroughly frightened, scrabbled for her wits. 'I have no idea what you are talking about. You are welcome to inspect my bag.' She opened it, her fingers trembling, to show him the contents: a purse, a wallet, a comb displaying embarrassing stray hairs, glasses and a make-up bag.

The man made a cursory inspection of the bag. 'You've got it on you then. I know the tricks of your trade. I could make you come with me to the police.'

'Oh don't,' Blanche pleaded. 'Please don't.'

To her surprise the man relaxed his frown. 'Normally, I would. I was going to nick you in the store. I was only watching to see what else you'd take. Then I saw you with those girls. Nice girls. I didn't want to shame you in front of them and now my shift's over.' The grey eyes had become more human. 'To be honest with you, I don't care what you take from them. Call themselves a co-operative? All my Aunt Fanny.'

Blanche was sweating so copiously that she was sure the large wet patches she felt under her arms must be showing through her coat. Her legs felt as if they might give way. She reached out and touched the man's sleeve.

'Thank you. Honestly, I don't know why I do it.'

'Greed mainly, isn't it, if we're being honest?' her nemesis suggested. 'Mind you, it takes spirit too. I couldn't myself. I'd be too frit.'

'I was too,' Blanche said. 'Frit – scared, I mean – of being caught.'

The man laughed. 'Not so's I noticed. Cool as a cucumber you were. You had that wee vestie thing off its hanger and into your pocket before you could say "Jack Robinson". I watched you slip it into your bag, sly as anything, before you went off into the Ladies. I can't follow folk in there but don't count on it next time. Young Sheila who took over from me today, she'd be in there after you like a bloodhound.'

Blanche thanked her lucky stars that her raid on the lingerie department had not coincided with young Sheila.

'D'you fancy a cuppa?' Startled into dumbness by this, Blanche simply stared. 'You look as if you could do with one and I'm parched.'

Side by side, they walked in silence up to South Kensington. Blanche was too unnerved to speak. She was wondering if the man was really a store detective – he could be an imposter who had observed her theft and was now enjoying exercising his male power. As if privy to her thoughts, he offered, 'I was an officer in the Met before I retired. Detective Inspector. Then my wife went and died on me. I took this job to take my mind off things. But today I was thinking I reckon I'll pack it in.'

'Oh, why?' unnerved as she was, Blanche felt it only polite to ask.

'It's depressing, if I'm honest. Folk like yourself, bored and in need of a bit of a thrill when there's plenty these days in real need. What d'you want little vesties like that for?' He sounded fierce.

'I don't know,' Blanche said. She could hardly tell him it was for a mythical French lover.

'Pretty woman like you,' the detective said. 'I used to say that to my wife.'

'She wasn't a shoplifter?'

At this the man laughed. 'She'd be rolling in her grave hearing you say that. Very moral, she was. No, I used to say when she was on about getting a new outfit, "You're lovely as God made you, you need no adornment."'

'That was nice of you,' Blanche said. Ken had not been a great one for compliments.

'That's not what Julie thought. She said it was me being a cheapskate. I'm a Scot, you can probably hear that, and she used to play me up, pretending I was mean.'

'But you weren't really?' He hadn't been mean to her.

'I'm not the best judge.' They had come to an old-fashioned tearoom that had survived the area's upmarket improvements. 'Here, will this do you for tea?'

They sat in the teashop window and he told her his name was Alan McClean. Blanche drank her tea, glad to be saying little. The shock of the discovery of her theft, followed by the shock of seemingly being let off, had left her numb. She was relieved when this ordeal by politeness seemed to be over and he asked for the bill. Her attempt to pay was swept aside. 'I reckon I gave you a fright. And it's decided me. I'm sending in my notice when I get home.'

'But what will you do then?' she asked, guiltily feeling that she was to blame.

'I'll think of something. There's always the garden. And there's the old people's home down the road in Parsons Green. My wife used to go in there to chat to the old folk that still had it in them to string two words together.' He passed a hand across his eyes.

Blanche had not liked to ask about his wife's death but this seemed to be an invitation. 'How did she die?'

'How? Banging on as usual about how I was to remember to take some bloody nonsense she'd got me to take for my heart and remember to see about changing my glasses. She was convinced I'd be useless alone.' He laughed; but his eyes, which she saw now were flecked with gold, became mournful. 'As to what she died of, cancer of the liver. That was cruel because Julie never drank a drop. Took her vitamins, went to the gym, never touched alcohol. It was me should have got it, not her.' He stood a moment, apparently watching a bus making a bad business of turning a tight corner. 'Cruel,' he said again. 'But then nature is cruel.'

'Is it?'

He laughed again the brisk dismissive laugh. 'I don't know. I don't know what I'm saying half the time. Julie always said that. She was the clever one. I just followed orders.'

'I know,' Blanche said. 'I did too.' She thought of Nan saying, 'We're all on our own in the end.' She didn't like to think of that. 'It's horrid being on your own,' she said. 'But I suppose we'll get over it.'

He looked at her and shook his head. 'No, we'll get used to it. We won't get over it.'

19

Nan was lying in her coffin. She had made it snug so that with a pillow propped at one end she could lie with her feet against the other to press out her spine as if in the most satisfactory of baths.

She had been observing her sage on his rock. He sat for long hours on his plateau, cross-legged and motionless, apparently contemplating the distance. *The whole business of expecting anything is an illusion*, he seemed to be saying. *Look at life squarely but ask nothing from it.*

I agree, Nan said, but she did not utter the words aloud. She wondered if he could hear her thoughts as it seemed she could hear his.

Don't ask, he seemed to say. *Don't ask and you might be told.*

The buzzer on the door went, making her start and crick her neck.

Or not, the voice added.

Nan struggled out of the coffin, rubbing her left shoulder to chase away any mischievous gremlin that might have crept into the joint.

'Yes?'

Through the distorting crackle end she just made out '. . . not disturbing you?'

'To what do I owe the pleasure?' she asked as Blanche emerged from the lift.

'I'm sorry. I *am* disturbing you.'

'You have already so you might as well come in.'

Nan made tea while Blanche paced about her sitting room.

'Sit down, for heaven's sake,' Nan ordered. 'You're making me jumpy.'

Blanche settled herself on the sofa. 'I like your . . . with the cushions?'

'Coffin,' Nan said, coming through. 'I'm wearing it in. Sugar? No, you don't, do you?'

'No, thank you. But you aren't about to die, I hope?'

'Hope's got nothing to do with it,' Nan said shortly. 'I like to be prepared.'

'Goodness!'

'Goodness hasn't got much to do with it either,' Nan said, annoyance at the assault on her peace making her relentless. 'The world's not a nice place, in case you hadn't noticed. We're all doomed for a certain time to walk this earth.'

Blanche felt crushed. She had come to Nan's because Nan was the only person she could safely tell of her shop-lifting escapade. She was aware that in doing this she risked causing annoyance; but a need to convey not only the fact of having been detected but the exhilaration pro-voked by the outcome had overridden reserve.

'I was caught shoplifting today,' she announced rather sullenly.

If Blanche had hoped for a reaction she was disap-pointed. 'I said it was only a matter of time. If I could spot you a trained eye was bound to soon enough.'

'He said I was practised,' Blanche said, now absurdly annoyed.

'Who's "he" when he's at home?" Nan decided to be nasty.

'I'd better go,' Blanche said. She put down the mug of undrunk tea. 'I'm sorry.' She began looking wildly for her bag.

'It's OK,' Nan said more gently. 'Carry on. Tell me what happened. I'm all ears.'

'Sounds to me as if you got lucky with your Alan Breck,' Nan said after she had heard Blanche's story.

'Alan McClean,' Blanche said. 'I was, wasn't I?' She considered this, feeling the rare satisfaction of one whom the fates, in their inscrutable calculations, have decided for the moment to let off the hook.

'And now you're wondering how you're going to see him again.'

Blanche blushed. 'Oh no. His wife died and he's clearly still very cut up about her.'

'All the more reason he'll be wanting a replacement,' Nan suggested. 'Men like being married better than women in the long run.'

'I can't see how he'd get in touch. He didn't take my number.'

So that's what's eating her, Nan thought. She's come here for advice. 'He must have told you something about himself.'

'Only that he lives in Parsons Green.' Nan waited, suspecting there was more. 'Oh, and his wife used to visit an old people's home there,' Blanche admitted.

'There you are,' Nan said. 'Find the old folks' home.

There can't be too many in the area. They'll know him through the wife.'

'Oh, but . . .' Blanche was now embarrassed. She hadn't herself recognised the direction in which Alan McClean had nudged her thoughts. 'I don't want to chase after him.'

'You do,' Nan said, 'or you wouldn't be here talking about him. And there's nothing wrong in that either,' seeing Blanche about to object. 'You're both lonely and missing your spouses and now with him knowing about your shoplifting you have a secret between you.' She knew there were few things more binding. 'How's your other fellow doing, by the way?'

'Which other fellow?'

'Your *grand amour*?'

'Albert, you mean?'

'Yes, him,' Nan said, amused. 'You don't want to give him up just because you've found this Alan Breck.'

'McClean.'

'When it comes to the fellers, the more the merrier, as my grandmother used to say.'

Nan didn't add that like the first Elizabeth her grandmother had used this ploy to keep herself safely single for the whole of her widowed life. Blanche, Nan surmised, needed a man to give her definition.

This was not something Nan herself had felt any need for. If anything it was she who had been the defining presence – certainly this was the case with her husband. And Hamish . . . he had not so much defined her as brought her out; they had brought each other out.

'Well,' Blanche said. 'I should leave you in peace.' She made no move to go.

Nan's mind unthinkingly brought Hamish up out of the salt deep where his young body, now long since bereft of flesh, lay. *Of his bones are coral made.* Coral was what time made of death's leftovers; it was what Shakespeare made of the boy's lost father, who is not lost, save to himself. But for all that Shakespeare knew there was only so much time granted to one lifespan.

'No time to be lost,' she said suddenly aloud.

At which Blanche jumped and got to her feet. 'I'm so sorry. I should go.' She scrabbled into her coat.

'Very good,' Nan said cheerily. 'Be off with you, then.'

With Blanche safely dispatched she resumed her position in the basket. *Lie back*, the willows murmured . . . *Lie here in our arms. We will hold you as the river runs by.*

Blanche walked back from Nan's. The sun, which had started the day behind banks of impressive cloud, decided to come out in style. Blanche shed her coat.

The stall holders were packing up, bundling unsold goods into old supermarket trolleys and plastic laundry bags. One, a sturdy dark-haired woman whose stall dealt in second-hand clothes, was chatting to a fellow stall holder and stepped back, treading with heavy boots on to Blanche's foot so that she shrieked and dropped her coat.

The woman bent to pick it up. 'Sorry, darling. I didn't see you there. Here.' She proffered the coat but all in a flash Blanche felt a deep repugnance for it.

'Take it,' she said. 'Take it, do.'

'You all right, darling?' The woman looked concerned. 'Your foot OK? I'm heavy – I must have hurt you.'

'Yes, I mean no, no really I'm fine. And I don't want the coat.'

'I'll give you a tenner for it,' the woman said. The coat had an expensive label. Clearly, this was one of those women a bit gone in the head through having too much money.

Blanche accepted the ten-pound note and walked on. She felt lighter. Jaeger, she had read somewhere, had folded. She had no need, she felt, of a coat from a firm that couldn't keep its end up.

20

Rose's mother back from Glasgow called at the shepherd's hut to collect her daughter. She found her directing the toys in *Matilda*. Rose had cast against type and a meek blue hare was revealing previously undetected depths of sadism as Miss Trunchbull.

'Do I have to go now, Mum? I've had supper.'

'Yes, please, love,' her mother said. 'Thank Minna for looking after you.'

'I don't need thanks,' Minna said. 'It's a pleasure to have Rose and she's always very polite.'

'I'd like her to thank you anyway, if you don't mind.' Rose's mother was annoyed by this intervention. Her daughter, her rules.

'Thank you for having me,' Rose said, bowing to the inevitable. Her tone was muted and her mother thought hopefully, perhaps she didn't have a nice time after all.

'How was it staying over in that hut?' she asked as they walked home.

'It was fine,' Rose said, cautious. In a seismic moment she had understood that her mother would prefer her not to have had too good a time with Minna. 'And I missed you,' she added, the brash burst of consciousness bringing tact in its wake.

'How was Minna's cooking?' her mother asked. 'I don't know how she manages without a proper oven.'

'It was OK.' Rose perceived that her mother was worried her daughter might prefer the food she had at Minna's, cooked on the exotic little stove, to the food she had at home. 'Nothing special,' she added.

'How was the book festival?'

The book festival was safer ground. 'It was amazing. And guess what, Mum, Elizabeth Pattern's going to send me her book herself because they ran out.'

'Ah, I did wonder. That'll be the package that's arrived for you at home.'

Minna had expected to miss Rose when she left. She tidied away the toys interrupted in their play and as she did so she talked to them. She was aware that anyone hearing this would wonder if she was maybe off her head. She wasn't at all – her mind was her own and all in one piece – but Rose's faith in the reality of her toys was so strong that it had come in an oblique way to inform Minna's too. That evening the toys' worn, well-loved faces, their shabby fur and crooked beaks, the ribbons and collars and home-made clothes and their intent unblinking eyes seemed to express a sympathy Minna was in need of. We know how you feel, they seemed to say. We miss her as well.

With nothing else to do, she took up *Swann's Way*. The grandmother, she read, was unable to give any gift that was not wholesome and uplifting. '*My dear,*' the grandmother had said to the narrator's mother, '*I could not allow myself to give the child anything that was not well written.*'

Minna agreed with this, though she was not sure that the grandmother would consider some of the books Rose read of much intellectual profit. And she admired too the old Frenchwoman's disdain for wealth. But the fact was that worldly wealth was useful. It would be hard, given Minna's slender means, to visit Rose in Glasgow or invite her to stay in the holidays.

As a child Minna had been taken by her parents on holidays to Weymouth and it had remained to her an idyll of wide golden sands, Punch and Judy shows and donkey rides. They had hired a little gaily painted beach hut decorated with a string of Union Jacks where she had scrambled into a green woollen bathing dress – why, she wondered now, did we have wool to swim in? – before running down to the shock of the cold water.

At night she slept beside her parents in a truckle bed in the boarding-house bedroom, hearing the keening sounds of seabirds and the occasional companionable hoot of passing ships. And when morning came and she woke with fresh excitement for the day ahead there were squashed-fly biscuits from a tin with 'Come to Sunny Dorset' written on the side and tea from a Teasmade.

A novel determination formed in Minna's mind. She would take Rose to Weymouth. It would require thought. There was not only the money she would have to find but she would have to persuade Rose's mother to allow this. But somewhere Minna had read some words which had stayed in her mind. *What you want with your whole heart you can always have.* She had not come across them in time to try their efficacy with John but she had squirrelled them away with a view to testing them out when a suitably urgent need arose.

'I am going to take Rose for a holiday to Dorset.' She

spoke the words aloud and, looking at the book open on her lap, thought, it's wholesome in Dorset. Proust's grandmother would approve.

Elizabeth Pattern had been as good as her word. A package was waiting for Rose at home and when she opened the book a letter dropped from its pages.

> *Dear Rose,*
> *Here as promised is a copy of 'The Lilac House'. I do hope you like it and when you have read it perhaps if you felt like it you would write and tell me what you think. I am always glad to hear from my readers.*
> *Love from Elizabeth*

'Love' from Elizabeth Pattern, who had not even added her surname. Rose, filled with wonder and astonishment, ran to give her parents this marvellous news. But before she reached the kitchen she caught the sound of raised voices.

Back in her room she heard the front door slam and from her window saw her father stride down the path and bang the garden gate. She stole into her brother's bedroom in search of company. But Justin, his mouth open, was already fast asleep.

Rose went back to her room and opened the book. Elizabeth Pattern had repeated the marvellous words of her note: To Rose, With Love from Elizabeth'.

The Lilac House, she read, *seemed to anyone who cared to look quite an ordinary house. But that was only on the outside. Outside it appeared to be a Victorian semi-detached house, with a little porch over the front door which was set with panes of coloured glass that sent darting patches of light on to the tiled floor inside. From the hall there rose a flight of stairs with just the kind of polished curving mahogany banisters that a child might like to slide down. And if you went through to the kitchen, you would find a large open room filled with curiously shaped bottles, and a big open range, where you could imagine a great fire blazing, and any number of pots and pans and cauldrons on the hearth.*

Hours later, Rose's mother found her daughter still reading.

'Lights out, love. It's way past your bedtime.'

'Can I finish the chapter?'

Rose's mother had been stoking her post-row resentment with a bottle of cheap white wine. She dropped heavily on to the bed.

'Mum, what is it?'

'Your father doesn't want us to go to Glasgow.'

'Oh,' Rose said. This seemed to her a good development. 'Why?'

'God knows why.' Her mother began to cry, big tearing sobs. All in a minute, she turned on her daughter. 'He claims it isn't fair on you, leaving your school and all your friends behind.'

This was confusing. Unused to such consideration from her father, Rose felt uneasy. 'Don't worry, Mum. I don't mind going to Glasgow. Honestly,' she lied.

Summer Holidays

21

Blanche had made a half-hearted effort at investigating the old people's home where Nan had suggested she might get news of Alan McClean. She had put 'Parsons Green' into a Google search and come up with a couple of possibilities. She had even dressed up one day ready to go and explore these with the faint hope that she might run into him. But in the end she hadn't gone. The recollection of the shoplifting was too mortifying.

The long summer lay depressingly before her with no Kitty and Harry to take, as she had been used to doing, to the seaside or to some country cottage. She rang Mary but Mary, she knew, was wary of her brother's wife and didn't want to get involved with family rows. 'Why don't you have a holiday anyway, Mum? You could go anywhere. I was thinking next Christmas you must come to us.' Somewhat strengthened by this Blanche decided to make other plans.

Nan's suggestion that she play up an imaginary French lover had been given substance by her cleaner. How Marissa had got hold of the idea that her lover was French Blanche couldn't for the life of her say. But Albert had gradually become an acknowledged presence in her flat so that it appeared entirely natural to say one day to her cleaner, 'Oh, by the way, I'll be in France for the first two weeks of August,' and for Marissa to respond, 'With your French boyfriend?'

'That's crazy,' Kitty heard her mother say. 'D'you think she's dementing?'

From the lowered tone and the unmistakable strain of annoyance, Kitty guessed they were discussing Blanche. Of no one but her grandmother did they get into that huddle or speak in that particular tone. She moved with extra stealth along the corridor to the kitchen.

'I don't see any sign of that,' her father said, torn between a wish to placate his wife and a faint return of filial loyalty. He had become increasingly unhappy about the breach with his mother but couldn't bring himself to offer the first olive branch.

'Then what on earth has given her such a mad idea, going right across France on her own at her age?' Kitty's mother said, and then had a new, disquieting thought. 'You don't think there's a man involved?'

'It's not all that far,' Dominic said. 'Her grandmother's house was somewhere quite near Paris.' He tentatively added that a man in his mother's life mightn't be such a bad thing.

But to Tina's mind a man threatened a further possible deflection of her father-in-law's estate. 'Bound to be a gold-digger.'

Kitty, when told of her grandmother's plan, had had a similar if less self-regarding reaction. 'It's a great idea, Granny, and you might meet a tall dark stranger.'

'I doubt that, darling.' Blanche was flattered nonetheless.

'He'll have silver-grey hair, like Richard Gere, and a face ravaged by sexual experience,' Faith decided later when Kitty conveyed her grandmother's plans for the summer. 'At first your grandmother will hate him and try to shake him off and then, when she's drunk, she'll trip on her high heels because she's not used to wearing them and fall into his arms and they'll end up in bed together.'

'She's quite used to heels,' Kitty corrected her.

Faith had taken to Kitty's grandmother at the encounter at Peter Jones and was hopeful that she and Kitty might somehow wangle a way of being included in the proposed trip to France. She conjured for herself a romantic encounter with a sax player, maybe filling in time as a hotel waiter, while Kitty's grandmother dallied with the silver-haired hotel owner. 'Where's she going?' The sax player had long hair and rode a motorbike and smoked. Kitty was welcome to his friend, plumper and playing something less cool, the harmonica, perhaps.

'I'm not exactly sure,' Kitty said. 'She wants to visit where she used to stay at her grandmother's house.'

'Where's that, then?' Or maybe a poet, Faith decided. And he didn't smoke but was a Buddhist.

Kitty's grasp of European geography was hazy. 'I think it's not far from Paris but I'm not sure where exactly.'

'How's she getting there?'

'Eurostar to Paris,' Kitty said. 'Then she's getting another train.'

'She'll be stopping over in Paris, then,' Faith determined. Paris was chic and a better location for her sax player or poet. Mentally, she ditched German for her prospective GCSE choice and decided on French instead.

22

Against all odds, Minna had got her wish. Unable to hold out against his wife's persistence, more powerful than the threats of his former mistress through proximity's greater opportunity for expression, Rose's father had stiffened his sinews to brave the move to Glasgow. So Rose's mother had been almost grateful when Minna had offered to take Rose away for 'a little holiday' while her parents travelled again to Glasgow, with Justin, to finalise the move.

After some desperate searching – for it was late to be booking and her resources on a state pension were straitened – Minna had struck lucky, with a rental of a nineteen-thirties showman's wagon.

Minna drove them to Dorset in her old Ford. Approaching the hamlet of Tolpuddle, she recounted the story of the Tolpuddle Martyrs. 'Six labourers there formed a kind of trade union to preserve their wages and were sentenced to seven years' hard labour in the penal colonies. There was a big march in their support in London.' It was John who had told her about the martyrs. 'One of the first public demonstrations and it got their sentence dropped in the end.' I am still serving mine, she thought. John had been big on the rights of man but he'd crumbled over the rights of mistresses.

They found their destination at the bottom of a steep track, parked in maroon magnificence by a grim-looking farmhouse. A pond lay in a dip below. As the car drew up beside the wagon a straggly troupe of geese appeared.

A couple of collies came bounding up, yelping. The geese were joined by some turkeys, who, ignoring the dogs, thronged round the car, their thin necks craning with curiosity.

It's like a child's picture book, Minna thought.

A woman wearing a workman's shirt appeared to welcome them. She took them up some wooden steps on to a veranda surrounding the wagon. Over the lintel a wooden plaque, once painted, now a relic of past glory, read, 'Max the Magnificent: Magician Extraordinaire'.

'This was his,' the woman explained. 'His full name, Maxim Lightning, was engraved on a window but it broke clean across one night in a storm. We found the pieces in the morning. My husband swore it was his spirit come back.'

Not wanting any shadow cast on her holiday choice, Minna tried to change the subject by asking after their hostess's husband.

'He passed last autumn,' the woman said in a voice so sepulchral that Minna wished she had stayed with the revenant magician.

The wagon was fitted out in grand style. The furnishings were covered in a faded gold velvet, the walls were lined with gilded mirrors, there were flower-shaped glass shades to the lights and cabinets of exotic woods faced with etched glass.

Rose was enchanted. 'Minna, look at these glasses.'

'They're for champagne.' Said to be the shape of Marie Antoinette's breasts, Minna remembered. John had told her that and cupped a warm hand round her own breast. Her left breast, the fuller one with the mole he had liked to kiss.

'It's *so* pretty here,' Rose said, opening the window.

Outside, large tin cans, the kind used for canteen purchases, filled with scarlet geraniums and French marigolds stood ranged along the terrace. In the distance the sea threw out, as if in honour of the dead magician, fantastical spangles of dancing light. Ducks were diving industriously for weed in the pond.

'*Ducks are a-dabbling, up tails all,*' Minna quoted, but Rose had disappeared to the bathroom, which was tacked on to the wagon by means of a makeshift bridge. Crossing it, Minna swayed and imagined slipping disastrously down into the nettles below.

'Look, Minna, the bath!'

A copper hip bath, buckled and green in places, was jammed into a corner. Overhead, like a vast sunflower, loomed an antiquated showerhead.

Rose tried the shower handle and produced a splatter of rust-coloured water. 'It works,' she cried.

Minna said she didn't like the look of the water but Rose was having no fault cast on their paradise. 'It's *beautiful*,' she declared. 'I want to live here for ever and ever.'

Together they unpacked the car. Minna ranged teabags, Nescafé, drinking chocolate, Marmite, Nutella, pasta, tins of tomato soup and baked beans along the kitchen shelf, while Rose arranged the toys along the narrow couch in the living room. There was some squabbling among the toys over their ranking, the black swan claiming superiority over the moulting yellow duckling. 'Quiet, Odile!' Rose said. 'One more squawk out of you and I'll put you in a drawer.'

'That's right, age before beauty.' Minna was feeling the exhilaration which is the reward of the successful accomplishment of any long-hoped-for well-executed plan.

23

'For God's sake, Alec,' Nan said again. 'Can you not for once get your bloody act together?'

'It seems not,' her son said at the other end of the phone. 'Bill'll be just as happy to go with you. Happier,' he suggested.

'He won't be "happier",' Nan said. 'He'll be disappointed. But I dare say he has to get used to that.'

'Life hasn't read the declaration of human rights,' Alec reminded her, this being a maxim that as a child he had had too often relayed to him. He rang off before Nan could marshal a suitable riposte.

Packing a case in preparation for the holiday with Billy, Nan wondered, not for the first time, by what incalculable system children were allotted to their parents. Was it some form of other-worldly raffle organised by an indifferent deity? More likely a diabolical one. It was her secret fear that her son was living out the genes of her absconding father, who, having impregnated her mother, had hung on to see his child born and then scarpered, to be seen only sporadically again.

'You father doted on you, Annie,' her mother had once said. Shrewd even as a small child, Nan had doubted it. What she was, she discerned, without then having the words for the insight, was someone who for her father counted and whom he wanted to impress. He had once sent her a present of a doll dressed in stiff pink net tulle. She had had no time for dolls, and particularly disliked this one for its dead lidded eyes. She had sent it out to sea on a driftwood raft and good riddance. Hamish had laughed fit to bust when she described this.

Virginia, who was spending a week in the Scilly Isles with a girlfriend, dropped Billy round at Nan's flat. She rattled through a list of things Billy was to mind out for: too much sun, too much sea, too much sugar, too many late nights. To each of these Billy offered vehement and voluble objections.

'There was no need for all that carry-on,' Nan said when Virginia had finally left, huffy and a little tearful. 'What the eye doesn't see the heart doesn't grieve after. Least said soonest mended. You could try being a bit nicer to your mum.'

Billy ignored this. 'Dad said we're going first class.'

On the train they played I-spy, noughts and crosses and battleships. Then Billy played on his phone and Nan looked out of the window, letting her thoughts ride. *Faster than fairies, faster than witches, Bridges and houses, hedges and ditches*, her mind sang. She allowed herself a pang of regret that few children nowadays would be familiar with *A Child's Garden of Verses*. It belonged, like the rhythm of the old trains, to a time past.

Alec had provided cash for a taxi from Weymouth station to the outlying village where Swan's Nest, the cottage he had rented, was to be found. Driving through Weymouth, past various supermarkets and then round the steep-hedged narrow Dorset roads, Nan began to wonder how they were going to shop. Not something that Alec with his fast car would have considered.

'Is Chickerell very far out?' she asked the taxi driver.

The taxi driver's shoulders made an ambiguous movement.

'Are there shops there?'

The reply was not reassuring. 'Where you're staying in't Chickerell. It's out a way on its own.'

He veered suddenly on to a main road, accelerated hard and drew up in a lay-by, spraying newly laid grit. Alongside the lay-by a run-down red-brick terrace bordered a deserted scrubby-looking field.

Swan's Nest was number 5, the last in the row. The taxi driver unloaded their cases, jumped back into the car, reversed sharply into the loose stones and drove off before Nan's instinct could stop him.

The front door failed to yield to her shoving. 'Here, Bill, give us a hand.'

Billy put his shoulder to the door beside her and the pair of them fell forward into a dank-smelling hall.

Billy ran up the stairs and Nan followed him to a room with some bunk beds. The windows of the second room looked out over the road and there was an old sponge left in the washbasin in the bathroom.

Billy held his nose. 'Pooh! It stinks!'

'This,' Nan said grimly, 'will not do.'

Visitors to Swan's Nest, though provided with few other perks, could, if so minded, avail themselves of a payphone which took only credit cards.

'Why don't you have a credit card?' Billy asked.

'You know why, I've told you a thousand times,' Nan

said, unfairly, since although she was often asked this question by others Billy had never before had reason to enquire. 'Running up debts for money you may not have is the devil's own work.'

'Do you believe in the devil, then?'

He was all set, she could tell, for a theological discussion and another time she would have enjoyed this. 'Call your father, will you? I'm going to give him a piece of my mind.'

'You can't.' Billy was expertly tapping in numbers.

'Can't what?'

'Give him a piece of your mind. Your mind's in your brain and if you took bits out you'd die.'

Alec's voice came on speaker. 'Hi, guys, everything OK?'

Nan snatched the phone. 'This place would be an apology for a bloody aquarium, never mind a holiday cottage. And I've told you before I don't want to be called "guy".'

Alec's tone became pained. 'It looked charming on the website.'

'It might charm a bloody swan – the hall's practically growing bulrushes and the bathroom stinks worse than the bottom of a pond. Did you book this?'

Alec admitted that his secretary had booked it.

'Well, you can give her – oh no, never mind. This was a last-minute offer, wasn't it?'

Her son didn't reply to this but asked what she would like him to do.

'There's no way we're staying here. I can feel the clothes on my back turning to mould as we speak. We'll have to go to a hotel.'

Alec suggested they find a hotel in Weymouth and promised once they had done so that he would call it and pay with his credit card.

'That's why credit cards is useful,' Billy said. 'They's useful in an emergency.'

'*Are* useful. And there was no need for this emergency. And you can stop teaching your grandmother to suck eggs and look up the local taxis, please. I need to get out of here before I grow webbed feet.'

The second taxi driver was more forthcoming than the first.

'You're well out of there. Chickerell's full of drugs – mind you, Weymouth is too, they all are, the resorts, these days, with the unemployed. Bloody rabble.'

Nan, whose sympathies were all with the unemployed, bit back a caustic comment. 'Is there a hotel you can recommend?'

'Five-star,' Billy said. He was checking his phone.

'Why not?' Nan said. 'I reckon we've earned it.' She winked at Billy, who grinned back, relieved that she'd recovered from her annoyance with his father.

'Don't know about five-star. The Jubilee's where they go for fancy dos.'

The taxi driver dropped them by the Jubilee Clock. 'The hotel's just around the corner there. "Jubilee" means fifty,' he said, addressing Billy. 'Bet you didn't know that. That clock was built to mark the fiftieth year of Queen Victoria's reign.' He nodded cockily at Nan. 'I used to teach at the College of Further Education before I took early retirement.'

'I knew that,' Billy said indignantly as the taxi driver

drove off. 'We did Queen Victoria's jubilee in Mr Adams' class.'

The Jubilee Hotel was a melancholy reminder that all things must pass. But after Swan's Nest Nan rather welcomed its faded grandeur.

'The carpet goes up the walls,' Billy pointed out in the lift. He had taken charge of the key and called out to her when he opened the door of their room. 'Wow, Nan, we've got a balcony.'

Excited, they both rushed to look down at holidaymakers eating ice creams and candyfloss, shouting, laughing, flirting and racketing. 'This is more like it,' Nan said.

She unpacked while Billy bounced on his bed. 'Can we go to the beach?'

'That's why we're here, you daft 'appeth. Put on your trunks, why don't you, under your shorts?'

'Are you going to swim?'

'Depends how cold the water is.'

'You learnt to swim in the North Sea. That's, like, arctic.'

'Maybe,' Nan said. 'I was a spring chicken then. I'm an old boiler now.' But she changed into her costume anyway.

Outside they bought a bucket and two spades from one of the shops selling seaside paraphernalia. 'Why are we getting two spades?' Billy wanted to know.

'I might fancy digging too.'

The beach was packed with recumbent bodies. Looking around her, Nan recollected a photograph in the *Guardian* of a beach in the seventies published to show how people today were more obese. 'Human beings aren't pretty on the whole,' she said to no one in particular. Billy, oblivious to questions of weight, was hard at it digging a hole.

'In my day we used to say we were digging through to Australia,' Nan observed.

Billy looked up in amazement. 'Australia's millions of miles down. You'd have to go through the centre of the earth. You didn't really think so?'

'I don't know if we did or not,' Nan said. 'I can't honestly remember.'

She had spread out their towels on the sand and lay back, cupping one hand round her eyes against the sun's glare the better to look at the sky. All but cloudless. In her peripheral vision she could see Billy's back, his thin shoulder blades raised at an angle, like wings. Angel's wings, she thought. We clip them, we clip their angel wings so they forget how to fly. Forget they ever could.

The image was so vivid that for a moment tears pricked her eyes. Life hasn't read the declaration of human rights, she reminded herself, as Alec had reminded her. Alec. What a puzzlement. He too had once had angel's wings. As a child he had cleaved to her, unwilling to let her out of his sight, sobbing when she had left him, heart in her mouth, at nursery. Once she would have said that she knew him better than any living soul and he her, and yet now . . . now he was someone who, however much she loved him – oh, and she loved him most dearly – she found incomprehensible. When had that happened, that unchartable slow unravelling process that had left them at odds, for ever wrangling; amicable, certainly, but with their old tie so attenuated, almost estranged?

High above, screeching herring gulls wheeled, beadily

scouring the beach for food to nab from careless holiday-makers. 'Look,' she threw out to Billy. 'Look, I'm so old the vultures are circling over me.'

Billy frowned. 'They aren't vultures, they're gulls.'

'Oh, you're no fun,' Nan complained.

She stretched out her arms, wheeling them across the sand to ease aching muscles. The business over Swan's Nest had left her physically tense. Just beyond her feet the sea was gently crashing on to one of the bands of shingle that lie along the Weymouth strand. *Like as the waves make toward the pebbled shore, So do our minutes hasten to their end.* Was this what dying was, a steady progress of waves washing you, finally fatally, up on to the farthest shore of eternity? Sometimes the waves were small and regular, easily negotiable; sometimes they were whoppers that could thrash and flatten you, pull you under to drag you over the harsh shingle, break your bones on the hidden rocks. *Not waving but drowning.*

But she hadn't drowned. She had come close to it but she had learned to swim with the tide, or against it when required. She had held her breath beneath the pressing weight of the seas when needful, bobbed up again and swum or floated on to more tranquil waters. Now she need only stay buoyant to see Billy launched. A spray of sand on her face made his presence palpable.

'Hey, watch out. That went in my eye.'

'Sorry. Come and see my hole.'

He had dug down far enough so that, crouched there, only his head and shoulders were visible.

'Strong lad. That's some work you've put in.'

It was too. Play was children's work.

'I'm hungry,' Billy said.

They were in luck. Just across the road, the other side of the esplanade, was a café, apparently famed since the time of King George for its fish.

Over their cod and chips, the latter for Billy in a red plastic bucket complemented by a red plastic spade (useless for digging), he asked again, 'Nan, did you really think you could get to Australia?'

One of the truths Nan had divined early is that it is the hardest thing in the world to grasp that other people see life from a perspective often quite unlike one's own. 'The trouble is we all see through our own leper's squint,' she had once said to her husband, who had confirmed the point by asking what on earth she was on about. She tried out the same idea on their grandson.

'What's a leper's squint?' he asked, as she had hoped he might.

'You know about leprosy?'

'When bits of you drops off?'

'Not as bad as that but horrible certainly. In the days when leprosy was common and people were afraid it was catching there were tiny windows made in churches so the lepers could see into the church while the Mass was being said. "Mass" is a name for a church service,' she added hastily.

'Why did they want to?'

'Why did the lepers want to see into the church?'

'Yes. What did they want to do that for?'

'In those days most people believed in God.'

Billy dipped a chip into some tomato ketchup while he pondered this. 'Why?' he asked again.

'That's what I was trying to explain. It was normal then to believe in God. Not being allowed to mingle with the other healthy people in the church they saw as a terrible consequence of the illness. Nowadays it's more normal not to believe. They – the lepers and the other folk – would have found it weird, as you would say, not to believe in God while I think you find it weird that they did.' Though of this she wasn't sure. Billy sometimes interrogated her views on religious questions. And she welcomed that. She was open to doubt herself. She continued on more substantial ground. 'You see, pet, in your way of thinking it's ridiculous to suppose that by digging a hole you could reach Australia but in my world I liked to imagine that I could.'

'Even if you knew you really couldn't?'

'Yes,' Nan said. Aside from loving him, this was what she liked best about her grandson: he was willing to explore things. 'Even though with another part of my mind I knew quite well that I couldn't.'

Billy's forehead wrinkled while he tried to absorb this idea and Nan, feeling she had provided enough food for thought, suggested that he might like to look at the dessert menu.

Billy was halfway through a banana split topped with mountains of whipped cream and Nan was finishing her coffee when a waitress came over. 'Would you mind if two people joined you? Only we're so busy there aren't any other tables free.'

A woman about Nan's age and a freckle-faced girl with plaits were hovering. The girl was eyeing Billy's banana split. 'Of course,' Nan said. She moved her bags and herself across to the seat nearest to the wall so the woman and the girl could sit opposite each other.

'That looks good,' the woman said to Billy. Her clothes might have been leftovers from a jumble sale but she had a gentle voice and a good-natured face.

Billy began to scowl and the girl looked apprehensive. Nan said, 'Are you on holiday here, like us?'

'We're staying in a magician's wagon,' the girl said proudly.

Billy looked up from the banana split as if preparing to dispute this. Nan said, 'That sounds like fun.'

'It's brilliant,' the girl said. 'It belonged to a magician called Max and it's all like it was in the nineteen-thirties.' She blushed at this effort of social exertion.

Billy was not going to be bested by some old wagon. 'We're staying in a five-star hotel.' He returned to scraping the dish.

The girl countered with 'My mum and dad are staying in a hotel. In Glasgow. We're going to move up there.'

Nan decided not to contradict Billy about the five stars. 'That's quite a move. If you live in England, that is.'

The other woman, who had been surreptitiously counting the notes in her purse, said, 'We live – well, at the moment Rose does – near Reading. I'm Minna. This is Rose.'

'How do you do,' Nan said. 'I'm Nan and this is Billy.'

'Bill,' Billy said. He ran a finger round the dish, chasing the last vestiges of cream.

The waitress appeared and handed menus to Minna and Rose and Nan asked for the bill.

'You can get the chips in a bucket,' Billy offered while

she was paying the waitress. 'With a spade. But it costs more.'

Observing the slight anxiety in the other woman's eyes, Nan said, 'They're the same chips and the bucket's not much cop, is it, Bill?'

Billy snatched up his bucket and clutched it to him. When they got outside he said, 'I wasn't going to give her mine.'

'Of course not,' Nan said. 'No one was suggesting you should.'

Aware that from an early age children are nagged by adults – themselves demonstrably inequitable in their behaviour – to share, she sympathised with children's natural unwillingness to do so.

24

Breakfast at the Jubilee Hotel the following morning was a success. Billy was impressed by the range of cereals, yoghurts, fruits, dried and fresh, glass pitchers of juices and milk with varied levels of fat content and the hotplates of bacon, sausages, scrambled egg, hash browns, mushrooms and tomatoes. He was especially taken with the toasting device and used up several slices of bread feeding the rotating grill.

Nan simply had coffee and a croissant, which Billy felt was a poor show.

'Aren't you having a cooked?'

'Not for me, thanks, Bill.'

'Why?'

Nan had not slept well. The hotel bedroom was too hot, the orange sodium street lights filtering through the curtains had kept her awake and long into the night she could hear the yells and screeches of laughter of Weymouth's youth and the crash of beer bottles breaking on the cobbles below.

'Just because.'

Billy turned his attention to one of the leaflets posted on diners' tables.

'*Sea Life; Weymouth's Biggest Attraction*,' he read out. 'There's sharks. Can we go?'

'Where is it?' Nan had her reasons for not relishing the prospect of a visit to Sea Life.

Billy consulted the map. 'The other end of the beach from here.' He handed her the leaflet promising *the experience of a lifetime* with penguins, sharks, seals and other sea creatures.

'Living creatures cooped up like that. Do you really want to see them, Bill?'

Billy pointed at a picture of an octopus. 'I saw a programme about them. They're as intelligent as humans.'

Nan said that in her opinion that didn't amount to much. She promised to think about a visit to Sea Life but pointed out that the morning looked to be fine; perfect for the beach.

Billy's plan for the morning was to build a system of waterways leading to a pebble-lined reservoir. 'When's high tide? I want the channels to fill up with water.'

'They've got the tides chalked up on a blackboard on the side of that place selling all that beach tat,' Nan told him. 'I saw it as we were passing. You can hop along and check.'

She settled herself on the spread towels and took out her book. But the sight of the sea stretching out in an evanescent spangle of light to the far horizon held her gaze and she let the book drop.

Since a girl, Nan had been fascinated by the horizon and the way that the seemingly palpable line along which, as if in a child's game, silhouettes of various craft were now slowly progressing both was and was not there. It was there by the virtue of the evidence of the eye and yet reason insisted – against, it must be said, all ocular proof – that this apparently sensible truth was a mere illusion. There was nothing there but the ironical effect of the slight but calculable curve of the surface of the Earth.

Out of nowhere a fragment of a line of a poem began to flicker into being. Rootling in her bag for her note-book, she realised that she had left it behind in the hotel bedroom and cursed. If she failed to commit these but-terfly incursions to paper they simply fluttered away into the beyond.

Nan dug in her bag for one of Billy's coloured pencils and transferred the fragile flight of words to one of the blank pages at the back of the book she had brought to read on the holiday. She had never got around to reading the novel she had bought long ago on the strength of the author's now-forgotten reputation. But a book called *Weymouth Sands* had seemed fitting in the circumstances.

But before she had read even the first paragraph Billy ran up with the freckle-faced girl they had met at the fish-and-chip café. 'She's going to Sea Life,' he shouted accusingly.

The woman who had introduced herself as Minna now appeared. 'I'm so sorry. We met Bill at the stall over there. Rosie told him we were going to Sea Life. Only we got an offer.' Anxiety clouded her good-tempered face.

Nan said, 'There's no call for apologies. I told Bill we'd go. There's no need for all this fuss, Bill.'

'You only said you'd think about it,' Billy reminded her angrily.

'It's just we had an offer,' the woman repeated. 'We're going tomorrow morning.'

'See!' Billy said, as if this confirmed a gross injustice.

'Lord help us,' Nan said. 'What a fuss. If it's that import-ant to you we can come along too.' She arranged with Minna to meet outside Sea Life the following morning.

Billy, who had looked slightly appeased, began, once

Minna and Rose had gone, to object. 'I didn't say I wanted to go with them.'

'Too bad,' Nan said. 'I've agreed to meet them now and it's thanks to Rose you're going at all so if I were you I'd pipe down.' He looked up at her and at the sight of his fierce brown eyes in his triangular little face her heart melted. 'Dope!' she said, kissing him on the crown of his head, where the pattern of his hair was heartbreakingly like his father's.

Minna and Rose discussed Nan and Billy as they walked back towards the part of the beach where they had left their towels. 'She seems friendly,' Minna suggested. In truth she felt somewhat in awe of the little woman who seemed so definitive; but she was relieved to have the company of another adult. Away from the shepherd's hut, she was overtaken by fears for Rose's safety.

'Did you like the boy?' she asked, hopeful.

Rose had registered Billy's hostility. 'I don't know.'

'It might be fun going round Sea Life with him,' Minna suggested.

'Perhaps.' Rose was aware that Minna was anxious not to have displeased her and just for a moment enjoyed the sensation of withholding her approval.

25

When Billy and Nan got off the bus near Sea Life it was to a strong fishy smell. 'Pooh!' Billy made a face.

'It's you as wanted to come,' Nan said. 'Now behave nicely, please, with that lass. She's shy.'

Rose and Minna were waiting for them by the entrance. Rose said, 'We got your tickets because we found out one of our coupons was for a family' and blushed painfully.

Anticipating some objection from Billy at being turned into an ersatz family, Nan said swiftly, 'That's very thoughtful, Rose. How much do I owe you, Minna?'

While the adults were swapping notes and change Billy and Rose exchanged glances. Finally, Billy said, 'There's sharks inside.'

'There's octopi too,' Rose said.

'It's *octopuses*,' Billy said scornfully. 'Not octopi. Everyone knows that.'

Rose looked crestfallen and Minna, who had completed her transaction with Nan, began to apologise. 'That's my ignorance, not Rose's.'

Billy became condescending at this evidence of his superior knowledge. 'They're as intelligent as humans, octopuses.' He looked at Nan. 'She thinks they're more intelligent. Except for children,' he added reassuringly.

'Sometimes,' Nan said. 'It depends on the child.' She

grinned at Billy and he grinned back, secure in the knowledge that she liked children better than adults and him most of all.

Feeling more comfortable, Rose said, 'We did a project on them at school. Wouldn't you love to hold one of their tentacles?'

Billy unbent enough to agree that this might be cool but added that he thought her teacher should have known it wasn't 'octopi'.

They passed into a thronging area where mounds of bad replicas of various forms of sea life were on display, arousing covetousness in the children and menacing the adults' wallets.

Nan steered Billy sternly through this temple of temptation. There was not enough money, she could tell, for Rose to be bought anything extra so she deflected his demand to buy a furry shark. 'Dad said he gave you spending money for me.'

'Maybe later,' Nan said. 'Look, there's where we can see the real thing.'

A sign directed them to the aquarium. The doors gave on to a long tunnel where behind imprisoning glass varieties of brilliantly coloured fish were performing a shifting kaleidoscopic ballet in the well-lighted waters. Now and again the ponderous shape of a shark loomed by, causing no obvious disturbance to the smaller fry.

'Why don't the sharks eat the other fish?' Rose wanted to know.

Billy, who felt he should have an explanation for this, retreated into knowingness. 'It's because they're all in captivity,' he hazarded.

They passed slowly through to a smaller aquarium. 'Look, look,' Rose called. 'Octopuses.'

The children pressed against the glass walls of the tank, trying to catch a glimpse of its occupants.

'They're shy,' Rose said. Being shy herself made her sympathetic to the retiring inhabitants.

'Sensible, more like,' Nan commented. The creatures in the tanks had awakened memories for her. 'I daresay they don't like people gawping at them.'

'I read about one that escaped from a zoo,' Rose said. 'Someone left the top off its tank and it got out and slithered down a tiny *tiny* pipe into the sea. They didn't know it could make itself so tiny,' at which Nan had a sudden intuition of being able to make an escape by reducing one's self into all but nothingness.

Billy, caught between interest and a desire to know best, said, 'I read about that. It was in London Zoo,' he added, guessing.

'I think it was in New Zealand,' careful Rose suggested.

Some other children arrived and began to jostle for position round the tank. The tip of a greyish tentacle appeared over a toy wreck, gestured a little and then withdrew.

'Yuk!' a small girl shouted. 'It's *disgusting*.'

Rose and Billy exchanged looks.

'My dad eats those,' an older boy announced.

'Yuk!' the girl said again. 'Yukky, yuk, yuk yuk.' She slid her eyes sideways at the boy.

Little flirt, Nan thought. The octopus declined to show itself further so she suggested that they visit the café.

Billy and Rose held the table while Nan and Minna

queued. Disgust at the reactions of the other children was fermenting an idea in Rose. 'We could escape them.'

'What d'you mean?'

'The octopuses. We could set them free.'

'How?' Billy was annoyed that he had not thought of this first.

'We could take the top off the tank. Like I read about.'

'We'd be caught,' Billy said, lapsing into a defensive prudence.

'We could get in at night,' Rose suggested.

'How d'we do that?'

'I don't know,' Rose agreed. She had hoped that the idea would fire him too.

Minna appeared with chocolate cake. 'Nan was getting some for Bill, so I thought, Rose . . .'

'She says, "A little of what you fancy does you good,"' Billy reassured.

From the café they moved on to the seals' pool, where feeding time was about to start. Nan settled herself on one of the high observation steps while Minna supervised the children, who were vying with a crowd of other candidates for the dead fish from the keepers' buckets with which to feed the seals.

The children were throwing raw fish into the pool and assigning personalities to the different seals when Nan saw Minna take a call on her phone. She talked for a moment and then looked up towards Nan as if for confirmation.

'What?' she called down.

Minna called out, 'It's our landlady. She's got a problem.'

'She has to go to London,' Minna said when she had climbed up the banked semicircle to where Nan perched, like a small brown bird, Minna thought. 'Her son's been taken to hospital so she has to go to London to look after her grandchildren. She's asked if me and Rose could see to the livestock. I said we would.' She looked uneasy.

Nan made her face into a question.

'I just wondered if you and Bill might like to come and stay with us there. She said she'd be delighted if you would because she'd rather not leave the main house with no one in it. There'd be no charge.'

Looking at Minna's expression, Nan made a snap decision. Billy would be furious at leaving the luxury of the hotel but the night spent there had tired her. And she had taken to Minna. She was, Nan could tell, a thoroughly decent woman, warm-hearted and plainly devoted to Rose.

Shepherding a sullen Billy back to the hotel, she reflected that it wouldn't do Bill harm to get to know Rose. Rose might be good for him, she speculated, and then rebuked herself. It was none of her business who he liked. This was her wishful thinking, wanting him loved and appreciated.

Nan had no doubt that Virginia loved her son, doted on him, even, but she was aware that her daughter-in-law didn't always understand him and often found him bewildering. But then, there was no God-given rule that parents and children should understand each other. It was the luck of the draw, apparently.

Billy showed no sign of being influenced by his grandmother's wishes and was frankly livid at this change of plan.

'Why we doing this?' he demanded. 'We was staying here for the rest of the holiday. Dad was paying so it didn't cost you.'

'*Were* staying, and it's called helping out,' Nan said, so firmly that Billy went temporarily quiet.

He gave vent to his fury, however, by screwing up his clothes and stuffing them into his suitcase on top of one of his remote-control cars so that the lid of the case wouldn't close.

'See!' he shouted. 'That's probably broke my best car.'

Nan decided to drop the grammar lessons for the moment. 'Your car'll be fine. You can repack that case and then find a taxi for us on that phone of yours.'

'Have you told Dad?'

'You can do that with one of your blessed texts. He's not going to worry – we'll be saving him a fortune. Besides which you'll be able to play with your remotes much better there, where there'll be space. Now get your skates on and find that taxi while I call down to Reception to settle up.'

It had begun to rain. The taxi driver, swearing audibly as he negotiated the running slime of mud and the many potholes in the steep track, drove them past rusting pieces of agricultural equipment entangled in what looked like uprooted fences and barbed wire. At the bottom of the hill a duck pond came into view. Beyond this the shot-silk sea unrolled to a cloud-stacked horizon.

The taxi swerved on to a patch of muddy grass, setting off a cacophony from the livestock as Rose came running towards them.

'Are you going to help us with the bags, then?' Nan asked the driver. He did so, plonking down their suitcase amid the goose shit. She rewarded him with a meagre tip. 'Don't spend it all on drink.'

'Well, now,' she said, to Rose, whose face was pink with the pleasure of being host. 'This is your magician's wagon, is it? It looks grand. Show us round, will you, pet?'

The first thing Billy saw on entering the wagon was the toys lined up along the couch.

'What are they doing?'

'They're my toys.' Rose became defensive.

'Why d'you bring all them?'

'As if it's your business, Bill Appleby,' Nan intervened. 'Why shouldn't Rose bring her toys on holiday? You bring your cars.'

'Only two of them,' Billy said. His fury at leaving the hotel had not abated. 'Anyway, fluffy toys is silly.'

Nan did not remind him of his recent clamouring to buy a fluffy shark. She could see Rose was trying not to cry and began to regret her decision. Why should the kids like each other anyway? 'Rose, lass, will you show us where you sleep?'

In the bedroom two berths were set into the wagon's sides; between them stood a built-in marble-topped table through which emerged an elaborate glass-shaded lamp in the shape of a bronze nymph. Engraved glass windows let in a cloudy green light; the ceiling, once gilded but with most of the gilt now erased, was coffered – like a Venetian church, Nan thought.

'D'you sleep there?' Billy asked Rose, nodding at one of the berths.

'You can sleep here too if you want. Minna says she can sleep in the lounge.'

'Where's my grandmother supposed to go?'

Nan was touched by this. 'Don't you worry about me,

pet. I'll be fine in the house. You can sleep there too with me if you prefer.'

Minna appeared behind them. 'Bill'll be all right here, won't he?' she asked, her eyes full of hope.

Nan, bracing herself for further dispute from Billy, was pleasantly surprised when he flung himself down, saying in quite a cheerful tone, 'What's for supper?'

'Sausages,' Rose said. 'And oven chips. And there's a telly with DVDs, so we can watch after supper.'

She's excited, Minna noted. It's better for her having company her own age. She tried not to feel hurt by this and almost succeeded.

Minna showed Nan to the farmhouse, where she unpacked. She was relieved, provided Billy was going to be all right, to have her own space and the lav nearby. She didn't envy Minna having that bridge to cross in the night. She took *Weymouth Sands* from her bag and reread the lines that had come to her on the beach. More words came to her and she wrote them down and dated the page. Maybe one day Billy would find what she had written at the back of the book and remember their holiday.

By the time she got back to the wagon Minna had made supper. The rain had cleared so they ate outside on the veranda under a washed sky while the ducks entertained them on the toy-town pond and the geese rooted about in the grass.

The children finished their supper and went inside to examine the collection of DVDs. Rooks were drifting in for the night to settle in elegant silhouettes on the branches of a tall ash. Behind the stand of trees the sun began its own apparent journey downwards, heralding the fall of night. Nan as she watched thought again how much of what seemed to be solid and tangible in the world was an illusion. '*When does the day begin?*'

She had supposed she had spoken this wordlessly to herself and was startled when Minna said, 'It's funny, isn't it – there isn't any one time when it becomes day or night. It's all rolling round and round, all the time.'

'They're not my words,' Nan said, a little taken aback. 'Lewis Carroll's.'

'I read the Alice books to Rose when we first met,' Minna remembered.

The children watched *Home Alone 2*. They had each seen it many times before and felt entitled to make disparaging comments. Then they were sent across the perilous bridge to wash and clean their teeth.

'But we can read, can't we, in bed?' Rose asked.

'If Billy's grandmother says it's –' Minna began, but 'Absolutely,' Nan interrupted. She was interested to see what Billy would make of this.

'What's that about?' Billy asked. He did not especially want to know but Rose's concentration on her book made him want to shatter it.

Rose had finished *The Lilac House* and was rereading one of her favourite Elizabeth Patterns. She put the book down, ready to defend her favourite author against potential criticism. 'It's called *Seal Lullaby*.'

'I can read!' Billy prepared to take offence.

'It's from a poem,' Rose explained. 'The title's the same as a poem by Rudyard Kipling. You know, who wrote *The Jungle Book*.'

'That's Walt Disney,' Billy said, scornful.

Rose was not above a bit of scorn herself. 'That's only the film. The story was written by a man called Rudyard Kipling. It's a book. Two books, actually.'

'Rudyard?' Billy said. 'That's a dickhead name.'

Minna and Nan were sitting by the stove. The late-afternoon rain had left a chill in the air and Minna had got a fire going. The blaze behind the glass pane threw out a warmth which mirrored their conversation.

'It's wrong of me,' Minna was saying. 'I try not to show it, but I don't know what I shall do when she goes. She's not my granddaughter, after all. She's not even a blood relative.'

'There's more than one kind of relative,' Nan said. 'There are kindred spirits, to my mind closer than blood ties often.'

'I was close to my mother,' Minna said. 'Closer to her than anyone till Rose. Or maybe one other,' she added, for Nan's seemed a safe pair of ears.

Nan demonstrated the truth of this by not enquiring into that last comment. Instead she said, 'I was close to my grandmother. She really saved my bacon.'

'How?' Minna risked. Perversely, she was now rather annoyed that her allusion to John had not been picked up.

'She saw me,' Nan said. 'My mother, bless her heart, tried her best but we were cut of different cloths. My grandmother didn't have to.'

'Didn't have to try?'

'No,' Nan agreed. 'She was a wicked old woman. Mind you,' she laughed. 'I'm said to be her dead spit.'

Her laugh is like the ducks' quack, Minna thought. 'But you're not wicked,' she suggested politely.

Nan didn't bother to answer this. 'It was she who taught me not to have principles.'

'But surely principles . . .' But Minna suddenly wasn't sure what was sure about them.

'Principles,' Nan said, conscious that she was about to be provoking, 'are usually a cover for some form of power play.'

'Oh no.' Minna was ready to be shocked.

'Think about it,' Nan said. 'Think of any person you know who's principled and you'll find a hidden bully.'

Minna tried to think as bidden. The truth was with flesh-and-blood people she felt ignorant and out of her depth.

'What my grandmother had was scruples,' Nan said, more approachably. 'Scruples are fine. They keep you to the mark – keep you from slipping. It's scruples, for instance, that stop you making it hard for Rose to move to Glasgow.'

'That's because I love her.'

'Oh, love!' Nan said. '*That* word.'

This so crushed Minna that she sat mute until Nan said, 'I don't mean that you don't love her – but people do terrible things in the name of love.'

Never seek to tell thy love . . . she thought. The word should be taken out of circulation . . . or you should be allotted only a lifetime's measure and when you had used up your allowance you should have to make do without or find other, less loosely peddled words.

'Yes,' Minna agreed. She was again thinking of John.

Nan allowed her natural clairvoyance to emerge. 'Think of the times men have said "I've never loved any-one as I love you" and gone straight back to their wives.'

At which Minna flushed. 'I will never love anyone as I

love you,' John had said, and gone straight back to his wife. She kept her burning face turned to the fire.

'A cup of tea?' Nan asked. She was aware of what she had just prompted and felt compunction. 'If you ask me,' she said, filling the kettle in the cabin kitchen, 'they're damn lucky to have you, that family.'

They won't thank her for it, though, she thought, but said nothing, knowing that this would be neither news nor comfort to Minna.

'What's it about, then, that poem?' Billy asked. He wasn't really interested but he was bored.

Rose put *Seal Lullaby* down again. 'I'll read it to you if you like. It's here in the front of the book.' She read the poem aloud in what Billy called to himself 'a girl's voice'.

> *'Oh! hush thee, my baby, the night is behind us,*
> *And black are the waters that sparkled so green.*
> *The moon, o'er the combers, looks downward to find us*
> *At rest in the hollows that rustle between.*
> *Where billow meets billow, there soft be thy pillow;*
> *Ah, weary wee flipperling, curl at thy ease!*
> *The storm shall not wake thee, nor shark overtake thee,*
> *Asleep in the arms of the slow-swinging seas.'*

The words had an odd effect on Billy, who decided that they were stupid. 'What's it mean, "flipperling"?'

'It's the mother seal's name for her baby,' Rose explained. She was starting to feel upset.

'So what's the book about?'

Rose was a well-mannered girl but had not yet learnt

the art of polite refusal. 'It's about a boy called Hamish who's trying to save some seal pups – his father sells the seals' skins. He's bullied by his father, who thinks he's drowned – only he hasn't really 'cos what has happened is he's fallen into the sea and the seal world, which is kind of a parallel world to our world. And then this girl called Catriona gets there too. I haven't got beyond that this time round of reading but I've read it before and she's OK because he's there and they kind of get on.'

'Why?'

'She's running away from her stepfather and he – Hamish – has had this hard time with his dad, who beats him. So they're both kind of escaping.'

'Oh,' Billy said. He played with the razor-shell bill of a bird that someone had stuck together out of shells. 'Have you heard of Kew Gardens?'

'No.'

'It belonged to a king. I go there with Nan.'

Rose understood that this was some kind of oblique vote of sympathy for the story. 'Is it a good place to escape to?' she asked.

It didn't cross Billy's mind that this is what Kew Gardens might be for him. He played some more with the bird's beak, calculating how far you needed to wobble it before it broke off. 'If you come up to London we can take you there if you want.' The razor shell came away in his hand and he looked at it, unsure whether to be pleased or sorry.

'Thanks.' Rose didn't think this was very likely but as well as being polite she was a perceptive child and was aware she was being paid a compliment.

26

Nan, adrift in a carrack on the high seas, knew she would soon be out of drinking water. Her lips were parchment but she must not take a drop more than was strictly needed – her supply had run perilously low.

A night noise struck the waters of sleep and the boat rocked and tipped her on to the dry land of wakefulness.

What might she have discovered had she only been able to stay at sea? And what, in the name of all that is curious, was a carrack? Not for the first time she thought how extraordinary to know so completely in a dream what you have never consciously known in real life. So-called real life, she corrected herself. At some point, in that common-or-garden everyday reality, she must have been told, or read, that it was something like a galleon, the tall-masted ship, the carrack, that she was sailing in and saw with such precision, right down to the rigging, in the dream.

Her waking mouth *was* dry. She reached for the glass of water by her bed. And found there was no glass to hand.

For a moment she was back in the sea floundering and then her mind touched land again: of course, she was in a strange bedroom belonging to a woman she had never met – and Billy was over the way in a magician's wagon.

For a moment she felt anxious. She hoped that her waking was not in response to some need of his. But then for no accountable reason she felt sure that he was sleeping soundly.

At the image of a sleeping Billy her heart, as it always did when her grandson came to mind, swelled, faintly painful. Sweetly painful. To be sure, there was not another love like it. Not, other than one, anyway, that she had known.

Nan let herself slowly down the side of the bed, which stood high up from the floor, and felt her way along the wall to the light switch. At the sudden brightness a bird just outside the window took off with a clack of feathers. She went to the window and looked out.

Moonlight was silver-plating the grass. A full moon, vast and auspicious-seeming, was hanging like a child's lost balloon in a darkly violet sky. She had stolen that image from someone. Who the hell was it? That was one of the snags of age, that who you were and what you had been and what you had done and what you had read, or been told, had become so interinanimate that there was no telling any more what was what. *Interinanimate*: there, a case in point.

But what does it matter? Nan thought, as she trod warily – mindful of hidden perils: malicious stair-rods, for example – down dust-carpeted stairs to a kitchen with a cold stone floor. And who would care anyway? Not Dr Donne, who was dead and, as far as she could judge, generous-minded.

The kitchen smelt of old cooking fat and the water from the tap tasted rusty. Nan swilled out her mouth and spat. Too thoroughly awake now to recover sleep she went to inspect the contents of the fridge.

The fridge told a sad tale. A tub of look-alike (but not, to her mind, taste-alike) 'butter', some old jars of jam, an opened pack of sliced ham, the edges gone crisp and curled, and half a lemon.

Idly, she conjectured that if you were to open simultaneously all the fridges in the UK probably over fifty per cent would reveal half a dried-up lemon, already a little blue round the edge with mould.

For some seconds she stood in the strange kitchen examining the notion of herself as half a lemon in a vast cosmic fridge and then rejected the image as a cliché.

Across the way Minna was also awake. She too had surfaced from a dream but the details fled as she emerged into consciousness. Needing to pee, she lay awhile in the narrowness of the couch, putting off the moment when she must make the crossing to the bathroom.

There is only so long anyone can lie in any degree of comfort with the pressure of a full bladder. Reluctantly, Minna rolled from the couch and felt about on the carpet for her dressing gown.

Opening the door, she was smacked by the wind that had got up and was making great rents in the clouds which were racing across the face of the moon, alternately brightening and blackening the night. A weird moon, huge and bronze-coloured, had risen. The makeshift bridge connecting the wagon to the bathroom swayed as she crossed, making her place each bare foot down with extra care. An owl shrieked nearby and there was a sharp answering cry of some small animal, a rabbit, perhaps: the owl's lunch.

Back again in the fug of the wagon Minna also went to

the kitchen. She was neither hungry nor thirsty but had an impelling desire for some material comfort against the dark. The dark held too many dangerous possibilities; too many unfulfilled promises. It whispered that dawn might never come and till the end of time – your time, anyway – you would have to make do with this forever-dark.

Minna made herself a Marmite sandwich, doubling over the thick crust end of the cut white loaf that Rose had requested. She chewed it, reflecting on the day that had passed and the oddness, yet satisfactoriness, of the new connection with Billy and Nan. Nan, she thought, was intimidating but also reassuring – a combination she had not met before. True, Nan had summoned up the ghost of John, but his haunting never quite left her and something, something she couldn't put her finger on, something about his ghost, seemed less devastating in Nan's presence. And Bill was such a nice normal decent boy – a companion for Rose.

In the bedroom Billy and Rose slept the matchless sleep of children who are as yet still free of the terrible know-ledge of the forces of darkness and the havoc they can wreak – save that of the blameless prophylactic darkness to be found in films or stories.

27

The wagon curtains were of a fancy lace which let in the morning light. Rose woke early, allowing the relief of not having to hurry up for school to course enjoyably round her mind. She settled the toys who during the night had fallen into disarray and reached down to the floor for her book. But catching sight across the room of Billy's sleeping form, she held off reading for a moment.

She was unused to being so close to a boy. There was Justin, but he was her brother and didn't count. She had friends at school who were boys but none she was friends enough with to spend a night alongside. Her friend Tabitha had boy cousins whom she spent holidays and fought with. For all the fighting, Tabitha seemed quite proud of having boys for cousins. Tabitha had elder sisters too and had started her periods.

Billy sighed in his sleep and turned over, apparently settling into deeper levels of slumber so that Rose was startled when, having taken up her book to read, she heard, 'So are we going to do it, then?'

'Do what?'

'Free the octopuses.'

'How would we?'

'Like you said. Lift the top off the tank, you said.'

'I said that was how Inky got away.'

'Who's Inky?'

'The octopus that escaped. In New Zealand,' she put in, because she had thought about it and was sure she had got that right.

'Doesn't matter where it was.' Billy was dismissive. 'A tank's a tank. We just need to get the lid off of it.'

'We'd need a bucket. Inky got down a pipe, they think, to the sea. We don't know there's a pipe at Sea Life.'

'A bucket, then.' Billy was beginning to lose interest. This was very like girls. They started things and then changed their minds. 'I don't care if you don't want to . . .'

Which ignited Rose's resolve. 'OK, then. How shall we do it?'

'We'd have to go back to Sea Life,' Billy said. 'With a bucket,' he added, in case she was going to remind him. There was no way he could see how they could push an octopus down a pipe.

'Wakey, wakey,' Minna called through the door, cheerful now the night had passed without doing its worst. 'Your grandmother is here, Bill. Breakfast time.'

After breakfast the children washed up. This was Nan's doing. Minna would never have inflicted any domestic task on Rose but Rose, as Nan guessed she would be, was thrilled to be asked.

Billy, used to his grandmother setting him chores, acted nonchalant. 'I always wash up at Nan's,' he told Rose, not entirely truthfully.

While this was going on Minna read and Nan sat listening to the mindless voices of nature: the dismissive laughter of the ducks, the nasal snorts of the geese, the cascading heavenly melody of the blackbirds and the tiny pips of clear crystal with which the swallows and martins were stringing the bright air.

The birds were the last custodians of freedom. You couldn't – or not yet – regulate the birds. And they are the final evolution of the dinosaurs, she reflected. More beautiful and older far than Johnny-come-lately *Homo sapiens*. Clever birds not to have over-evolved. 'You know your own measure,' she remarked to a house martin which swerved by chasing insects.

'But how we going to get them to go back there?' Billy asked again. They had finished the washing-up. Rose was tidying the shelves and he had returned to their plans of octopus liberation.

'I don't know.'

'You ask. If I ask Nan'll say no.'

'Minna might say no too.'

'She won't,' Billy said, who had picked up Minna's concern for Rose. 'She'll want to do what you want.'

'Doesn't Nan want to do what you want?'

Billy considered. 'Mostly she does. But sometimes,' he added, with his strict regard for truth, 'she just doesn't want to do what I want and she doesn't care.'

'She's very clever,' Rose observed. She knew that Minna was not what people call clever but on the whole she was glad of that. She admired Nan but Minna was more like another child.

Billy had no views on whether or not his grandmother was clever. 'She smacks me sometimes,' he announced. 'And she's teaching me to lie.'

He had expected a reaction to this but Rose only said, 'She can't smack you, smacking's illegal.'

'The boy in your book's dad hit him.'

'That's in a book. You can't for real nowadays.'

'She does, though.'

But Rose knew he must be lying. 'Minna says even the Bible lies,' she told him, in case he might feel guilty. She was being kind but she also wanted to establish that Minna had a certain authority too. Minna might not be clever like Nan but she also knew things.

Nan had naturally noticed what Minna was reading. If it had surprised her she did not admit this to herself. She had not read Proust, preferring to nurse a prejudice against him for not owning that he was gay. She had him down as one of those self-indulgent men who bang on endlessly about themselves and their tedious inner lives and so she was slyly pleased when she observed Minna put the book down.

'I keep starting this and then having to go back and start all over again,' Minna said. 'It doesn't stick. I hope I'm not getting Alzheimer's.'

'If everyone who couldn't get along with Proust was an Alzheimer's case half the reading population would be in the loony bin,' Nan suggested.

'I read all the Russians, though,' Minna said, boasting a little. 'All of them: Tolstoy, Dostoyevsky, the lot. It took me over three years.'

Minna, Nan could tell, was not one of those people who embellish and somewhat in spite of herself she was impressed. She had had Minna down as something less . . . she couldn't for the moment have said what . . . salient, perhaps.

'What brought that on? If you don't mind me asking,' she added, remembering herself.

Unequal to explaining the background to her hard pilgrimage to Proust, Minna began, 'I've read all kinds of things,' and then found herself blurting out, 'It all started after an unhappy love affair.' Never before to anyone had she mentioned John.

'Ah,' Nan said, recovering her incurious self-image.

But now the cat was out of the bag Minna wanted to pursue it. 'We had started to live together and it was . . .' how to describe the incomparable? '. . . wonderful,' she finished lamely. Oh the remarkable delight of daily waking with limbs entwined, the simple humble everyday things, like fresh-ground coffee (never, before John, had she drunk it) and reading the *Guardian* (never, before John, read it) and going for walks on a Sunday down the towpath and then a drink at the local pub or to the cinema to see foreign films with subtitles in which adultery was not a matter for shame but considered art. An image came to her – Monica Vitti staring into the middle distance murmuring, 'Perché?' And then . . .

'And then,' not looking at Nan, 'he went back to his wife.'

With the words the shock of it blazed up anew, seeming to scorch her being all over again, almost as painful as when it had occurred in time. More agonising, in some ways, because time was always somehow recurring . . . only over time do you learn that there are things that never get better.

'I'm sorry,' Nan said. 'That's hard.'

'I thought I was going mad,' Minna said. 'I did go mad, in fact.'

Stark staring raving mad. She had howled and roared and scarred and starved herself – and no one could help her. Not the doctors, not the counsellors, not the well-meaning but woefully inadequate priest, not, God help her, the countless bogus 'healers' with their tinctures and chants and dubious Eastern philosophies and false tales of 'cure'. Not even nature with its austere promise of renewal, for renewal was the very thing she dreaded. It was in books she had found sanctuary at last. Books, where she found colleagues, fellow travellers, allies, comrades: people who felt and suffered as she had done, was doing. And then, like a miracle, there had been Rose.

Her phone rang. 'I was wondering how you were.' Rose's mother's voice was reproachful. 'Only Rosie promised to call me.'

'Oh, I'm so sorry,' Minna said, dismayed that she had not reminded her charge. 'It's the signal here. We're in a dip. I'll get her now.'

When Rose came out on to the veranda to speak to her mother she brought with her the book she had been reading. She put it down on the table where Nan was sitting and took up Minna's phone.

Minna had gone inside to give Rose some privacy. Not wishing to seem to be eavesdropping but not wanting to bother to move, Nan picked up Rose's book as a distraction.

Billy was playing with his remote on the veranda when his father also rang. 'How you doing?' he asked Billy. 'Only I've finished up here and I thought I might bomb down to find you.'

'Suit yourself,' Nan told her son when Billy passed her

the phone. He would anyway, she thought. She was annoyed at his assumption he could come and go as he liked with Billy but she knew too that Billy would want to see him, would be glad.

'My dad drives a Ferrari,' Billy boasted to Rose when they were sent to collect their bathing things from the bedroom.

This meant nothing to Rose. 'Could he take us back to Sea Life in it?'

'If I ask him to.' Billy was pleased to be the one with control of a car.

At the beach the children played separately. Rose spent the morning building a mighty castle while Billy constructed an extensive waterworks. He capered manically about shouting derogatory words at the unresponsive tide until it swept a dead crab unannounced into his reservoir and he spent an enjoyable time chasing after Rose with the pincers. After a while they reached a truce and together buried the corpse with a lolly stick for a tombstone.

'Have you ever eaten a crab?' Billy asked, and when Rose shuddered said, 'She loves them,' nodding at Nan.

'Just the ticket,' Nan said. 'When I was a girl we used to line-fish for them for our tea.' Hamish had once called her 'hermit crab' because she preferred her grandmother's house, his house, any other house but her own.

After lunch – sandwiches bought from M&S – the children, with no spoken agreement, began to play *Master-Chef*, concocting exotic dishes out of seaweed, shells and sand.

Minna acted as judge while Nan, who made more than

was necessary, Minna thought, of her dislike of TV cooking programmes, went off beachcombing.

Her trousers rolled up to the knee and the sun on her back, Nan walked barefoot in the shallows. She was glad of this opportunity to be by herself. Her apprehension that time was short had grown. Some words from long ago had returned to run again through her mind. They were there as her eyes trawled the bottom of the sea for likely stones: *What is a woman that you forsake her?*

The name Hamish had leapt out at her from Rose's book. It had been a jolt and there had been that strange coincidence of the Kipling poem. She was no great Kipling fan but these words of his had long spoken to her.

Nan was a quick reader and she had sped through much of the book while Rose talked to her mother, reassuring her, Nan could tell – for she could perfectly well read and simultaneously catch the gist of a conversation – that she was having fun and at the same time missing her mother, a fair feat of tact for a ten-year-old lass. When she had finished on the phone Rose had gone back inside and Nan had continued reading.

To say that she had not thought about Hamish over the years would be a nonsense. There was a sense in which at a subtle level he was with her all the time. But never, since his death, had he been so present – more than present, so alive in her mind.

The conversation with Minna about her lost lover must have opened the sluice gates against which the pale washed-up body of her own drowned love somewhere endlessly knocked. And now the gates had reopened and he had come crashing back.

What is a woman that you forsake her . . .
To go with the old grey Widow-maker?

Nan sat down on a patch of dryish shingle and emptied her trouser pockets of their collection of wet stones. She had walked some way around the bay and although she couldn't pick out the others for sure the Jubilee Clock marked where they were to be found. A jubilee marked the passing of fifty years. It was fifty years since Hamish drowned. She examined the stones carefully one by one, then gathering up some shingle for support, piled them up into a small cairn.

By the time they were driving down the track to the wagon the early-evening sun was painting patterns of crimson light on to the surface of the pond. Around it a device was whizzing, causing commotion among the ducks. Alec was on the veranda watching.

Billy almost fell on his face, rushing up the steps. 'Dad! You've got a drone!'

'Hi, guys.' His father landed the drone expertly beside him.

'Hello, Alec,' Nan said coldly.

He was her son, and for that reason she was always pleased to see him; but she was not pleased to see the drone.

Minna was not pleased to see the drone either. She had been enjoying her burgeoning relationship with Nan and was feeling proud that she had made a bit of a hit with Billy at the beach. She had awarded him top prize for his *MasterChef* pomegranate-and-prawn soufflé and had been relieved by Rose's conspiratorial smile of approval and rewarded by Billy's obvious pleasure at the accolade. And now here was his rich dad providing drones and loud male company and Rose would be put in the shade.

'Can I have a go with the drone?' Billy asked. He was actually dancing up and down, Nan noticed, in excitement.

Rose, who had followed more soberly up the steps, made to go inside.

'Who is this?' Alec asked, grabbing her arm. 'Who is this pretty maid, William?'

Oh no, Nan thought. Please, Alec, don't be arch.

'This is Rose,' she said briskly. 'And this is Minna and they have very kindly invited us here as their guests.' She levelled a look at Alec. Especially kind, the look said, after that hole you found for us in Chickerell.

Alec, practised at ignoring his mother's looks, took refuge in being charming. 'And very lucky you are too,' he said annoyingly. 'This is a terrific spot. Clever you to find it,' addressing Minna. He smiled, beguiling her.

Minna, unused to praise, visibly melted. 'We are very glad to have your mother and your son here, aren't we, Rosie?'

Rose made an indistinct murmur and went into the wagon, where Nan followed, to be met with an angry face. 'Is that man staying?' Rose demanded.

Bloody Alec, Nan thought. Just as the lass and Bill were beginning to get along. 'Shall we make supper together?' she suggested.

Rose was bitterly regretting that they had invited these interlopers into her paradise and she was not going to be mollified by being invited to open some stupid cans of tomato soup. She did so in silence and Nan, noting the set of her shoulders, gave a swift sympathetic pat and let her alone.

Supper was a jumpy affair. Billy sulked when Nan said he couldn't fly his drone and then Nan sulked when Alec overrode her. Unused to manoeuvring the drone, Billy landed it in Rose's soup, which splashed on to the broderie anglaise dress that her mother had bought her as a parting gift for the holiday. 'To wear if you go out somewhere special,' her mother had said. The lacy dress had not so far seemed suitable for holiday wear but Rose, suddenly missing her mother, had run inside and put on the frock.

'It's my best,' she said, trying not to cry. 'And tomato stains never *ever* come out.' She hated these people.

Nan shot another angry look at her son and took Rose inside. 'It'll come out fine,' she said. 'You change into your night things, pet, and I'll see to your dress.' Bloody Alec, she thought again, arriving like this and taking over.

She took the white frock through to the sink, where she had been rinsing a couple of pebbles from her beach trove. Large smooth pebbles of pale sea-scoured marble. Relics, she had speculated, of some old shrine or temple, long washed into oblivion.

Setting the pebbles aside, she heard the voice: *There is no safety*, it said. *There is only shifting sand and air and water. They must take their chance. They have their own innate strengths and flaws. You cannot forever be watching over them.*

28

Nan was adamant that Alec could not sleep in the house. She vetoed Minna's timid suggestion that their absent host wouldn't mind. 'It isn't polite without asking and we're not troubling her, with her son so poorly.'

Alec, who understood his mother's reasons for saying this, laughed and said he would get a room at a local hotel. He and his mother had more in common than either acknowledged. He too preferred not to share. But also he had come down to Dorset to impart some news which he suspected – no, was sure – his mother would deplore and he didn't fancy being alone with her. The effect might be to make him blurt it out, to get it out of the way. It would be better for him for his mother to hear his news with Billy present when for his son's sake she could be relied on to hold her tongue.

He was aware of the strength of his mother's love for his son; and for the most part he was grateful, more so, perhaps, than he let on. Like many men who have apparently escaped the terrible hold of the umbilical bond, Alec was wary of giving his mother too much credit – or letting her know that he did.

Nan had kissed Billy goodnight and left it for his father to put him to bed, ignorant of the new assault being prepared on her peace. If Alec was there, she thought, Bill would be happy and she could retire alone with her thoughts.

She went across to the house, taking with her the marble stones.

Her supper had been disrupted by the business of Rose's frock – but it was not so much food she felt a need for. Alec had brought wine with him but by the time she had finished cleaning the frock and soothing Rose it had mostly been drunk by himself and Minna. Minna had apparently fallen for her son's smooth talk and annoyed by this Nan had baulked at asking him to open another bottle.

The house smelt of dust and neglect. For a moment Nan regretted leaving the others behind in the wagon. She went and poked about in the cupboards in the gloomy kitchen. A number of sticky bottles containing inches of ancient squash but nothing stronger till she opened a bottle with a Ribena label. Sloe gin. Or Ribena gin, maybe. She carted the bottle up to bed.

Nan was sixteen when she properly met Hamish. She had seen him around ever since she could remember on her regular visits to her grandmother's – a black-haired boy with eyes the peculiar seraphic blue of the Celtic tribes. He was a couple of years her elder and had grown to be a broad-shouldered young man, one of the gang of local youths who hung about, smoking and spitting into the sea and laughing raucously about nothing. Clever young Nan on the whole despised them.

Nan's mother was what nowadays would be called an alcoholic. In those days she was simply someone who coped with an errant husband and not enough money with the anaesthetic of drink. No one blamed her for it – she was never so far gone that anyone felt a need to call in

Social Services – but it was not an environment that offered much to Nan.

Her grandmother's natural resilience had bypassed her only daughter and resurfaced in Nan, who was only too glad to escape when she could from her mother's squalid Newcastle flat to her grandmother's house at St Abbs, where her mother's brothers, hardier specimens than their sister, had settled nearby and she felt more at home than at home.

She helped out with the mail-order business which her enterprising grandmother had set up, commissioning fishermen's jerseys from the fishermen's wives which she advertised in women's magazines and sold on at inflated prices. And when Nan wasn't packing up the woollies – which often on account of having been made by a smoking fire amid a croftful of children needed a damn good wash before being dispatched to buyers – she wrote poems in the draughty bedroom from which, sitting on the window ledge, she had sight of the endlessly various sea.

As long as she could remember Nan had loved the sea with an ardour that as a young girl slightly frightened her. She was conscious when she walked, sometimes perilously, along the top of the harbour wall, followed by a train of screeching herring gulls, of a troubling desire to hurl herself into the waters – or to swim far out, buffeting against the cream-capped waves till her strength gave and her body sank unprotesting, fathoms deep, under the weight of the sea.

She was not suicidal; that she was sure of. She simply had this urge.

St Abbs is famed for its lifeboat and for its saying that

those who man it never turn back. It was from this life-boat, on its way to a craft in trouble, that Nan's grandfather had been swept overboard and drowned. The young lads of St Abbs were waiting their turn to make their marks as their fathers and grandfathers had done before them, pitting their own mortal powers against the heartless power of the North Sea. In the absence of ships in peril and when not earning their living on the fishing smacks they drank and smoked and showed off by diving through the complex of rock formations that decorate the clear depths around St Abbs.

It was while swimming in Broadhaven Bay one unusually hot summer that Nan really met Hamish. He bumped up against her body, having just swum through the remnants of the wreck of the *Ringholm*, an old ship known to the locals as the Peanut Boat after the cargo she was carrying when she went down.

As his wet frame surfaced beside her his hand had grabbed her right breast.

'Oi!' Nan had yelled. 'Get off!'

Hamish, like most of his peers, was only apparently a lout and had been embarrassed. He pulled off his mask and apologised awkwardly, explaining that he hadn't seen that she was there. The apology was accepted – Nan's protest being more a matter of form; he was more flustered than she was – and she agreed to cement her forgiveness with a drink at the local pub.

She had set out that evening dressed to the nines in a spirit of girlish conquest, ready to break this brash boy's heart; and she had come home shaken to her core with her first real taste of sexual desire.

Lord, Nan thought. Here I am in a strange woman's bedroom, on the other side and the other end of the country and at the other end of my life and yet . . . and she felt that desire run through her body again, right down to her toes. How astonishing that it was still there. She took another swig of the Ribena gin.

Had her grandmother, never a vigilant guardian, failed to notice the nights her charge had spent out, climbing down from the bedroom window on the shaky drainpipe and dropping to the ground? Or was it, she wondered now, with her grandmother's tacit permission that, nightly, she had run like the wind down the cobbles to the harbour to be crushed half to death in Hamish's tobacco-smelling arms. My God, how they made love that summer . . . and the summers that followed. Insane for each other's bodies, they found every possible way to meet. Scenes flooded back to her: wet shingle pitting their naked flesh on Coldingham Sands as they clung to each other swearing love eternal beneath the indifferent stars, rocking violently on cold tarpaulins on a boathouse floor while rain banged down on the roof as if in sympathy with their love-making, once in the harbour master's office, penetrated with keys borrowed from his son, their friend and ally. Another time, she remembered, in the sea, not too successfully: 'Bastard won't stay in,' he had said, and they had laughed and laughed about it. The laughter was almost the best of it, the proof of what they were for each other, two strong young beings full of the glory of being alive.

Alone in the strange bed, Nan, recalling the gladsome couple she had once been part of, laughed again aloud.

Every holiday after that, whenever she could get away

it had been her and Hamish, laughing, drinking, kissing as they walked the clifftops alight with gorse – because when the gorse is out, and it is always out, kissing is in season – and whenever they could, wherever they could, making love.

The Easter when she turned eighteen and was about to go back to take the A levels which were to be her passport from the muddle of home, he had said, 'I don't suppose you'll be coming back here much when you go to the university, Annie.'

She had denied this vigorously, proclaiming loyalty, asking if he didn't believe her, and he had smiled a smile which she still found painful to recall. 'Reckon you will come back, then?'

She understood why he doubted it; but for all his fears she had been true. She gone back faithfully every vacation, leaving, not too regretfully, her more sophisticated Oxford friends, and always it had been the same, the sense of affinity – the feeling that here was her truest reality. Everything else was simply a preparation for putting the future on a sounder basis. Always she had promised and kept the promises to return.

And then the Easter before her finals she had stayed behind to revise.

She hadn't phoned. She had written to explain, a quite innocuous letter but – rereading it when his mother returned it to her – there was no denying it was uncharacteristically colourless, saying she felt she should 'put her head down' and work. But assuring him that once the exams were over she would come up and be with him. Surely, she must have promised that . . .

Was there some ambiguity in her words that he had discerned? She couldn't now tell – she had long ago thrown out the letter, afraid of the grief latent in its sparely written pages. The fact was she hadn't phoned.

Had she no longer wanted – or wanted as ardently – to marry him? Again, she couldn't at this distance in time tell. No more than she could tell whether or not, had they married, it would have been a success. There was no telling, a little drunkenly Nan reflected. There was never any telling about anything.

In any event, Hamish never replied. He was no great letter writer and hers would have been a disappointment. He might have put off replying, not wanting to seem to sulk or stand in her way (he respected her intelligence – her 'book learning', as he put it, intending the words ironically, teasing her with a supposed gap in their social status or perhaps wanting, just a little – because, for all their seeming sharedness he couldn't have been, could he, quite without a sense of the difference between them? – to bring her down). Or he might have been too hurt or too annoyed. He might – because he would of course have noted that she hadn't phoned – have simply thought, To hell with her, stupid cow. He could be like that too, she remembered.

What she also remembered was how, hearing nothing, in youthful pride and some resentment she had left him to stew in his own juice – as she would have put it – while she laboured with Anglo-Saxon and timed herself writing pithy essays, getting in practice to impress the examiners, who cared not a jot about her then and for whose opinion she cared still less now.

Until suddenly missing him badly, with that fierce physical need of which she was now feeling this ghostly return, she had changed her mind and without any warning had taken the overnight train up to Berwick, finally arriving in St Abbs on that maddeningly slow bus the following morning to learn that Hamish and some friends had gone the previous night for a drunken swim, that Hamish had not returned and was feared drowned.

29

Alec arrived early next morning, eager now the moment had come to unburden himself of his news. He brought with him a packet of chocolate brioche he had bought at the local Co-op. A bribe, Nan thought, and not a great one. It had dawned on her that her son had come for a reason.

The reason was dropped with false casualness over the brioche breakfast. 'Looks like I'll be moving to Singapore sometime this autumn.' Billy's father smiled at his son to cover his nerves.

Innocent of what this might entail, Billy prepared to be proud of Singapore.

'Why?' Nan asked.

'It's a new office,' her son said brightly. He was not feeling too bright. The fear of his mother, which he was always a little keeping at bay, was constricting his heart now. A more self-aware man might have recognised that the move to Singapore was in part fuelled by a wish to escape this fear. 'I've been asked to head it up.' He detailed the ins and outs of the business the international commercial law firm had invited him to set up. 'It's a great opportunity,' he said, in the dispiriting knowledge of how his mother would receive this.

The iron was entering Nan's soul. 'It's all settled, I take it?' He was her son and would know she was angry; and she knew too that he knew she would try to conceal her anger for Billy's sake.

'Pretty much, bar the shouting,' Alec said, resorting to meaningless verbiage. All he wanted now was to get away.

But if Nan could do nothing to avert the larger dereliction she could at least block the lesser one. 'Well, if we're to lose you so soon it's as well you're here now to have fun with Bill.' She stared hard at her son. 'I dare say that hotel room will be free so you can stay on a bit.'

'Can we go back to Sea Life?' Rose asked.

Nan had been successful in removing the stain from Rose's frock and Rose had awoken in a happy mood. She liked Billy's father, who was so much better tempered than her own and brought chocolate brioche for breakfast. She was even prepared, with encouragement, to like the drone.

'Can we, Dad?' Billy asked.

Alec looked sideways at his mother to see if this was likely to cause more problems but getting no guidance said, 'I don't see why not. Sure.'

It was agreed that Alec should take Minna and the children back to Sea Life. Nan said if they didn't mind she'd stay put.

'We'll bring you back something nice,' Rose said, climbing into the back of Alec's Ferrari. She didn't want anyone feeling left out.

Sea Life was not as busy as on their former visit. Alec, anxious to be seen to be generous, gave in to the children's pleas for a Sea Life toy. They lingered in the aquarium tunnel, where Alec, with a need to get Minna on side, regaled her with the plot of *Jaws*.

Billy, who was a devotee of David Attenborough and knew far more about the habits of sharks than his father, listened in restrained silence until Rose nudged him. 'What about the octopuses? Shall we go?'

The children careered down the tunnel to the room where the octopus was housed. There was no sign of life behind the toy wreck and the room save for the two of them was empty.

'Quick, quick,' Rose said. 'Get the top off.'

There was a stool available for smaller children to stand on in order to get a better view of the contents of the tanks. Billy stepped on it to reach to the top of the tank, where there was a cover which could be removed.

'Hurry, hurry,' Rose cried wildly. Her cheeks were burning with excitement.

But Billy was suddenly blindsided by the catastrophe that is reality. 'We haven't got a bucket,' he said. 'We said we needed a bucket.' He climbed down off the stool and kicked it away.

'We can leave the top off,' Rose urged, still in the heady grip of their plot. 'It could get out by itself, like Inky.'

But a much larger, more serious matter had caught up with Billy and he turned away from Rose to hide his smarting eyes. 'It was a shit idea,' he said, and ran out of the room. He felt humiliated and was furious with Rose, who had suggested this stupid plan and was probably now telling his father. He hated Sea Life. He wished he'd stayed behind with Nan.

'Everything all right?' Alec had arrived and found Rose standing alone by the tank. 'What have you done with Bill?'

But Rose had been visited by a darting intimation of the cause of Billy's changed mood. 'He went off,' she said, not looking at Alec. When Minna appeared, panting a little, she went over to her and took her hand.

Minna, sensing an awkwardness, felt – as she did on such occasions – responsible. 'Are you all right, sweetie? Where's Bill?'

'Billy's gone off,' Rose said. 'I don't know where.' All at once, both she and Minna wanted Nan.

Alec, as it happened, was also feeling the lack of his mother. His anxiety over her reaction to his move had clouded his own sense of guilt about his son, whom he loved in his own way. He had been planning to organise visits to Singapore for Bill where he would treat him lavishly with the extra money the new position provided – he had even toyed with an idea of moving Bill and Ginnie out there permanently, to be closer to him. But he knew in his heart that he would not get around to it and that his mother's care for his son was invaluable and that Bill – maybe even Ginnie too? – needed her nearby.

So far as he was able to, he loved his mother and wished they could get along better – but the very nature of that love, together with his sense of never quite getting it right with his son, made him want to keep his distance. He had wanted to give his son a good time but now something had gone wrong and he was at a loss to understand what or why.

'I need the toilet,' Rose said, this being a distraction she had learnt to employ on awkward social occasions.

Hearing the car doors bang and then raised voices, Nan thought, Oh Lord, it's *that* kind of a day. Billy had been tracked down at Sea Life, they had all had a drink at the café but the life had gone out of the party. Matters were made worse when Billy discovered he had lost his toy shark. When Rose, wanting to make things right, offered to give him her octopus he had declared rudely that he didn't want a 'stupid octopus' and that 'only girls' liked furry toys. After that it seemed best to leave.

Nan was still sitting on the veranda, where she had settled when they had left, from where – drinking coffee amid the agreeable sounds of gently guttural rooks and piping swallows and martins – she hadn't, except to brew more coffee, moved.

Her own day had so far been spent in reflection. She had recovered from the shock of her son's announcement and other, more tender, feelings towards him had re-emerged. One way or another they would manage it between them, this move to Singapore. And – who knew? – the expanded horizon might be good for Billy. She mustn't impose on him her own concerns over his father's neglect. If she were to be fair – and Nan mostly struggled to be fair – she had not done such a great job with his father. Her irritation with Alec might with equal justice be turned against herself.

But she had lived long enough to be sure that the whole business of meting out blame was a mistake. Blame was a displacement activity, a means of avoiding the recognition that very little in life was in your control. Things happened and you got along with them, or not, and getting along with them was generally – unless you were talking major iniquity, Hitler, for example – the better path, provided getting along with them was not confused

196

with giving in to them. You could learn to get along with things on your own terms.

Yet seeing Billy's face white with repressed tears she let those wisdoms go hang as she gathered his thin body in her arms and rocked him to her, wishing she could take all the hurt to herself.

30

Blanche had last visited Paris just before Ken died. He had booked a smart hotel in the Marais and they had done the usual things, queued for the Louvre, visited the Pompidou Centre, even, a little to her embarrassment, taken a trip down the river to the Eiffel Tower. And 'Shall we go up?' he had said when they got off the boat and because she could think of no reason not to they had queued and ascended the famous tower. In truth it had bored her, but Ken had liked it. And she had liked that – she liked him to be happy.

As she made her way through the carriage to her seat on the Eurostar Blanche wondered if maybe some intimation of his death had prompted her husband's suggestion of that trip. But that wasn't Ken. Ken wasn't given to psychic intimations. He was a solid down-to-earth man who loved his food and drink and would have been, she surmised now, too frightened of dying to resort to it as a prompt for his holiday plans.

Her mind arabesqued – as she begged the man whose aisle seat was next to the window seat that her ticket proclaimed hers to excuse her – to how they had dined so expensively at the restaurant at the top of the Pompidou Centre with the night sights of Paris laid out before them. And how afterwards Ken had almost hurried her back to the hotel, where they made love in the crisp clean sheets of the hotel bed. Was that the last time they did so? she continued to wonder as – excusing herself again to her neighbour – she parked her coat on the overhead rack and arranged her bag and her magazines before finally settling into her seat. They had by then got out of the way of love-making. Not that there was ever much. But Paris had reawakened some life. Getting out of a rut, Ken would have put it – had he spoken of it at all.

She grinned, freer to be indulgent to her husband now he was no more, and her neighbour mistaking this as intended for him smiled back. Heartened by this encouraging start to her holiday, she sent a text to Kitty.

Aboard the Eurostar and about to set off for Paris, adding, *Wish you were with me*. Too bad if horrible Tina read it. With all the latest terror attacks in Paris Tina, she was sure, would consider any desire to take Kitty there tantamount to a declaration of an intent to murder.

The hotel Blanche had booked for herself was on the Left Bank in the arrondissement of St-Germain-des-Prés. If this was an act of rebellion against Ken, she was not consciously aware of it as she walked, pulling her case, from the Métro down to her hotel.

The hotel was in the old Parisian mode, with flamboyantly flowered garishly coloured wallpaper and carpets, also with a floral theme, which in some mysterious way added up to a sense of style. A rickety lift took her four floors up to a bedroom – extravagantly mirrored and with a bed with an old-fashioned bedhead – quite unlike the smart streamlined up-to-the-minute hotel she had stayed in with Ken. Here there was even a bath, a discreet Parisian bath squashed into a tiny tiled bathroom. Ken had been a shower man but Blanche loved baths.

Her stomach was clanking with hunger and she left her case unpacked and went out in search of lunch.

She found a café-restaurant with tables outside and took one boldly, not waiting to be placed. A glamorous young waitress, her hips bound tight in a long white apron, appeared and began to spread the table with a clean cloth. She handed Blanche a menu and a wine list and rattled off the specialities for the day.

Gratified that her French still held up enough to follow this, Blanche ordered a salad and a glass of Sancerre.

The salad was good and the wine still more so. She ordered a second glass and then, having drunk it and paid, she sauntered along the rue Jacob, her limbs loosened by wine. On a whim she turned up a side street and found herself in a tiny square, made more charming by the four plane trees decoratively clustered around an ornate lamp post.

To add to the atmosphere of a *fin-de-siècle* painting there was a florist displaying a delectable range of flowers: deep-blue delphiniums, golden rod, burnt-orange and crimson roses stood in old metal watering cans while ice-cream-coloured stocks in enamel buckets sat alongside baskets of mauve and purple lavender and a mass of sweet peas whose distinctive spicy scent was suffusing the warm air.

As Blanche breathed in the mingled scent of flowers there came back to her an image of a flower-seller doll her mother had bought for her on a trip abroad with her soon-to-be stepfather. A rosy-cheeked doll with a stiff striped skirt, a black bodice, a lace blouse and a flat straw hat who carried little panniers of tulips, mimosa and carnations. How surprised she had been by her mother's present and how very dearly she had loved that doll, which was, she saw now, in the nature of a bribe. What was her name?

Still trying to recover her doll's lost name, Blanche noticed a plaque on the wall which informed her that she was standing by the last dwelling place of Eugène Delacroix, where on 13 August 1863 the artist had died.

Blanche and Ken had variously visited the musées d'Orsay, Picasso and Rodin on their Paris visits. Ken, as he liked to say, could take or leave art but he went with Blanche and stood or walked dutifully beside her while she worked her way through long galleries, guidebook in hand, trying to absorb the visual treasures displayed there. When Ken, as he sometimes did, referred to her among their friends and acquaintances as 'arty' she felt embarrassed and brushed this off as an example of Ken's nonsense (she knew that he meant it affectionately but still she had wished that he wouldn't). She would never have dreamt of describing herself as cultivated but within the limits of her own understanding – well, she wasn't ashamed of it and why should she be? – she did like art.

And here was an artist whose work she didn't know. The effect of the wine and the colours and scents of the flowers had given an extra fillip to her mood for adventure. She paid the modest entrance fee and bought a guide.

It was, she read, the last of Delacroix's studios, rented late in his life when his health was failing. Here he lived, the guide explained, wifeless and childless with only his housekeeper, Jenny, for company, married, Blanche imagined, to his art. She wondered how that would be, what it would mean to have only paper and paint and canvas to commune with. No children but only housekeeper Jenny. But why not? A kindly practical Jenny and all the paintings were arguably better company than her own barren state.

It was a sensitive face, she decided, assessing Delacroix's self-portrait. Slightly leonine, fastidious, a little haunted. The face of someone who maybe took things hard. Perhaps – though this was ridiculous, she knew – he might have understood how she felt. For the first time it struck her that the dead might become friends – or if not friends then allies, maybe? Yes, she liked that – allies.

Her new ally's studio stood within the garden and was almost empty of other visitors. Blanche looked about, taking it in: a simple room with a lofty ceiling and wide windows filling the room with the artist's requisite north light. Examples of Delacroix's work were displayed on easels or hung around the walls.

On one wall a larger canvas than most depicted an older woman sitting with a younger, an open book between them. Both women seemed absorbed.

'*The Education of the Virgin Mary*,' Blanche read. So that must be Mary's mother, St Anne.

How interesting that Delacroix should want to catch these women at this pursuit. Not, as they were usually depicted in other paintings, being advised by awe-inspiring angels that they were to carry the seeds of divinity but quietly, unostentatiously, reading together. Jesus's grandmother as a teacher, passing on her own quiet pleasures to her daughter.

Into Blanche's mind filtered another image of St Anne: the Leonardo in the Louvre, far lovelier and more gracious than the smug-looking Mona Lisa. Ken had liked to pronounce that in his view the Mona Lisa looked constipated, and she had laughed dutifully because she didn't want to hurt his feelings, though the truth was she found his humour infantile.

The fleeting feeling of relief at her freedom struck her again – followed hard on its heels by a gulping sense of loss. She did miss him – dear Ken.

Back at the entrance she bought some cards: *The Education of the Virgin*, a study of Dionysus feeding a tiger, a delicate watercolour of some poppies for Kitty and a strange arrangement of some purple flag irises with a drawing of a skull by it for Nan. Nan would approve of her striking out like this in Paris. Rather guiltily, she realised she had forgotten Maggie, who would be expecting a card.

As if struck by a plank, a great tiredness hit her and rather than plunge into Paris as she had intended she turned back, wanting the refuge of the hotel.

A sanctuary. Her room had been tidied, the bed made, the towels replaced. She stripped off her dress and lay on the bed in her underwear and read about Delacroix until she drifted off.

When she awoke – how much later she had no idea – she could hear people chatting below in the street. The tiredness had gone and she felt replenished. She dressed and went out again.

Outside she encountered a boutique advertising 'Sales' in its windows. Well, hadn't she packed lightly with an eye to this possibility?

She tried on a cream skirt and examined her reflection. Not bad for sixty-two. Her legs appeared long and shapely but maybe that was the mirror. They did things to the mirrors to flatter your reflection.

A recollection of her shoplifting caught her and a fizz of fear ran through her limbs. How alarming that in the blink of an eye you could become someone unlike yourself. Or unlike the self you thought you were, she supposed she'd better put it, as into her mind unbidden came the accent of Alan McClean. *What d'you want little vesties like that for?*

Did he think about her? Probably not – or only as that mad greedy woman he had caught stealing.

After a good deal of clambering in and out of clothes Blanche settled on a blue linen shift and a faded denim jacket. The selection had taken time and when she emerged from the shop she heard a clock sound seven, followed by first one and then another set of church bells.

She ate a good dinner that evening and sat outside with her coffee, smoking against the possibility of biting insects, hardly thinking, letting her mind drift. That night she slept long and well and woke too late the following morning for the hotel breakfast. Too bad; she would have her coffee in the Louvre.

Light of heart, Blanche set off up the rue de Seine towards the river. At the top of the street she crossed the road on to the pont des Arts. And there below her was the Seine, its grey-green water lapping as boats laden with tourists plied their way up and down its course. People of all shapes and ages in various states of undress were sunning themselves along the embankment. Turning about, she saw the topmost section of the Eiffel Tower, like a child's pencil drawing against the cerulean sky. That was another life. I shall never go there again, she thought.

The bridge's wrought-iron lamps were wreathed in clusters of padlocks pledging the eternal faith of romantically minded couples. A young man beneath one was chatting up two young women, a cigarette in one hand, his other ironically clutching his heart in a gesture designed to make them laugh. Another man was challenging a crowd to spot his sleight of hand with coins and cards. She liked the fierceness in his eyes willing his audience to dare to prove him wrong . . . the quickness of the hand deceives the eye, she thought, liking everything she saw around her. I am myself and a part of all this, she thought, continuing over the bridge and passing through to the old cobbled complex of the Louvre.

Beneath an arch an elderly hippy, his thin grey hair in a straggly ponytail, was strumming a guitar and singing in a faltering tenor 'When I'm Sixty-four'.

Yes, Blanche thought indulgently, I will help – to feed you, at least – and not bothering to count them, she dropped some coins into the open guitar case.

Ahead, the morning sun was being refracted from the glass panes of the Pyramid on to ornamental basins of water. Around the water's edges children ran, sometimes stopping to pull off shoes in order to dip their toes into the water, while adults lingered or lounged, smoking and chatting or simply enjoying the warmth and the view.

Paris is a moveable painting, Blanche decided, feeling a little elated at her play on the reference and rejoicing in the fact that the night before she had thought to buy a ticket on her phone and was therefore able to beat the general queue. Ken would be proud of me, she thought as she showed her phone at the entrance until it crossed her mind that perhaps he might feel some chagrin that she was managing so well on her own.

She decided to give coffee a miss – the crowd was overwhelming and she had to almost beat a path to the Leonardos.

Blanche skirted the dedicated worshippers of the *Mona Lisa* and slid her way through the cluster of people standing before the painting she had come to see. A painting of a trinity, not *the* Trinity but another less advertised triad, the holy trio of St Anne, with her daughter, Mary, and her daughter's boy child.

She stood absorbing the scene with no Ken to worry about. Ken hadn't much time for what he called God Squad stuff. She was not religious either – had never been to church since leaving school – but she often liked the holy subjects she saw in paintings. Certainly, she liked this one. She stood studying it now.

St Anne, mother of the Virgin Mary, was sitting with her grown child on her lap, contemplating her daughter and the child her daughter in turn had borne. Mary, enlapped and enfolded by her mother, was oblivious to all but her baby boy, to whom she was reaching out in a beseeching gesture of love. The little boy was playing with a lamb, a creature as innocent as himself of its untimely destined end.

Blanche as she stood there observed how Mary's boy was looking back and up at his mother while her own mother, the boy's grandmother, gazed down on the two of them.

And it seemed to Blanche that before her eyes the gazes of the three melted into a kind of moving reflection – mirroring and binding the three figures impalpably together in a never-ending play of encircling love.

St Anne's feet, she saw with a new consciousness, were planted solidly on the ground, as if to bear the combined weight of her daughter and her grandson. Long elegant feet. An elegant face too with that bony nose and archaic smile. Infinitely more speaking, she thought, than the Mona Lisa's. For while in its reserved beauty it undoubtedly had a tincture of mystery about it, Anne's smile was not an enigma. Not to Blanche. Quite clearly she could see in it the fond pride of a mother in her beloved daughter and the pride of a grandmother in her brand-new grandson.

But she could see in the smile too – the thought like lightning struck her with an almost physical pain – the harrowing foreknowledge of all that lay ahead for this pair, in all the world closest to her heart, her dearest and most precious flesh and blood.

Alone in the crowded salon of the Louvre, Blanche silently began to weep.

She woke the next morning ravenous and almost ran down the flights of stairs to where the hotel breakfast was being served.

A smart black woman took her order and brought a tray bearing jugs of piping coffee and warm milk, a basket of fresh baguette and croissants, a glass dish of apricot jam and some little cracker-shaped foil-wrapped portions of *beurre doux*.

Across the room a group of American women were

discussing whether or not to take a cab to the Arc de Triomphe. 'The fare won't be more than ten dollars apiece,' one of them declared. 'Probably cheaper than going on the subway.'

'What was the arch put up for anyway?' one asked.

Another woman gave it as her opinion that it was to 'mark the end of World War One. When we liberated them, you know.'

Blanche, with her old guidebook to hand, smiled and checked the entry on the Pompidou Centre, where she was planning to start her own day.

She walked there along the Seine, stopping to look at the devastations the fire had made of Notre-Dame. Charred but still noble it stood there, defying the forces of destruction. 'Good for you, Our Lady.' She spoke the words aloud and a couple of British tourists, discussing the time the repairs were going to take, turned and stared at her. Probably have me down as a madwoman, she thought, and the idea amused her.

What in the world has become of me, mad, drunk and dangerous to know? a loftily satirical voice enquired. A shoplifter too, another voice sneered. Oh, but that was awful! How could she have? As if fleeing the physical manifestation of a spectre, Blanche hurried on.

She arrived sweating at the Pompidou Centre, where she took the escalator, observing how the Sacré-Cœur looked more than ever like an over-done meringue as she rode upwards to the galleries. Here she strolled, only half examining the works of art, letting the thoughts prompted by the previous day's excursions percolate.

Her encounters with the image of St Anne had touched

the wound that was Kitty and Harry. Grandmothers had no rights, or none that had any influence over action. But a grandmother could care, as Leonardo – she felt sure – had understood, every bit as deeply as a mother for a child.

What did Anne think, she wondered, of her grandson's life choice (if 'life' choice was really the right term in the context)? The very experience of being long enough in the world brought you versions of wisdom – as well as a fair share of silliness and prejudice, Blanche reminded herself – out of which Anne must have longed to encourage her grandson to adopt a less self-destructive line. A grandmother, she thought, is unlikely to be in favour of the needlessly heroic – or is maybe more likely to see how the likelihood of it might arise.

Blanche's knowledge of the Bible, as with her knowledge of everything learnt at school, had lapsed into a murky vagueness. But somewhere, though she couldn't have given chapter and verse, she recalled an incident when Jesus had sharply rebuked his mother and made some harsh pronouncements about the need to distance oneself from constraining family ties.

Perhaps this was a reaction to the tendency in mothers to be sure they know best, a maternal possessiveness that maybe in Mary had produced a peculiarly potent strain. A strong-willed young man like Jesus of Nazareth might react to a mother's intransigence over his wellbeing as a cue for wanton self-sacrifice. Jesus, Blanche speculated, pausing before a drawing of a guitar, was probably one of those adolescent boys who refuse to wear a coat when the weather is arctic for the very reason that he has been assured by his mother that by not doing so he will surely catch his death.

That is what St Anne is seeing in Leonardo's painting, she decided. Anne has a premonition of the desperate clash of wills that is to occur between her daughter and her grandson – a clash foreshadowed in that gaze of ardent maternal love – that will lead to a horrible quite unnecessary tragedy. One that she can do nothing about.

Pleased if at the same time disheartened by her radical reworking of Christian theology, Blanche turned her attention to the picture before her: Braque's *Man with a Guitar*. There were many versions on that theme displayed in the gallery. The artists of the period evidently had a thing about guitars.

Her mind conjured up the man with the pathetic grey ponytail in the courtyard of the Louvre. What forces of loss and failure had driven him there to eke out a living with his guitar? Or was he in his mind still a virile young man, still following a romance of living by his art?

Will you still need me when I'm sixty-four? might be a plea addressed to God, or anyway to the god in charge of fate, as much as to a sweetheart. Was there a god of fate? No, the Fates were women, weren't they? She rummaged in her mind for more information but nothing came. Nan, she thought, would know.

31

Nan had been relieved to note that when Alec had left them to return to London Billy appeared to recover his spirits. Although, Nan thought, little pitchers were deep so you could never tell. But she was pleased that her hunch about Rose had not been wrong. The upset at Sea Life had apparently created some kind of bond. The two children had built a hideout where they assumed in turn the role of Maxim the Magician and brewed noxious potions from plants and duckweed. Brown and freckled, they rushed about shrieking and casting on each other terrible transforming spells. When not at the beach the pair of them spent their days immersed in their alternative world.

And she and Minna had rubbed along, once she got Minna to drop her habit of always deferring.

'I suppose,' Minna had said during a conversation about the children's impending SATS in which she had aired her anxieties about Rose's maths, 'I suppose they must have educational experts who know what they're talking about.'

Nan gave such pieties short shrift. 'It's not education, it's a system of indoctrination, designed, if you ask me, to stop children thinking for themselves.'

And Minna had said apologetically, 'I'm no judge. I don't have a degree.'

'I don't have one either if it comes to that,' Nan had retorted.

She wasn't about to go into her flight from Oxford on the eve of her finals. Water under the bridge, she would have said. But if the water had ever flowed on, now it appeared to be flowing back, bringing with it flotsam.

She had not returned to take her degree after that long trek to St Abbs, where she had received the fateful news that her young lover had died. He and the other lads had gone to swim through the wreckage of the Peanut Boat and – for whatever reason – Hamish had never resurfaced. He had died in the waters of the sea where they had first met. Died in the waters into which she herself had so often felt the urge fatally to plunge. Died where she longed to join him now with every fibre of her aching body and every impulse of her sorrowing mind.

Was it grief or guilt that had seemed best honoured by her refusal to continue on the path she had set out on? Set out secure ("secure"! how laughable that idea seemed now) in the knowledge that with her degree she could make a good career. For that had been the plan: to teach English Literature to girls who like herself had brains enough to take them beyond the circumstances into which they had been born.

Alongside this, she had blithely imagined herself and Hamish in the house they always said they would buy, their house, they called it, a fine local grey-stone house which he would put to rights with his clever capable hands. A rambling draughty house atop the cliffs with a patch of land to keep hens or a goat or maybe a donkey for the children or to make a garden large enough for the large family they planned to have to muck about in. A home by the sea where Hamish could with her encouragement and his industry (an industry that it was part of her role, she knew, as the pushier one, to promote) in time maybe save enough to part-own a fishing smack – her uncles had done it and they might take Hamish on board; a home where they would bring up a troupe of water babies as able in the sea as on land, and where at night she would tuck them into their cots and beds and read to them poems and stories to ensure that their hearts and minds grew as sturdy and resilient as their young limbs would in the clean air and the sunlight.

All this, the sea took from her that fatal evening.

What is a woman that you forsake her,
And the hearth-fire and the home-acre.
To go with the old grey Widow-maker?

The words rang as clear in Nan's mind as they had when her lover's sea-swollen body was at last washed ashore. For days she had walked barefoot along the clifftops or in the salt waves along the sea's margin – the sharp gorse and thistle or the biting shingle on her cold flesh were what she felt were needed as she mourned; mourned for her love who was gone for good.

Gone for bad, more like. It was not Hamish who had been the forsaker.

'No,' she said more peaceably to Minna. 'I never finished my degree.'

If Minna's reading had not so far bred the confidence to differ openly with a character as firm as Nan's it had quickened a natural sensitivity. She was alive to what not to pursue. 'But you've done fine without one,' she suggested.

'Well enough,' Nan agreed.

It was true. She had done all right, taking jobs as a secretary – she had proved a demon typist – rising to a PA, which is how she met Terence, who chose her over another, better-qualified candidate to run his burgeoning architects' practice.

'What made you pick me?' she had asked him when later they were on more intimate terms. And he had said, 'You put me right over the Planning Act, if you remember. A boss needs a PA who can pick up a dropped stitch.'

And she and Terry, living and working together, had been all right, in their way. There was none of the passion there had been with Hamish. But perhaps she had not wanted that again (the burnt child dreads the fire). Still, there had been mutual respect, good humour and an easy-going generosity.

Terry had never interfered. Never enquired what it was she was doing when she withdrew to the comfortable study – her 'brown study', she had named it – that he had designed for her in the terraced Chiswick house so unlike that rambling house by the sea that was never to be hers.

She has no house to lay a guest in –

He had never objected to the evening classes she took in order to keep her brain ticking over, as she put it, or her trips abroad. (Though those must have been a godsend to him, she had recognised when the truth about his sexuality emerged.) From time to time he had urged her to get the degree she had foregone – for that hitch in her history she had revealed to him if not the reasons which had led to it – but she had never felt inclined to go back. Never go back, she would have said, had been her guiding watchwords.

In my end is my beginning . . . The line, from being so often and so facilely trotted out, had almost lost its virtue for her; but she seemed to be living to gather the truth of it now.

Time, mindlessly heedless of those who must abide in it, galloped towards the end of the week at the wagon. The children, as yet ill acquainted with this implacable natural disaster, played as if they could play for ever. Their land-lady rang to say she would be back from London on the day of their departure and the news was a signal to the women to begin to tidy: to shake sand out of shoes, scrub at tar stains, pack up clothes that were not going to be worn again.

'Rose is going to miss Bill,' Minna observed.

It was their last evening, the children had disappeared to their hideout and the two women were sitting out on the veranda. They had been reading but Minna had finished *Swann's Way* and Nan had abandoned *Weymouth Beach* and was musing.

'And Bill will miss the lass,' she said. It crossed her mind that it would be charitable to say that she would miss Minna. 'I shall miss being here,' she managed. And that *was* true. With the children thick as thieves and Minna so deep in her book there had been space for Nan's long poem to begin to etch itself on to the back of her mind. 'I'm very grateful to you for suggesting we stay here,' she volunteered.

Minna was pleased at this. But she had acquired a sense of how to treat Nan so she didn't, as she might have done, immediately thank her for this token gratitude. 'Having Bill here to play with Rosie's allowed me time to finish this.' She gestured at *Swann's Way*, which she had laid reverently beside her. 'It took some getting into but . . .' hesitating – then, 'you might like it, you know.'

Nan's first instinct was to dismiss this. But she had been impressed – though she would never have mentioned it – by her companion's absorption in the book and she was aware too of her own tendency to indulge her prejudices. Over the years she had come to enjoy this habit: it was good fun to play at scoffing at Proust, who was such a bastion of a certain kind of literary taste.

She was aware that she had constructed for herself a personality based on a propensity to go against the prevailing grain. Her grandmother's advice had found fertile ground in her own innate character. That and the life fate had dealt her had led her to build for herself an inner citadel and really only Billy was permitted inside. And defences, built over years, were not so easy to surrender. *We would rather be ruined than changed*, she thought, sharply rueful. There had been other ways of life once open to her.

Not for the first time she considered whether part of her cussedness (for she knew that was the face she often showed to the world) was born of the decision to abandon Oxford and all that that life might have entailed. All ways of life have a cost, she reminded herself, and smiled inwardly because she knew too that self-knowledge, for all it made life more interesting, didn't of itself bring about change.

But lately – the conversation with Minna had under-lined it – she had begun to experience a desire to be done with all such nonsense, to let her hermit-crab shell and all its accretions be washed away – to become her naked self. What ever, in the world, that was or might be. Still might be, maybe . . .?

'OK,' she said. 'Chuck it over and I'll give it a whirl. I can't say the one I've been reading is much cop.'

'What's it about?' Minna asked, passing her the book.

'As to what it's about,' Nan said, 'I couldn't tell you. But I've a feeling it's heading towards the mystical.'

Retreating back into her shell, she couldn't help mak-ing 'mystical' sound almost like a term of abuse.

The children were shy with each other when the final moments of departure came. Minna had offered to drive Billy and Nan to Weymouth station but it was out of her way and Nan felt that a taxi made the parting simpler. She allowed Minna to help her with the cases to the waiting taxi and gave Rose a fond hug. 'Goodbye, lass.'

Rose was looking forlorn. The holiday which had stretched before her with such promise had ended too abruptly and she was experiencing the horrible shock of finality. It didn't help that after a couple of overcast days the sun was shining baldly in a brilliantly clear sky.

'Come and see us in London,' Nan rashly offered, and wondered why in God's name she had done so.

'Can we?' Rose asked Minna and, seeing the question in Minna's eyes, Nan unthinkingly came out with 'You could always sleep on my sofa. I'm sure Bill's mum would be glad to have Rose.'

That was daft, she reflected as the taxi drove up the pitted track, for other than Billy she hated the prospect of company in her tiny flat.

Minna, having dropped Rose at her house, returned to the shepherd's hut and unloaded the toys from her car.

'Well now, toys,' she said, arranging them with care around the room. 'We're back.'

The drive had been a long one. For all it was light still, she lit the oil lamp and, cold with fatigue and a renewed apprehension of being alone, poured a large whisky.

The holiday had been a success. Better than her best dreams. She could be proud that she had given Rose that. But the move to Glasgow was now ahead, with no ameliorating prospects to soften the coming parting.

I must pull myself together, Minna thought. She looked at *Within a Budding Grove*, which was waiting for her. Proust had been one thing while she had Rose, and Billy and Nan. Alone again, and out of practice, she felt a want of living comfort.

The books which Rose had finished had been packed away in Minna's case ahead of their departure. Minna took up an Elizabeth Pattern. The letter which the author had written to Rose was inside. Rose had shown it proudly to Minna but wanting to be reminded of their day in Oxford and in need of some sense of a sympathetic sentient soul Minna took it out and read it again.

32

Blanche had not considered what she would do after her stay in Paris. She was slightly amazed at her own willingness to see how the mood took her and just take it from there. This was unquestionably a departure from the Ken days: Ken never moved more than a mile without a well-considered much-discussed plan.

She had explored the parts of Paris she had formerly never ventured into, allowing herself the disloyalty of rather welcoming the absence of Ken. And one day she passed an art shop, where she found herself buying a set of pencils and a sketch pad.

She had spent several afternoons after that in the Jardin du Luxembourg, sketching the people on the park benches, even returning to the art shop to buy watercolours so that she could try her hand at painting. But after eight days she said farewell to the hotel and took the Métro to the Gare de l'Est, where she booked a ticket on the TGV to Reims.

Her feeling of competence had grown. She had found on the internet a modestly priced hotel on the broad avenue that leads up to the cathedral. She checked in, saying she would be staying for a couple or so – she wasn't yet sure how many – nights. She might have noticed that the daringness of these off-the-cuff arrangements was not unlike the thrill produced by shoplifting.

The hotel was high and narrow; there was no lift and Blanche's room was at the very top. She climbed five flights of stairs, heaving her suitcase, to find a room smaller than at the Paris hotel but with windows that looked two ways.

An eyrie full of light. It was clean and had a double bed and while there was no bath, only a shower tucked into the corner of a tiny bathroom, it would more than do.

Blanche's decision to revisit Reims had been sparked by the Leonardo painting. The smile on the face of St Anne had illuminated a memory. She had been taken as a child by her grandmother to see the famous cathedral where the kings of France had been crowned. The memory was misty – a dim recollection of high columns, vaulting ceilings and a large reposeful silence. But what had strikingly come back to her was the smiling face of an angel who stood sentinel at the cathedral entrance.

Her grandmother must have liked it because she recalled her pointing to the angel. 'Ma chérie, regarde le sourire de l'ange. C'est très beau, n'est-ce pas?' And Blanche had held the angel's smile in her mind when she was sent back to that school and to what always seemed to her the lightless friendless cold which was England. And then she had forgotten it.

The woman who had once been the child Blanche now walked, bearing these tissued memories, up the avenue towards the twin-towered honey-coloured cathedral around which birds with scimitar wings were making ellipses against the soaring sky. Their thin high voices etched the ears of the plodding earthbound humans. She passed a woman pointing them out to her children, 'Look, darlings, swallows up there.' Her husband or partner corrected her. 'Not swallows, I think you'll find, swifts.' One of the children rolled his eyes and the woman killed the man with a glance. Blanche winked at the woman as she passed and then hurried on, embarrassed at her boldness.

At the cathedral's front she stopped to inspect the facade. Three doorways, each set into a deep arch and within each a profusion of stone figures. Where was her angel?

Here in the arch of the central door was an angel with comely rounded cheeks and a severed right hand. In spite of the injury, he was smiling. But this wasn't her angel. She moved along, searching almost frantically the medley of religious effigies.

Here was Mary receiving news of her pregnancy with a stupefied stare, as well she might; here was Peter with his keys. Oh, but here was her angel, the left arm handless but for all that held high, as if in greeting, the smile more reserved than that of his beaming colleague, gracious, humorous, ineffably understanding and quite unchanged. Remarkably so, given that it must be fifty years since she saw him last. But there, while she had moved on, he had stayed faithfully in the depths of her mind, patiently waiting for her to remember him.

She took some pictures on her phone and sent one off to Kitty with a text: *A smiling angel for you, my Angel. Best Love, G xxx*

Inside, she was met by the smell that as a child she had supposed must be the odour of sanctity. A distinctive musty smell quite peculiar to holy places. After the heat outside the cathedral was blessedly cool.

Blanche bought a guide from the kiosk and read that

the beaming angel was the Archangel Gabriel. But the other more gravely smiling angel, *her* angel . . . another recollection began to surface: some photos in her grandmother's album: smudged sepia photos of a wrecked cathedral with a great gash in its walls. Troubled now, she read of a German bombing raid in 1914, how the head of her angel had been a casualty and the shattered parts had been recovered and kept safely until the pieces could be restored and the head, remodelled and still gallantly smiling, returned to its place on the angelic form.

Before her tall grey-gold columns lanced by the afternoon sun rose loftily upwards, their fronded capitals recalling the trees on which they were modelled. Blanche walked down the aisle to the transepts. High up on each side the ancient stained glass, held by a web of stone in the rose windows, offered a vision to the faithful of a better life to come. She sat down and half closed her eyes so that the window opposite became a mandala of blues, magentas, purples and red tinged with green and white. For a long time she sat there, wordlessly absorbing the deep quiet, the rainbow colours of the glass, allowing the long-unremembered fragments of her life to float back.

That night she drank champagne in a fine flute, for after all this was champagne country, and for the next few days she went to pay her respects to her angel and to the cathedral he guarded so benignly with his missing left hand. What had he been holding before the bomb knocked it from his grasp? A flower, a lily, probably, Blanche decided. Beyond the flimsy guide she had sought no further information. It wasn't the facts of history that she wanted.

Over the next few days she spent whole mornings wandering round the cathedral, or sitting in the apse, observing how the light through the harsh patterns of the contemporary stained glass bathed the stone with great daubs of soft crimson and blue. *Roses are red, violets are blue,* her mind reminded her, *Sugar is sweet* . . . but sugar was no longer acceptably sweet as in the old world of the rhyme.

Once, very early in the morning, when the doors had just been opened and she had supposed that she was alone in the cathedral, the organ suddenly gave out a tremendous blast of sweet thunder and she all but wept at the glory of the sound.

Sometimes towards evening she lit long tapering white candles; for Kitty, for Harry, the odd one for herself and one – after a period of inner questioning – for Dominic: Dominic, her baby boy, for whose life she had once prayed. Ah, but she thought, grown more reflective in the space granted by the cathedral, it was easy enough to pray for a baby who had had no time to thwart you. But it would be wrong, she reproved herself, if – for the forbidding man he had grown into – she lit no candle now.

As the days passed with no other occupation but these it seemed that she was living out some gently restorative meditation. And when the time seemed right she packed up and took a bus to the village where her grandmother had lived and died.

She was worried that the blue-shuttered house in the little country village might have changed. But it was much as she recalled it: smaller, but she was ready for this, knowing how things lodged in memory will always expand to fill out their significance. And the garden – pushing herself up on tiptoe to peer at it over the stone wall – that was almost as she had remembered: the beds of white peonies, the rambling-rose arch, the box-edged beds, even the swallows seemed the same in their endless pursuit of flies.

Blanche stood there, quietly watching. Swallows were faithful birds. Time after time they returned to their old haunts to breed. These might be the offspring of the birds she had seen in that long-ago spring. They swooped so low she could see their neat pale bellies and dull crimson throats. Soon they would be collecting on the telephone wires, lining up, ready to make their departure for another world.

She pushed herself up again, stretching higher still, and there was the old brass tap, as it had been when her twelve-year-old self had watched enchanted as the cold water sluiced Albert's bare young back.

Where was Albert now? Probably a bald slippered old man with a paunch.

Kitty would want her to go and find him. 'He will fall in love with you, Granny,' Kitty would say, because that is what happened in the romantic films she was so fond of, 'and you will have a *passionate* love affair.'

The scent of the summer flowers and the thin cries of the swallows metamorphosed into the signatories of heart-break. All the hideous hurtful missing of Kitty came overwhelmingly back. She still hadn't sent her the card. Why not? Kitty would imagine she had forgotten her. But she knew why. She hadn't wanted to scratch the wound. And that's what bloody fucking Tina's done, she thought, rage flaring up again, blasting her recovered idyll. She's made it too painful to think about Kitty.

Fired up anew to fight this assault on her love, she found a café, ordered a kir and searched her bag for the postcards from the Delacroix studio.

'*Darling Kitten,*' she wrote. '*I'm having a fabulous time in France, revisiting places I loved as a girl when I was about your age. This is a painting by an artist I discovered in Paris. He's very famous but as you know I'm an utter ignoramus, so I've only just found him. He loved flowers and these poppies made me think of you. I hope you are having a wonderful summer. Much love, G. xxx*'

Reading this through, she underlined 'fabulous'. Good, she thought. Tina will read that and be annoyed.

She wrote the card of Dionysus with his tiger to Harry. '*This is the god of wine. I like the way he is feeding it to his tiger.*' This with luck would irk Tina too. She could hardly miss the reference to wine.

The card to Nan was harder to compose.

'*Had a great time in Paris and visited this artist's atelier. I thought you might appreciate the skull with the flowers.*' She had the other postcard in her bag too, the one of St Anne teaching her daughter to read. She considered adding some thoughts about the latter. But there wasn't room on a card and she hadn't the words. '*Hope your summer is going well*' hardly seemed the right note for Nan but after hesitating over an alternative she wrote it anyway.

There was a modest inn in the village and she took a room there. A simple room with a bed with an old-fashioned white lace coverlet and the tall grey-shuttered windows that are the hallmark of rural France.

That night Blanche slept fitfully and awoke to find it was only 2 a.m. Wide awake, she went to the window, where she had left the shutters open. Stars like millions of tiny fragments of crushed crystal had been embedded deep into the sky. From a nearby copse a bird called, a weird clattering sound, and the word 'nightjar' came unbidden to her mind. She had never to her knowledge even seen a picture of a nightjar. Out of the darkness an arc of falling light grazed the darkness, gave off a little flourish and faded into a swirl of pale ashes. Blanche knelt on the bare floorboards and closed her eyes.

Travelling back on the Eurostar, she tried to evaluate her spell abroad. It had been a tonic and she could mark up her venture as a success: she had discovered allies – Delacroix and Leonardo – and recovered her angel; she had found her grandmother's house, where she had wished on a falling star.

And for the rest of her stay the wish had offered the promise of the possible. But as the Eurostar plunged into the long tunnel that connects the mainlands of France and England she experienced a sharp drop in spirits. It was horribly reminiscent of the despair she had experienced on returning to boarding school.

Autumn Term

33

A week or so after her return to London Blanche rang Nan. 'I'm back from France,' she said brightly. And waited.

Since delivering Billy to his mother after the Weymouth holiday Nan had been absorbed in her long poem. Composing time was mostly spent horizontal in her willow casket, where words drifted down to her from sources into which she chose not to delve. But she was sitting ram-rod straight at her desk, having just typed the final line of a stanza, when Blanche rang.

To Nan's surprise she felt quite pleased at hearing Blanche's voice. 'Come over,' she said. 'Come and tell me all about it.'

Blanche, who had braced herself for Nan to be unwelcoming, was also surprised. 'When should I come?'

'About six tonight?' Nan suggested. Alec had sent her some wine, supposedly a thank-you for taking Billy on holiday but actually, Nan surmised, propitiation for his plan to move to Singapore. It was expensive wine, not the kind she was likely to broach alone, and Blanche was an excuse . . . Nan checked herself . . . no, not an excuse, an occasion to do so.

'I drank champagne in France,' Blanche said. They were drinking Alec's Chablis from Nan's unbreakable tumblers.

Nan understood that in saying this Blanche was not

intending to show off and resisted the temptation to say, as she might have done, Very lah-di-dah. Instead she said, 'I've never got along with champagne. It gives me a headache.'

'It can,' Blanche agreed. 'It has to be good,' and then, fearing a snub for this admission of a sophistication that Nan might not share, added, 'I only drank some because I was in Reims – champagne country.'

'Ah, Reims,' Nan said, letting the champagne flow down the river, 'with the affable angel.'

Blanche was so delighted that her angel would need no introduction that she got out her phone, searching for photos.

Cathedrals for Nan had other associations and she had her own pictures in her mind. 'I don't need to see those, thank you. What took you there?'

Blanche explained about her grandmother. 'She was a Catholic and very devout. My mother didn't bother at all with religion; she was a great disappointment to my grandmother. I didn't either except when I stayed with her. We always went to Mass.'

When she was staying with her grandmother her grandmother had used to send her to bed up the dark-oak twisting staircase that smelt always of polish, saying that while she slept a host of angels would cluster around her, watching over her throughout the long night. She had believed in those angels and had slept so securely in the knowledge of their presence.

'My grandmother believed in angels,' she said aloud, and then wished she hadn't, expecting Nan to mock this as a childish superstition.

But Nan only said, 'People believe in far more improbable matters than angels.'

Blanche was a little reassured. 'She used to say we all have a guardian angel.' She laughed nervously. 'Not that I believe that now.' A needle of guilt pricked as she said this – as if she were betraying her smiling angel.

Nan looked at her hard. 'I don't see why not. Plenty do. Blake saw angels all the time.' As a lad, on the common at Peckham Rye – *a tree filled with angels, bright angelic wings bespangling every bough like stars.* 'He talked to the Angel Gabriel.'

Blanche considered saying, He's on the other door, but thought better of it.

'I expect it's one of those things that exist if you believe in them,' Nan continued. 'Like quantum mechanics – or placebos,' she added, less poetically.

'Do you believe in them?' Blanche risked.

Nan considered how to answer this. In her mind's eye she saw Blake's angel-filled tree as a flowering hawthorn, its white blossoms caught in the transforming everyday miracle of the incredible morning light. 'What I think is that over the ages enough people have seen them, talked to them, been affected by them – and painted and composed and written of them too – for them to be some version of reality. I respect that.'

She didn't mention her sage – he was her business, and whatever he was she was sure he wasn't an angel.

'After Reims I went to find my grandmother's house,' Blanche said. She felt more confident now. 'It looked just the same. The garden did, anyway.'

'And did you see what's-his-name?' Nan asked.

Blanche was about to answer when she remembered

that she had not in fact told Nan about the flesh-and-blood Albert, the young man in the workman's *bleu de travail*. She had merely borrowed his name.

'Albert?'

'Him.'

'No,' Blanche said. 'I didn't.' She wondered how Nan could know she had met Albert in that garden.

Nan could not have supplied Blanche with an answer to that question, which might have easily been a lucky shot in the dark. 'That's a shame.' She felt a certain artistic interest in Albert, having had a hand in his creation.

'You sound like Kitty,' Blanche said. 'She would love me to meet a tall dark stranger and have a love affair.'

It struck Nan that Kitty might have a point. Ken sounded to her a bit of a stick-in-the mud. 'How's your other lover doing?'

'You mean Alan?' Blanche blushed.

'That one. Alan Breck.'

'Why do you keep calling him that?' Blanche asked.

Nan laughed. 'I'm sorry, that's me playing silly buggers. Alan Breck is a character in a book I like. I know your Alan has a different name.'

'He's not "my" Alan.' Blanche took cover in being indignant.

'Have some more wine,' Nan said. She was practising being less tricksome and was amused to see how Blanche was taking it.

It was Kitty, Nan guessed, whom Blanche had really come to talk about. Kitty had got her way and was about to start, with her friend Faith, at St Anselm's, the Catholic comprehensive. She and Blanche had communicated on their phones and Blanche reported that Kitty sounded excited if a little scared.

'I still hope I haven't done the wrong thing,' Blanche said, for what might have been the fourth time.

Nan had resolved to be patient. 'You can't know. She'll have one sort of a time there and she would have had another sort of time at that other school she was down for. There'll be pluses and minuses both ways. All ways of life have a cost,' she threw in for good measure, and added, because Blanche wasn't Billy, 'I don't mean to sound like a cracker-barrel philosopher.'

Blanche was no judge of philosophy and was comforted by Nan's observations. 'I miss her,' she said. 'I miss her hideously.' All her brave adventures in France seemed no more than fool's gold.

'Of course you do,' Nan said. 'It's wicked what they've done to you – and to her. But your Kitty sounds like a resourceful girl. It's a pain that she has to – and I'm not saying it's all for the best or any nonsense like that – but my hunch is she'll find her own ways to see you. It'll be easier now she's at the secondary.'

'She's got a friend going there with her.' Blanche felt a little cheered. 'Faith. I liked her.' She didn't add that Kitty had informed her that Faith thought she was 'cool'.

But Nan had intuited this. A well-dressed indulgent grandmother was an asset, the value of whom any intelligent young woman would be quick to recognise. 'Good,' she pronounced. 'Everyone needs an ally. Faith will help.'

As it happened, a little later that same evening on the other side of London Faith cropped up in a conversation between Tina and Dominic. Tina had embarked on a lament about the new school's many drawbacks when compared with the virtues of the Dean's School. She had worked herself around to the potentially undesirable influence of Kitty's friend.

'I'm not saying Faith's not lovely,' she volunteered. 'It's just . . .'

'What?'

Dominic was not quite alive to his wife's concerns, which had to do with the fact that Faith's father was black and therefore Tina felt constrained from openly expressing any reservations about her. Tina was sure she was not a racist and would have been appalled to have been considered one. But the colour of Faith's skin was inhibiting Tina from speaking her mind. It was thanks to Faith that Kitty had wheedled them into allowing her to attend St Anselm's and some of the spleen Tina felt for her mother-in-law had spilled on to Faith.

She fell back on 'She's just not very interested in reading and music, that sort of thing.'

Dominic laughed the blokeish uncomprehending laugh that particularly annoyed his wife. 'She seemed to like music OK when she stayed here.' Faith had played very loud music on her phone and he had been sent to ask the girls to turn it down.

'You know what I mean. Those clothes she wears, some of them are quite inappropriate, and all the make-up and the nail varnish . . .' she trailed off uncertainly.

Dominic, who had been taken with Faith's multicoloured nails, began, 'I don't know that nail varnish –' but his wife interrupted.

'You know fucking well what I mean. If she'd gone to the Dean's School . . .'

'She'd be mixing with the right sort from the top drawer, I suppose?' Dominic risked a foray into sarcasm, provoking a furious scowl from his wife.

Tina had grown up in a family which had mercilessly mocked her for being conscientious over her homework. She had won her way to a Russell Group university from a notorious state comprehensive with a record of low A-level grades, had worked her socks off while there and taken a good degree and followed this with a Master's in Social Policy. All this she had funded herself, taking on tedious jobs which, through strict economies, kept her just out of debt until she found a job where she could set about paying off her loans. And she had worked hard and risen to a senior position at GlaxoSmithKline. Dominic had sailed into the same university via an expensive public school and parents who unquestioningly settled his student overdraft.

It did not occur to Tina that what she desired so urgently for her children was the very condition she most resented in her husband, whose parents, to her mind, had spoiled him. His mother, certainly, had coddled him.

'Well, if you have no ambitions for your children . . .' She left the consequences of this paternal dereliction hanging in the air and went upstairs with her phone for company to run a bath.

Nan and Blanche, but mainly Blanche, had polished off the bottle of Chablis, and Blanche, who was wary of outstaying her welcome but wanting not to lose Nan's company, offered, 'Could I take you out to eat?'

Nan consented on condition they split the bill and in the mild early-autumn air they strolled down the road together to the local tapas bar.

It was a quiet evening with few diners and a solicitous waiter appeared swiftly to invite orders for drinks.

'Shall we have some more wine?' Blanche asked.

Nan, who liked to keep her wits clear, was about to say, Not for me, but observing Blanche's expression, changed her mind. 'I dare say another glass won't put me under the table.'

When the waiter had brought the wine and taken their orders Blanche took a postcard from her bag and passed it wordlessly across the table to Nan.

Nan studied the picture for some time before turning it over to read the artist's name. 'Delacroix? Thank you for your card, by the way. I should have said.'

Blanche didn't ask whether Nan had liked the skull and irises. She was more eager to hear what she made of this picture. 'What do you think of it?'

'Interesting subject.' Nan was cautious. She guessed that something about this picture had kindled the glint in Blanche's eyes.

'It's the Virgin's mother, St Anne.'

'Ah.' Nan had already worked that out.

'There's another painting I saw. Well, I'd seen it before, but . . .' Blanche heard herself begin to gabble. She paused to gather the words to convey what in Paris had seemed to her so precious. 'There's a Leonardo in the Louvre, not the *Mona Lisa*, another . . .'

Nan listened without comment as Blanche tried out her thoughts about St Anne.

'. . . What he saw – I mean what Leonardo saw – I was thinking,' Blanche tried to summon her complicated thoughts, 'is that St Anne, as the grandmother, has to bear the knowledge that, in spite of what she can see, because she is older and wiser and maybe knows more about how the world works, she is powerless to do anything . . .'

'You mean powerless to stop a young man in the pride of life choosing wilfully to go to his own death?' Nan summed up for her.

'Yes, sort of, yes,' Blanche said. Her seemingly novel insights spelt out sounded pathetic and confused.

But Nan was reflecting. She had seen the other version of this painting, the cartoon at the Royal Academy, and she too had been taken by a feeling she had not had words for, or perhaps not thought to analyse at the time. She had been struck by the study of the irises and the skull that Blanche had sent her from France. The fragile but imperiously coloured flowers juxtapositioned with the stark memento of death was not the kind of picture she would have expected to receive on a card from Blanche.

'You know,' she said, unthinkingly reaching across Blanche to help herself to more wine, 'I think that's spot on. It gives that whole story a domestic dimension which you get in the early bit, with the babe born in the barn and the shepherd folk and so on, but which they made so high-falutin with all that fancy theology later on.' She took a reflective sip. 'I never liked the idea he was supposed to die to save us all. It's maudlin. And theoretical,' she pursued. 'It's a male kind of a notion, making a moral out of a myth.'

'Do you think Leonardo had a grandmother?' Blanche was too gratified by Nan's approbation to comment on it.

'Bound to have had, I suppose.'

'It would be nice to think they were close.'

Nan fell silent. She was trying to recall something she had read about Leonardo being like a child who wakes too early in the dark. But it wouldn't come. Blake was only eight years old when he saw the angels in the trees on the common of Peckham Rye.

'Maybe the point of grandmothers is to keep the child alive after death,' was all that she could manage. She couldn't for the moment have said herself what she meant by this.

34

Rose's mother had returned from Glasgow in the summer, having made a decision on a house and arranged a survey.

'What's it like?' Rose had asked, excited in spite of herself.

'It's got a swing,' her brother said.

Justin had gone with his parents up to Glasgow and as a result had, to Rose's mind, acquired a new bumptiousness. Although Rose had loved her time away with Minna, her brother had had their parents to himself and it was only natural that she should feel a little jealous.

'It's got a swing and my bedroom's got a window into the garden,' Justin said, slightly taunting.

'We thought you'd like the attic room, Rosie,' her mother interjected, seeing a fracas looming. 'It's lovely, it has windows that look both ways.'

Rose consented to look at pictures of the house on her mother's phone. Her brother's projected room had French windows but the attic room was larger and had a sloping ceiling and funny windows. 'We thought it was like *Anne of Green Gables*,' her mother suggested placatingly. 'Dad says he can whitewash it for you, if you like. And we can put up some pretty curtains.'

'I'm getting wallpaper with trains on it,' Justin announced.

*

Some weeks later, when the new term at school was under way, a well-dressed well-made-up young woman appeared at the gate as Rose and Justin were playing after supper in their front garden. The woman caught Rose's eye and beckoned her over.

'Are you Nick Cooper's daughter?'

Rose, who knew not to talk to strangers, nodded cautiously and the young woman produced an envelope. 'Can you see your dad gets this?' She smiled at Rose; the smile was not an agreeable one.

'My mum's inside,' Rose said.

'It's for your dad. It's confidential.' The woman smiled the unreassuring smile again and Rose was left with the envelope.

A little later when their father arrived home from work Rose and Justin were still in the garden.

'There was a lady who came and said to give you this.' Rose produced the envelope on which 'PRIVATE' was written. She observed the expression on her father's face become shifty.

'Oh yes,' he said, and the tone of his voice was also odd. 'That must be about a job we're advertising at work.'

'Is she your secretary?'

'No,' her father said quickly. 'Or, yes, kind of. So, she was, that's true, yes, but now she's kind of filling in.'

Justin stopped what he was doing – which was collecting snails in a bucket ready to throw over his sister at a suitable moment – and stared. He had rarely, if ever, seen his father like this.

'So I needed to look at some papers tonight,' their

father, too explanatory, went on, 'and she's run them out here for me.'

'She smelt,' Justin said. 'She stank, the lady.' He pranced about, swinging his bucket of snails and holding his nose.

'She didn't,' Rose objected. 'That was her perfume.'

Her father crammed the envelope into his pocket. 'Is Mum inside?'

Rose looked at her father's face. A wash of sweat had broken out on his brow. 'She didn't see Mum,' she advised him.

Blanche had not risked taking her Paris drawings along to show Nan when she went to see her at the end of the summer holidays. She would have liked to do this – she was eager for comment, as those in the first stages of artistic endeavour often are. But she was aware that her drawings were not up to much and she was alive to the fact that Nan was not the sort to bestow false praise. But as they walked back up the Portobello Road after their supper at the tapas bar she did tell Nan about her sketches in the Jardin du Luxembourg.

'I thought I might enrol in an art class,' she concluded. 'Life drawing, maybe. Though what I enjoyed most was drawing the pool with the trees and plants all round it.' There was something about the leaves, she half thought.

'I read somewhere that drawing is an antidote to dementia,' Nan offered. 'I can see how that might work the brain, translating from the eye to the hand.'

'I hope I'm not dementing!' Blanche was a little put out.

Nan laughed. 'I wasn't implying . . . of course you're not. I was just saying . . .' but she felt that she couldn't be bothered to say quite what it was she was just saying.

She didn't much want to talk at all, as she was mulling the conversation they had had over supper. She had been stirred by Blanche's observations about the Virgin and her mother and the light this shed upon Anne's love for her grandchild, a love that perhaps acted as an image for the love of all grandmothers, everywhere. But there was more in all this which she couldn't quite tease out but which she felt she had half uttered with the strange words she had come out with about keeping the child alive after death.

Blanche's revelation about her drawings fed into these ruminations. For certainly, Nan was thinking, to draw or paint or write words or music of any quality you must preserve a child's vision, even through that valley of death which is the incremental death of innocence. For wasn't the progress into adulthood, her mind ran on, itself a kind of death, if a death that was necessary for the birth of new life and new possibilities? But a death that at another level must also be resisted so that – almost she could see it – a kind of sacred space could be preserved.

In the past weeks, lying in her willow coffin, she had spent much time with the sage. He had sat there on his rock, as it were beside her, saying little but keeping she now felt a kind of protective guard. Quite distinctly it came into Nan's mind that he was engaged in watching over her. It was a subtle act, not a controlling care . . . but the precise nature of what she was reaching to define was for the moment to elude her for she and Blanche had reached the place where the Portobello Road is crossed by Elgin Crescent, the physical parting of their ways.

In this part of London, which prides itself on sharing

the cosmopolitan customs of Europe, the shops stay open late. The red-headed florist on the corner was shutting up for the night, tipping water from the buckets down the drain and preparing to ditch those flowers that wouldn't survive the night.

'Thank you, Nan,' Blanche said. 'That was a lovely evening.' She looked over to the florist. 'I'll have those,' she called out, 'if you don't want them.'

'Thank you too, Blanche,' Nan said. For once she didn't add any quip but added, 'You should come to Kew Gardens with me and Bill some time. There's plants aplenty there you might like to draw.'

'You can have these,' the florist called from across the road, holding out a spray of beech leaves and some Michaelmas daisies.

Blanche looked across at her. Under the first glimmer of the yellowing streetlight the florist's russet hair was making a halo. In her olive-green overalls and dark orange cardigan, with her offering of tawny leaves and pale mauve blooms she appeared to Blanche a painting in waiting.

'Thank you,' she called back. 'I'll take them.' And 'Thank you,' she said to Nan. 'I'd like that. Will you call me?'

35

'Are you OK, sweetie?' Minna asked.

The move to Glasgow, if all went to plan with the survey, was scheduled to take place just before Christmas – a daft decision, in Minna's view. Nowadays she and Rose rarely spoke of the move. What was done was done – but the prospect hung before them, casting a spectre over their remaining time.

Minna had tried her best to make sure Rose's time at the shepherd's hut was still fun. But it was not as light-hearted and inventive as in the past. And for the past week or two Rose had seemed oddly reserved and had not been interested in playing their usual games. These days the toys' faces seemed to Minna to wear doleful expressions, reflecting her own sadness that Rose was moving away.

It was a dreary day. September had passed into October; the sky was white and unyielding and a pitiless rain had set in. Rose's demeanour, as she came through the door, seemed of a piece with the melancholy weather.

Lethargically, she began to peel off her coat, which caught on the bunched sleeve of her jumper underneath. Suddenly, she began to tug violently at the coat sleeve. Her pale little face on which the freckles stood out in blotches was creased with a tension that broke Minna's resolve.

'Sweetheart, whatever is it?' she couldn't stop herself crying out.

Justin had been put to bed and Rose's parents were eating supper when Rose, in her pyjamas, had crept along the hall to where her father's jacket was hanging. Her heart thudding, she had felt into the pockets and found the mysterious envelope.

She had not known what to do with the appalling images she was faced with. Pictures of her father, pictures . . . such disgusting pictures, which, try as she might, she couldn't erase from her mind. She had spent the night of their discovery too stricken for tears. The following nights were a miserable mishmash of tears, patchy sleep and nightmares and, as the weeks passed, frequent trips to the bathroom.

'Rosie seems to have picked up a bladder infection,' her mother said to her father one evening. 'I'm thinking of taking her to see Dr Chen.'

Her husband had grown even less communicative. He was drinking immoderately in secret and this, and the worry of Emma, meant that his sleep too was disturbed. The photos delivered by Emma had been taken over a weekend when the office had been sent on an HR exercise – building trust and intercollegiate dependence – at a Holiday Inn. The pictures were intimate, explicit and would be quite impossible, if revealed to his wife, to explain away. Entangled in the sticky web of his own predicament, he said only, 'Right.'

'What do you mean, "right"? Your daughter's not well. Are you listening, Nick?'

But he wasn't listening, except to the minatory voice of hindsight.

Poor Rose had been struggling with the burden of her shocking discovery. She had not looked at all the pictures; she saw two or three and then, engulfed by a feeling she couldn't describe, it was all she could manage to somehow guide them back into the concealing envelope with a shaking hand and slide the envelope into her father's pocket before scurrying to her room. But she had seen enough to bring on a blast of irrevocable enlightenment.

And in the familiar safety of the shepherd's hut, worn out by the effort of keeping this dangerous secret and in terror of the uncharted world which threatened her former security, the struggle with the malicious coat sleeve finally broke her down.

'I don't want to go away,' she sobbed in Minna's arms. A mixture of shame and a kind of desperate loyalty to her father meant that even to Minna she couldn't divulge the real cause of her grief. 'I don't want to go to Glasgow. Can't I stay here with you?'

'Sweetheart' was all Minna said, rocking the child in her arms. 'I'm sorry, my lamb.'

Later, after reluctantly sending Rose home, Minna went across to Frank's. 'What else could I say to her?' she asked when she had described the scene.

What she had said to Rose was, 'Sweetheart, it will get better. You will find new friends there and the schools in Scotland are supposed to be wonderful. And we'll still see each other.'

'Fair enough, as it goes,' Frank said. 'But as to it getting better, you don't know that. You'll have to keep your word and make sure you do see her.' He topped up her whisky. 'When are they due to move?'

'Christmas holidays, I think,' Minna said. 'It depends on the survey on the house they want to buy. A dotty time to move, if you ask me.' As if they would ask her.

'Well then, there's half-term to come still,' Frank said. He agreed that it was thoughtless to move kids bang in the middle of a school year but he didn't bother to say this. He was not a man who bothered to say things that wouldn't help. An idea came to him. 'You could take her to London to visit that boy she liked and your new friend Nan.'

Billy was round at Nan's helping to stick labels she had printed out on to the envelopes that he had gone with her specially to buy.

'Are these really all your friends?' he asked, looking at the several packets still unopened.

'My friends are scattered so we mostly talk on the phone or email.' Nowadays she preferred it that way.

'Where you having the party? They're not going to all fit in here.'

'We'll hire somewhere,' Nan said. 'You and Dad can help me look. And you can be in charge of decorating it. What shall we have?'

'Balloons,' Billy thought. 'Load of balloons, with helium so we can let them off after. And can we have garland things made of flowers? And lanterns with real candles?' He had once as a very small boy seen Chinese lanterns swinging in a line in a summer breeze at night by the river at a party. His father had taken him there. His father always laughed when Billy referred to this and said that it had never happened. But it had happened. Billy could still smell the warm wool of his father's coat as he lifted him up to see the lanterns in the dark.

'Yes,' his grandmother said. And she smiled. 'Garlands made of flowers would be grand. And lanterns. Plenty of those. Maybe spring flowers, given I'm an April birthday.'

'But April's not for ages,' he said, a little puzzled. He counted on his fingers. 'Six months.'

'Oh, you know me, Bill. I'm a terror for wanting to get things sorted.'

'What's this?' He was looking at some lines printed on the front of the invitations.

'Just something I wrote,' Nan said. 'What do you think of it?'

Billy screwed up his face and read the words, silently moving his lips. Since the summer there had been no more visits to Miss Rainwright's office. His new teacher appeared to like him and he had abandoned, she noticed, his experiment of being dyslexic. 'What does it mean?'

'What does it mean to you?'

He was about to answer but the phone rang and Nan picked it up.

'I just wondered,' the voice at the other end said, 'if maybe we could take you up on your kind invitation to come and stay.'

The survey on the Glasgow house had thrown up questions – the roof was possibly unsound and there was a query over the likelihood of getting planning permission. When presented with the suggestion that Minna take Rose to London to visit Billy and Nan, Rose's mother had been more than accommodating.

'To be honest, you'll be doing us a favour. Justin is staying with his friend he knew from nursery over half-term and I promised to take Rose up with us this time as she didn't come last. But it's easier if it's just me and Nick.'

'As long as you're sure Rose wouldn't rather go with you' was tactful Minna's response.

But Rose's mother said she was sure Rose would like to see her holiday companion again. She was rather keen to get her husband on his own to find out what was eating him.

It had taken some nerve on Minna's part to call Nan. The passage in time since the summer had eroded her confidence and she had had to steel herself to lift the phone. But she did it for Rose's sake.

Her anxiety proved unjustified as Nan was cordial, even welcoming. 'I've been wondering how you and the lass were getting along. Bill's with me now, as it happens. I'll have a word with his mother but they're not going away and I'm sure half-term will be fine.'

'Oh, that's very kind.' This was the first good news Minna had had since the end of the Weymouth holiday. 'I'll check the dates and ring you back – if you're sure?' she inevitably added.

Half-term

36

When she opened the door of the flat Minna had the oddest sensation that Nan had somehow shrunk. But it was the Nan she remembered who said, 'Well, don't just stand there, then, come on in out of the cold.'

Nan's flat was much as Minna had imagined it would be. Small but orderly. If she was a little surprised to see an efficient-looking printer beside the desk, she didn't even register the low cushioned couch which lay nearby.

Billy, who was there to greet the visitors, pointed it out. 'That's Nan's coffin.'

Unlike Blanche, Minna at once grasped the significance of the coffin and knew not to make a drama of it. Instead she said, 'What beautiful workmanship. Is that reed?'

'It's willow. It's all handmade.' Billy was proprietorial about a project he had been in on at the beginning. 'I sit in it to watch telly,' he confided.

Rose said nothing during these exchanges. Billy and Nan, while recognisable as the people with whom she had spent a happy holiday, now seemed to inhabit a different plane. A plane from which she was separated as irrevocably – had she ever encountered the story – as is the dead Achilles from the live Odysseus when the latter views across a trench filled with blood his old battle comrade exiled in Hades.

She stared at Nan's coffin, which had been decorated by Billy with paper flowers and a Chelsea rosette. It seemed to her weird but she didn't think more about it. She found it less tiring not to think much at all.

Minna and Rose ate at the flat a supper specially chosen by Billy – pasta and chocolate eclairs – and then they all walked round to Billy's house with Rose's bag.

Virginia, Nan noted, had got herself up. She was looking flushed and pretty and greeted them most hospitably, presenting their young guest with a set of towels with pink roses printed on them and a little cake of scented soap.

'These are your towels and this is your own special soap. We've been so looking forward to your stay, haven't we, Billy?'

'It's rose soap,' Billy said. He saw that Rose had hardly reacted and was concerned that his mother should have credit for her preparations. 'We got it special with the towels for you at M&S.'

Rose smiled palely. 'Thank you,' she said. 'They're very nice.'

Nan made no mention of Rose as she and Minna walked back to Nan's. She had been quite shocked when she saw the child, whom she had last seen pink-cheeked and freckle-faced, with her plaits flying as she and Billy zoomed in and out of their hideout. Now she appeared stoop-shouldered, preoccupied. Closeted, Nan thought.

Minna said nothing either and they exchanged idle chat until, back in the warmth of the flat, Nan suggested a cup of tea.

'I brought a bottle of Scotch, if you fancy some of that?'

Nan had only once drunk whisky since Hamish had drowned. At his wake and for some days after she had pushed the boat well and truly out – and when she had resurfaced and begun, soberly, to rearrange her whole being to make a life without him even the smell of the spirit had revolted her.

When her grandmother died she had downed a token tot, as had seemed fitting in honour of one who had been her true kin. But not a drop had she taken since. Nor had she had the least desire to do so. But Minna needed a drinking companion. 'OK,' she agreed. 'If you're having one I don't mind.'

Rose had been given Billy's bed and he was in a camp bed on the floor beside her. He and his mother had discussed where their guest should sleep and Billy, recalling their time in the wagon, decreed that Rose should sleep in his room and have his bed. This act of nobleness had been his own idea but Rose had seemed so mindless of the sacrifice that he felt bound to point it out.

'I said you could have my bed,' he announced. By the night-light goose, a present from his father, he could just see Rose's profile. She was lying on her back, apparently staring at the ceiling.

Rose said nothing and Billy began to feel cross. Why had she bothered to come if she wasn't going to enjoy herself? 'D'you want a teddy?' Rose had brought with her none of her own toys and perhaps she was missing them. He extracted the shabbiest and dirtiest of the several teddy bears who privately shared his bed and offered it up.

Rose ignored the teddy and Billy, feeling slighted, took it back. Going to bed had not been fun, as it had been in the wagon. Rose had shown no interest in his pictures of the shrunken heads which he had shown her as a special privilege. She had not read. But nor had she wanted to play the game they had invented of seeing how many times they could turn around under the bedclothes at the bottom of the bed while holding their breath, which he had looked forward to reviving with her. He farted and giggled and turned over to see if she was enjoying the fart too. To his alarm he detected that she was crying.

It was a muffled crying but unquestionably he had heard a hiccupping sob. He sat up unsure what to do then slid out of the camp bed and wriggled in beside her.

Rose whipped her body away from his to face the wall. After a few moments Billy put his arms cautiously round her stiff back. 'There, there' was all he could think to say, the words Nan had said to him countless times.

37

'How's your cool grandma?' Faith asked. She was round at Kitty's, casting a remedial eye over her wardrobe. 'These'll have to go,' she pronounced, holding up a pair of jeans.

They were a pair only very recently bought for Kitty by her mother and Kitty quailed at the prospect of having to lose them. 'Why?'

'Wrong length.' Faith held the jeans up against herself. 'I s'pose you could cut off the bottoms.' She was doubtful that this would achieve the correct look but she was conscious that Kitty came from a problem family and didn't want to seem too discouraging. 'D'you want to come round mine tomorrow so I can do your hair?' Faith's own hair was a glowing aubergine.

'Will it wash out?' Kitty asked. 'Or my mum'll go mad.'

Faith shrugged. She was used to her own mother going mad and considered that this was a necessary part of a parent's upbringing. But she was aware that her friend had a tougher nut to crack than her own mother, who for all their arguments was proud of her daughter's fighting spirit. Faith saw it as a duty to strengthen Kitty's armoury. 'It'll wash out for sure but so what if it doesn't? They can't exactly send you to prison.'

This cavalier reading of parental rights was one of Kitty's several reasons for admiring Faith. But still she said, 'They can make my life a nightmare, though.'

Faith shrugged again. Learning to ignore parental shit was a central part of a girl's training. 'So . . .?'

'Granny's going to art school,' Kitty said, retreating to Faith's earlier question. 'Or art class, anyway.'

'What she paint?'

'Nudes when she's at the class.'

Faith made a grimace. 'Gross.'

'I know. But what she likes best to draw are flowers.'

Faith had already determined that her best subjects at St Anselm's were to be Computing, Design and Technology and Art. Her father was in IT; she had grown up playing on an Apple Mac and was competent in all its most advanced graphic programs. Her long-term plan was to become a graphic artist and she could see potential in Kitty's grandmother as a patron, possibly even a colleague if she shaped up. 'My mum's boyfriend sent her a load of flowers, which make her sneeze. We could take them to your grandma if you like.'

'Won't your mum's boyfriend mind?'

Faith made another shrug. 'Serve him right. He should know Mum's allergic.'

The half-term in London had not gone well for Rose. Nan and Billy had taken her and Minna to the Natural History Museum, where she had been polite about the blue whale. She had been polite about the healthy baked beans cooked without sugar that Billy's mother had prepared for their lunch, though Billy had advised she could leave them and they could have proper Heinz baked beans later when they went round to Nan's. Rose had even been polite about Billy's cars and had sat on the sofa and watched patiently while he made them whiz around Nan's living room and crawl up the walls.

Nan had observed Rose and concluded that she was not so much watching as focusing on the cars to make time pass. She was not confident that all that was up with Rose was, as Minna had confided, this move to Glasgow. Something had hit the girl hard. For one thing, according to Minna, she wasn't reading.

She tried saying, 'I read your *Seal Lullaby* while we were at the wagon. Are there other books of hers you can recommend?'

Rose turned to her a slightly less wary expression. 'She's written loads.'

'Any you specially recommend?'

'There's *The Lilac House*. Minna's read that.'

'Maybe I'll read it too. Tell me about it.'

Nan would never as a rule have made such a direct request but the words had come out before she quite meant them to and they seemed to touch some spring in Rose. Her face worked a little and then she began to speak, rather as a sleepwalker speaks in a gap of lucidity.

'It's about a house which seems ordinary. It's in Oxford (that's where Elizabeth Pattern went to live when she was about my age). It's old and all the paint's lilac and there's stained glass in the front door which makes these patterns on the floor in the moonlight. They're magic, the patterns are, because really the house belongs to the Lilac Fairy, but you don't know that for ages . . .' She stopped. 'If I tell you it'll be a spoiler.'

'That's OK,' Nan said. 'I enjoy things more when I already know the story.'

Rose looked doubtful and Nan, trying to be encouraging, said, 'I know that sounds odd but I'm like that. I promise you it's true.'

Rose shrugged. 'Basically, this girl – she's called Tilly – goes to the house because her cat's gone missing and she's asking everyone round about. She's called Julia – the cat is – because Tilly got her in July.' Rose explained.

'Good thinking,' Nan said.

'She's a kind of lilacky grey, the cat,' Rose went on, 'and she's been kidnapped by the Shadow King, who's stealing all lilac things from the world, which isn't just things that are the colour of lilac but all the things that the Lilac Fairy sort of . . .' She hesitated.

'Stands for, perhaps?' Nan asked.

Rose blinked and for a second her eyes cleared. Then she said, 'She looks after vulnerable things.'

'Like Julia?' Nan enquired.

'Like Julia,' Rose agreed. 'Anyway, if you get into the house when there's a full moon and step inside one of the patterns made by the glass in the door then it kind of melts into a whole different world. Tilly goes there by moonlight and she steps into this sort of shadow land and she meets this boy called Arthur. But then she gets caught by the Shadow King and she's nearly taken over. She starts to become all shadowy, as though she's fading away, so you can see through her so she stops being all real.'

'Hmm,' Nan said. 'That doesn't sound too funny.'

Rose's eyes, which had been almost perpetually lowered since she arrived in London, grew suddenly very wide. Then she said dully, 'It's all OK in the end.'

'What happens to Arthur?' Nan asked.

'He's all right,' Rose said in a little hard voice.

'I wonder why?' Nan allowed herself to pursue.

'Because he's a boy, I expect,' Rose said, which to Nan seemed quite shockingly unlike the girl she had met only a couple of months earlier.

The four of them had eaten supper at Nan's and the children were about to watch the DVD of *Mary Poppins Returns*, which Minna had brought with her as an offering. Billy was ensconced in his usual berth in the willow coffin and Rose was sitting behind him on the sofa when Minna murmured to Nan, 'Can I have a word?'

They went into Nan's bedroom. 'She'd like to stay here tonight,' Minna said. She looked worried. 'I've said I didn't think it was possible. I'm sorry, this trip isn't doing what I hoped – I hope we're not ruining Billy's half-term.'

Few people could, or would, have seen through Nan's tough-seeming, take-on-all-comers patina; but at heart she was one of nature's introverts and too much of any company, however agreeable, left her wrung out. The last thing she wanted was for extra bodies taking up space in her tiny flat.

'Of course the lass can stay,' she said immediately. 'But in that case I'd better ask Billy too. They can squash in in here on the bedroom floor beside me.'

Minna began to say, 'Oh, but won't that be too much for you –' but Nan stopped her.

'If I send you back to Virginia's for a sleeping bag and anything Rose will need for the night that would be a help.'

Minna set off to Virginia's and Nan lay down flat on her bed. She had begun to feel quite ill with the draining effect of being sociable. From the sitting room she could hear the voice of the new Mary Poppins issuing from the TV and began idly to wonder what the producers had done about that spoonful of sugar.

When Nan finally hauled herself up from her bed, a little dizzy, and returned to the sitting room she saw that Rose had climbed in behind Billy in the willow coffin. Slightly taller than him, she was half leaning against his back, her chin resting on his shoulder. Nan stood in the doorway looking at them. Mary Poppins had departed to her other world and the sky was full of balloons. The light from the TV screen and the refracted glow of the London street-lights outside illuminated the room so that beyond the two children sitting in her coffin she could see on her desk the photo she had taken of the scholar's rock.

You might try thin air, the voice said. *There is no safer ground.*

'Rose, is it OK by you if Minna sleeps over at Billy's house?' Nan asked and knew that Billy would ask why.

'Why's she doing that?'

'Because it's more comfortable in your spare room and Rose may like to stay over with us. Would you, Rosie? If Bill stays over too?'

'Where'll I sleep?'

'If you prefer,' Nan said carefully – she felt as if she had her hand out, cajoling with a tempting morsel a frightened wild animal – 'Minna can come back here and you can sleep by her in the sitting room. Billy sleeps on the floor by

262

my bed. You can sleep on the sitting-room floor with Minna or with me and Bill. You say what you'd like best.'

There was a pause, in which Rose began to chew one of her plaits. Billy started to exclaim but Nan said, 'Hang on a moment, pet. Rose is trying to think.'

'Can I sleep with you and Billy in your room?' Rose asked.

'Absolutely,' Nan said. 'And would you like Minna to sleep here too?'

There was another pause. 'Don't you like it at my house?' Billy wanted to know.

'Rose might like a change,' Nan said. 'You like a change. You like to sleep here sometimes. I was thinking you might like a change tonight.'

Rose waited a moment longer. Then she said, 'Did you speak to Minna?'

'Yes,' Nan said. 'I rang her. She's round at Billy's mum's now. She says you're to do just as you like. She's easy.'

Rose went over to the window and looked out at the cityscape lighting up before her. 'Is that the Post Office Tower?'

Billy joined her, keen to show off his knowledge. 'And that's the Shard. There are sixteen churches . . .' He began to count them. 'Nan, is it sixteen or fifteen?'

Rose turned back from the Shard, the Post Office Tower and the fifteen or sixteen churches. 'I think I'll be all right here with you and Bill.'

Mostly pleased but keen to establish his prior claim, Billy suggested, 'I could sleep in your coffin, Nan.'

'There's only one person ever going to sleep there and that's me,' Nan said, and Billy, oddly relieved, said, 'I didn't really want to.'

Virginia ran Minna round with a sleeping bag and Rose's night things and clothes for the morning. She seemed pleased to be entertaining Minna, and Minna, once she was sure that Rose was settled, said she'd welcome the luxury of a larger bed. She was not quite comfortable about leaving Rose but she sensed that Nan was oppressed by the numbers in her flat and was concerned not to further impose.

Having thankfully pared her guests down to the two children, Nan set them to prepare their makeshift beds and was heartened when they began to play the game they had invented in their hideout by the duck pond.

'I, Maxim, the mighty magician, transform you with my powers to a caddis worm,' she heard Billy say in a spooky voice and was relieved when Rose laughed.

Whatever's amiss with the child, she thought, being with Bill will at least maybe put it out of her mind, for the time being anyway.

'You were snoring,' Billy said when Nan awoke the next morning. Both children were standing at the foot of her bed. 'You were snoring like a piggy-wiggy.' He made loud snorting sounds and fell backwards on to the floor, convulsed with laughter. This was an accusation he had made before and Nan had always vehemently denied it. 'Rose heard you.' Billy pressed home his case. 'She *was* snoring, wasn't she?'

Rose giggled and agreed.

'Cheeky monkeys,' Nan said, torn between relief at Rose's improved looks and chagrin at the indignity of the charge. But in the bathroom she had to laugh at herself. Who cared if she snored?

The children had woken happier. They embarked on a game which involved rolling each other up on the bed in Nan's duvet and then unrolling themselves off the bed on to the floor. Nan could hear them shrieking excitedly as she lay in her bath.

'Can we go to Kew?' Billy asked when she emerged damp from the bathroom.

It was a brilliant day, blue and golden, made more splendid by the rich colours of the autumn leaves. Perfect, they all agreed when Minna reappeared, for a picnic in Kew Gardens. Nan and Minna prepared sandwiches while Billy and Rose continued their raucous game.

'She's perked up,' Minna remarked. 'I'm ever so grateful.'

'That's Bill.' Nan felt a grandmotherly pride. 'Nothing to do with me. How did you get on with Virginia?'

'Oh, well enough,' Minna said.

Virginia had been rather too ready, to Minna's mind, to confide that she found her mother-in-law tricky. Minna sympathised with this: she had spent enough time with Nan to feel grazed by her sharp edges. But Nan had befriended her when she had had no need to – and Minna had seen too that Nan's asperity and snappishness were aspects of a strength that her family too casually relied on.

In fact, what Virginia had been most keen to confide was that she had a new relationship.

'I don't quite know how to break it to Nan,' she had said, looking arch, and Minna, puzzled, had said, 'I really can't imagine she would disapprove.'

'I just wish that girl would get over bloody Alec and find someone else,' Nan said, cutting Marmite sandwiches.

Minna took a risk. 'I think perhaps she may have done.'
'Really?' Nan was agreeably surprised.

Minna considered whether to say more but decided that she had been primed by Virginia to break this news. 'I think maybe he's a she,' she volunteered.

Nan put the bread knife down. 'You don't say. Well, that makes sense. I hope she's a better bet than Alec. I thought we had more apples . . .'

She made no further comment and if she was hurt at this revelation reaching her via Minna, she wasn't, Minna could tell, going to let on.

Perhaps it was this discovery of confidences exchanged behind her back that made Nan more taciturn than usual as the four of them travelled by bus to Kew. It was the way, Minna reflected. Strong characters tended to be taken for granted. They got kicked in the teeth as much as weaker characters but they made less fuss about it. Possibly they even got kicked in the teeth more because of a notion that this was something they could take.

Virginia's excitable late-night confidences had left Minna tender towards Nan. She had wanted to say, I'd like to see how you'd have got on without her for all that she might occasionally grate on you. But it wasn't her place; more important, it wouldn't help. Nan did what she did for Billy and Virginia in the way that she, Minna, did what she did for Rose, because that's what you did when you loved someone. Expecting recognition was a mug's game.

The bus moved off from a stop. Approaching Kew Bridge, Minna began to recall a song her mother had liked. *Come down to Kew in lilac time, in lilac time, in lilac time.* It wasn't lilac time now but perhaps she might come again one day and see the lilacs in bloom. Envisaging her mother's sweet powdered face as the bus crossed the bridge over the Thames, Minna suddenly had the clearest vision of John. He had come to tell her he was going back to his wife, his face screwed up and his eyes filled with an unspeakable anguish. All at once she felt alight and filled with a marvellous all-conquering energy.

Poor love, she thought. My poor love. You weren't equal to it.

38

Blanche had waited for a call from Nan to say that she and Billy were off to Kew and might she like to come too. The prospect of going there to draw had taken root. It seemed presumptuous to go without Nan to a place that she had suggested they visit; but to wait for an invitation that might never come was silly. And the October day looked as if it would be so very fine.

She had packed up her sketching equipment ready to cart it to the car when Kitty rang.

'Hi, Granny, I'm round at Faith's and we thought we'd come and see you.'

'Kitten, angel, how wonderful to hear you. But I'm about to go out.'

'Where are you going, Granny? We could come too.'

So Blanche arranged to meet them at Kew station.

She was startled, though not alarmed, when a green-haired Kitty emerged arm in arm with a purple-haired Faith. The girls were dressed almost identically in jeans and trainers. Kitty was wearing Faith's black leather jacket while Faith was wearing a biker's jacket borrowed from her mum.

'Hi, Granny, we're the Avocado and Aubergine sisters.'

'Hey there, Avocado and Aubergine,' said Blanche, honoured to be let in. 'Great hair, girls.'

Faith returned the compliment by saying that Blanche's

denim was cool and Blanche thanked her instincts that she had thought to put on the Paris jacket.

'I've come to Kew to do some sketching. You two can draw too, if you'd like to. I've masses of paper.'

'We know, Granny,' Kitty said. 'I told Faith you're an artist now.'

'Hardly an artist, darling. But first I want to find somewhere.' Blanche had been consulting the Kew website. 'There was an intrepid artist explorer called Marianne North who went all over the world painting plants and flowers. She left Kew her work.'

'I told Faith you like flowers.' Kitty was keen that her grandmother and her best friend should get on. 'She was going to bring you some.'

'Lilies,' Faith said. 'But they were rubbish. They came from my mum's crap boyfriend.' On second viewing Kitty's grandma seemed even more sophisticated than before and Faith was experiencing a rare blast of shyness.

'That's sweet of you, Faith.' Blanche was also feeling shy. Kitty's friend seemed so sure in her judgements and she was anxious not to let Kitty down. 'Lilies are lovely. *Consider the lilies of the field* . . .' she quoted.

In the days when her father still lived with them Faith had been packed off regularly to Sunday school. She had been taught that the lilies of the field were anemones, the bright red and blue flowers that were cheaper than the tall scented ones with the pollen that made her mother sneeze. 'I don't think they're those lilies,' she advised.

Blanche and the two girls entered Kew by the Victoria Gate. They studied the map and then walked along the path till they found the Marianne North Gallery. Inside, their eyes were met by 'a foretaste of paradise', as Blanche, some years later, was to describe to her husband.

On every last inch of the walls and all around the lintels of the doors brilliantly coloured paintings of exotic plants twisted and trailed and glowed.

'Wow!' Faith said. 'That's blowing my mind.'

It was blowing Blanche's mind too. She stood gazing, overcome by the splendour of the artist's vivid palette, by her skill in depicting the varied leaves, blooms and seeds and by the sheer scope of her work.

Out of the blue, the name of the flower-seller doll she had loved as a child came back to her. Fleur. Of course she had named her Fleur. How funny that she had forgotten that. Maybe, a thought began to insinuate, maybe her mother had, a little, understood her after all.

'Look up there,' Kitty said. She pointed to where the words 'Sacred Plants of Hindus' were inscribed beneath the rail of the ornamental balcony that ran around the upper level of the richly decorated walls.

'They make medicines from plants,' Faith said. 'My dad's girlfriend is Indian. She's a dermatologist and she says all the healing medicines they use mostly come from plants.'

In their shared appreciation of Marianne North earlier shyness had evaporated. Blanche, with a girl on each arm, sauntered back towards the cafeteria-cum-shop by the Victoria Gate.

'I need to go to the shop,' Faith said. 'It's my mum's birthday next week.'

She rejoined them with a pashmina and a book of reproductions of the Marianne North flowers. 'Pashminas are back. Not that Mum would notice they'd ever gone out. That's for you,' she said, presenting Blanche with the book.

Blanche was so touched that she flushed. 'Oh goodness, Faith, really you shouldn't . . .'

'It's better to receive than to give,' Faith said. She had learned that too at Sunday school.

They bought sandwiches and as the girls ate, Blanche, encouraged by their questions, described her time in Paris.

'I want to go back to Paris,' Faith said. 'We went when I was a kid to Disneyland but I'd rather have gone to the Louvre.'

Kitty, who had begged and pleaded to go to Disneyland, prayed that her grandmother wouldn't give her away.

'Perhaps one day you two will come to Paris with me,' diplomatic Blanche suggested, and with a surge of delight realised that this was no longer a fantasy but might one day be possible.

'Now,' she said when they had finished their sandwiches, 'I may not be Marianne North but I am going to find somewhere to sketch.'

'If a thing's worth doing, it's worth doing badly,' Faith pronounced. 'My dad always says that.'

They passed the Palm House and were striking off across the grass towards the Brentford Gate when in the near distance Blanche spotted a group of people by a bench. Before she had consciously registered them, she recognised Nan.

Blanche's first instinct was to wheel away, unannounced. She had asked Nan to let her know when she was next going to Kew and here Nan was and, patently, she hadn't invited Blanche. But then she reproved herself for being silly. Naturally, Nan had other friends.

'Hi,' she called. 'Hi, Nan!' and she waved.

As it happened, Nan's feelings on seeing Blanche were somewhat similar. She had not forgotten inviting Blanche to Kew and had considered whether to let her know that they were going to be there. If she had held back it was for Minna and Rose's sake and her concern was justified as she caught a glimpse of Minna's apprehensive expression as Blanche approached across the grass.

'This is a friend of mine coming,' she said. 'I don't know who the two girls are but I expect one's her granddaughter.'

Nan made introductions and Blanche began to apologise, saying that she didn't mean to crash a party but she couldn't, having seen them, go away without saying hello. The four children eyed each other. Rose and Billy were at the age which, having just grown out of it, Faith and Kitty were liable to despise.

Billy, hovering, asked, 'Can me and Rose go and play?'

The two of them ran off but soon they had run back again and there was quite a bit of coming and going while Nan offered cakes and juice to the two girls and Blanche and Minna engaged in a stiff exchange.

The October sun was making a gold halo of Blanche's hair. Sizing up this interloper in her chic French denim, Minna felt more than usually shabby. Blanche was also feeling awkward. Minna, she guessed, was one of Nan's intellectual friends who would think her ditzy and for the very reason that she felt uneasy she lingered longer than she wanted to. But at last to everyone's relief she said, 'I really came here to draw – your idea, Nan – so if you don't mind. Do you want to come with me, girls?'

Kitty said she and Faith would go for a wander and the three of them could always hook up later on their phones.

'If all else fails meet me at the Victoria Gate when the park closes,' Blanche requested.

Which was when, after getting up from the bench and looking about her, Nan asked, 'Where have those two got to?'

Blanche had already set off with her sketch book but Faith and Kitty were finishing up the teacakes.

'They can't be far. They were playing under that tree over there,' Minna said, pointing to a weeping hickory. 'Billy came back for his water.'

'He took two bottles,' Faith observed. 'He took the whole packet of biscuits too.'

Something in Faith's manner suggested to Nan that here was a kindred spirit. 'What do you mean?' she asked.

Faith's natural vigilance had picked up covert signals between Billy and Rose. Her first thought was that these concerned her and Kitty's coloured hair – but they didn't seem the kind of kids to care much about hair. It was more as if they had some scheme they were carrying out while the grown-ups were distracted. She herself was experienced in such enterprises.

'I think they might have took off somewhere,' she said.

It was Minna's turn to ask, 'What do you mean?'

'He was collecting up stuff to eat,' Faith elaborated. 'Tuck,' she added helpfully – these badly dressed ladies

273

were usually grand. She judged that she may as well let them have the worst of it. 'He took a bag too, from there.'

Nan and Minna looked at the rug, on which they had laid out the picnic things. Rose's backpack, which she had insisted on bringing, was gone.

Rose had woken after her night at Nan's flat feeling a little restored. She could not have said why she had asked to stay there – but it might have had something to do with the size and snugness of Nan's flat reminding her of the magician's wagon, which was on the far side of her lost childhood. At this point Nan was sound asleep and snoring.

Billy and Rose had shared a good laugh over the volume of snores and then all of a sudden Billy had asked, 'Are you still going to Glasgow?' and out it had come.

'No,' Rose said, a decision forming as she spoke. 'I'm not going to Glasgow.'

Billy had taken this news as it came; he had no reason to be interested in Rose's family's movements and perhaps for the very reason that he didn't enquire Rose enlarged. 'I'm going to run away.'

'Where'll you go?' Billy asked, now curious.

And Rose, remembering their conversation in the wagon, said, 'Couldn't I run away in Kew Gardens?'

Billy was all in favour of a plan which he had apparently inspired. While Rose packed her pyjamas, her toothbrush and her spare clothes he raided the fridge for cheese and lifted a couple of apples from the fruit bowl. He also magnanimously loaned Rose twenty pounds, given him by his father to spend over half-term.

'You can send it back,' he said. 'Once you get to where you're going.'

It is likely that if it were not for Blanche's intervention Rose would never have pursued her idea. Beyond the inchoate impulse to get away it was not a well-formed plan. But when the tall lady with the two snotty girls with their coloured hair and heavily made-up eyes pitched up, Rose had felt a renewed surge of unhappiness. And with it a renewed urge to flee.

'Get my bag,' she had whispered to Billy from beneath the weeping hickory and he had flown past, impersonating a plane, and fished it up while Minna had all her attention set on managing Blanche and Nan was preoccupied feeding the two girls.

The man sometimes referred to himself as a tramp because it gave him a title and a status of a sort. But he didn't do much tramping. He had abandoned his given name and these days he preferred to be known as Lighting – an old nickname from happier times, a consequence of a spell when he'd worked the lighting equipment at a theatre long since closed down.

Lighting had discovered the haven of Queen Charlotte's Cottage the previous winter when the bad frosts had set in. In palmier days he had also worked as a security guard and when all other benefits of the job had disappeared the knowledge of the methods to disable different alarms remained. During his homeless years he had acquired another asset. A colleague, also much sunk in life, had been a key cutter trained in key moulds and had passed on his skill in exchange for Lighting's own expertise in alarms.

He had had a piece of luck when a workman attending to a report of damp had mislaid the back-door keys to the Cottage. By the time the workman had discovered the loss Lighting had taken a mould and stealthily replaced them.

The former royal residence was closed to visitors during the winter months; with the forged key and the alarm disabled Lighting had spent the worst of the winter nights inside taking cover from the weather. He had looked forward to returning to his winter quarters and had only the night before climbed into the Gardens from the river side to renew his residence there.

The sound of alien voices had at first dismayed him: he feared that his sanctuary was under threat. But he soon discerned that these were children. Kids were a pain but at least you could scare them. But with kids there would be people come looking, parents, keepers, very likely.

It had been Billy's bright idea to go to Queen Charlotte's Cottage. Rose's recalling their bedtime conversation in the wagon had reminded him how he had told her that Kew Gardens had once belonged to a king. The position of the old royal summer house on the outer edge of the Gardens and the fact that it had been a habitable dwelling made it an ideal place to hide.

It was sheer luck that they had got inside. Lighting had gone out for a smoke – he was careful not to attract attention by smoking indoors: a lingering smell of tobacco would be a give-away to anyone checking on the Cottage. He had not locked the door but closed it to, to enable him to slip back with the least kerfuffle should any snooper come by. Billy and Rose had arrived in the slice of time when the house was unlocked and unpeopled.

'Don't let's,' Rose had said when the door swung open. She tugged at Billy's sleeve, begging him to leave. The brave spirit which had urged her to run away was already ebbing. 'There's probably someone inside.'

'Where else we going to go?' Billy boldly pushed open the door. He hadn't cottoned on to the enormity of what they were doing and was enjoying executing his plan.

Lighting was not innately a bad man; but life had not treated him well and his better side had been eroded by serial disappointment. A gambling habit, made worse by the blow of being made redundant, had lost him friends, house, wife and children and by this time he was insulated through a long run of ill fortune against any fool notions about the milk of human kindness.

'What you two doing here?' he asked. He had tracked the children easily to their hiding place behind a curtain.

Rose was already strung out in a state of nervous excitement. When the smelly man with the angry red face threw back the curtain she was stricken with a fear that froze all capacity for response. But Billy answered the question. 'She's running away from home.'

'Oh, you are, are you?' the man said. 'So no one knows where you are?' He was wearing an old bus conductor's hat, which gave him a faint air of authority.

Rose said quickly, 'They do,' as Billy at the same time asserted, 'No.'

'So which is it?' the scowling man asked. 'Do they or don't they?'

'They don't,' truthful Billy said. He couldn't under-stand why Rose was denying this when all their efforts had been to escape unnoticed. He inspected the man's cap. 'Are you a keeper?'

'That's right.' Lighting was relieved that he now had a story. 'You can come out of there.' The children emerged, fearfully on Rose's part.

Lighting looked them up and down, assessing them. He had disliked children since his own two had rejected him and here was a chance to get his own back. 'You two could be in big trouble, yeah?'

Rose been told about men like this – they gave you sweets and then they did things to you – and she wasn't taken in by the cap, which was battered and dirty, as were the broken fingernails on the man's swollen hands. 'We didn't mean it, we'll go. We're sorry,' she said. Sick with dread she began to edge towards the stairs.

Lighting recognised the blind terror in her eyes. On balance he was pleased to find someone in as bad a state as himself whom he could hurt. 'I don't know about that,' he said, stepping in front of her and hideously wagging his head. 'If I hand you over it'll mean the police and maybe prison. This is breaking and entering, right?'

A warm trickle began to seep from the top of Rose's left thigh.

'It isn't,' Billy said stoutly. 'The door weren't locked. It's not trespass if you don't do any harm.' His father had told him that. 'And we can't go to prison,' he added with an extra spurt of confidence. 'We're too young.'

The boy spoke with neither fear nor contempt and Lighting decided to ignore him. He bent and peered at

Rose, shoving his face close to hers. 'Why you running away, anyway?' His breath smelt foul and his eyes were red-rimmed and watery.

The taut crossed wires of half-grasped knowledge that had been holding Rose together snapped. Hot urine ran down inside her jeans as tears flooded her face. 'My mum and dad are splitting up,' she cried wildly.

Billy was taken aback. He was annoyed and a little hurt that he had not been privy to this information. His own mum and dad had parted before he even remembered so he was an expert.

Lighting surveyed the girl, wet at both ends, with disgust. He found her abject shuddering repulsive. For a second he was overwhelmed by a vision of putting his big cracked hands round her little white flower-stalk neck and squeezing it till she shut her mouth and turned red and then blue and then shaking her body off and dumping it in the river. He stood grinding one fist into the palm of the other hand, looking down at the terrified girl.

'We'll give you twenty pounds if you don't say.' Billy's clear voice was not so much defiant as firm.

'I don't know.' Lighting began to recover his usual state of low-grade resentment. 'I'll think about it.' An ear infection untreated had left him quite deaf so he missed the announcements being made over a loudspeaker outside. 'How about thirty pound?' he suggested.

Billy heard the announcements and held his ground. 'My dad's a lawyer.'

Lighting had not survived homeless for five years without a saving canniness. From the kid's manner he might be the son of a judge, or some other establishment wanker.

'Right,' he said. 'Give us the money and I'll say nothing. And you say nothing either, right, or we'll both be in the shit. Right?"

Billy had Rose's backpack open to find her purse. He found the note he had loaned her and handed it to the keeper man. 'Deal?'

'The bag too, yeah?' the man said. 'Give it here.'

The backpack had been a birthday present to Rose from her father. It was an expensive designer bag, which her mother had been not at all in favour of, but Rose had begged and begged her father for it because it was covered in red and pink roses, her special flower. Seeing her treasured bag dangling from the man's hairy fist, Rose collapsed into a paroxysm of weeping. Billy tried to seize her arm to lead her away but before he could do so the man startled him by grabbing his hand.

'You be good now, son,' he said, retrieving a self he had long since said goodbye to. He shook the boy's hand. 'And look after the girl. You're a gentleman, right?'

He showed them to the door, where he tapped his nose in a gesture he had once seen in a film. 'Deal, right?'

It was Faith who found the pair of them, a little way from Queen Charlotte's Cottage, hand in hand like babes in the wood, she said afterwards to her mother. She had been taken by the image of the royal dwelling she'd seen on the map by the Marianne North Gallery and, believing that it was the kind of place where an enterprising kid might go to hide, had gone to investigate.

'They're going crazy back there looking for you two.' Her sharp eye took in the wet patch at the crutch of Rose's trousers. 'Come here.' She grabbed Rose and walked her round the back of a bush. 'Take those off,' she ordered. Rose obediently peeled down her jeans. 'And your pants, get them off too.'

'But what'll I wear?' Rose, cold, her legs stinging from the urine, and traumatised by the encounter with the terrifying man who had snatched her treasured rose bag and might as easily have snatched her, began to sob again.

'Here, have this,' Faith said, taking the pashmina she had bought for her mother from the bag. 'You can knot it round you – and have this over to keep it up.' She pulled off her little knitted top. 'It's tight on me so it'll fit you fine.' She threw Rose's wet pants under the bush, inspected the jeans and then flung them after. 'And stop crying,' she ordered, in the tone that she knew worked with herself. 'You're a big girl now. I don't know what you've been playing at but we're going to say you got all wet playing by the lake. Right?'

'She got all wet playing by the lake,' Faith primed Billy. 'Are you listening to me? You didn't want to get into trouble about her getting wet, right, so you hid, yeah? Got that? They'll still be pissed with you but they'll be so glad to see you worst case you'll just get a big telling-off.'

Billy gazed in admiration at this angel of salvation. He'd given the keeper his word and, unpractised at lying, had been puzzling what to say. 'Right,' he said, nodding. 'Right.'

Faith appeared, holding a subdued Rose by one hand, just as the adults were in consultation about whether to call the police. 'Found them,' she carolled, as if, Minna said afterwards, it had all been a game of hide and seek.

There was a good deal of questioning and a certain amount of reproach and some stern words from one of the keepers, who had gone to the trouble of having announcements made, about the dangers awaiting children who ran off unaccompanied. Billy kept staunchly to Faith's story and Rose said so many times that she was sorry that no one felt much like punishing her further with more questions. As Faith had predicted, everyone was so relieved, the two escapees got off lightly.

There wasn't room for everyone in Blanche's car so Blanche drove the four children back to Nan's while Nan and Minna got an Uber on Blanche's account. 'It's not an occasion for being thrifty,' she counselled Nan.

Kitty sat in the front next to Blanche while Rose in the back of the car squashed in between Billy and Faith. Faith nudged her. 'You all right?' she asked. 'Get you home, get you into a nice hot bath, yeah?'

'It's not her real home,' Billy said – but in a shaft of enlightenment that nothing in his later life would better, added, 'It's her London home, where she always lives when she stays with us.'

39

There was quite a celebration at Nan's flat when they all got back from Kew. Blanche and the children, directed by Billy, stopped off at Virginia's to pick up clothes for Rose and Virginia said that it was lucky they had called by as she might be out that evening – was in fact planning to stay at a friend's – so could they take a key to give to Minna so she could let herself in?

Nan opened several bottles of Alec's wine and Faith rang her mother to say she and Kitty wouldn't be back as they were having a sleepover at Kitty's gran's – which was close enough to the truth because Kitty's gran was declared by the company unfit to drive by that point in the evening and it was agreed that she and the girls should stay the night.

Billy rang his mother and reported, 'Mum says they can stop over at mine,' adding, 'Faith can sleep in my room.' He was staying, along with Rose and Minna – who was not willing to be parted again from Rose – at Nan's.

Faced with the reality of a crowd in her flat, Nan found that she didn't after all so much mind. Faith and Kitty played music on their phones and Rose and Billy danced with them, wilder and wilder, and then Minna, who turned out to be a nimble mover, taught them all to skip jive.

Minna and Blanche got pleasantly tiddly together and Blanche was singing '*Au clair de la lune*', and justifying it as teaching the two girls French when Nan and Billy, under a blurred half of a moon, walked them down the hill to Virginia's.

But Nan was glad that Rose elected to sleep by Minna on the sitting-room floor and that it was only Billy that night in his usual place by her bedside.

'Nan,' he said.

'Yes, pet.'

'What you wrote on your card for your party. Was that about Kew?'

'What makes you think that?'

'I don't know. It made me think of the ballan wrasse.'

'It's about that and other things – how the people and things we love go on existing even when we can't see them.'

'Nan?'

'Yes, pet.'

'Is that true?'

'I hope so, my love.'

She lay there listening until she heard the subtle shift in his breathing which signalled he had passed into sleep. She wondered what had really gone on with the pair of them at Kew. She didn't buy the tarradiddle about the lake. That girl who had found them didn't look as if she came down with the last fall of snow either. But even to herself she didn't want to enquire further. If he didn't want to say what had gone on, well, that was fine. He's learned to lie, she thought, bless him.

She turned on her side, drawing her knees up to her chest as if waiting to be born again.

After some moments she was swimming with Hamish

through an arch and she knew it as the strange rock for-
mation off the coast of St Abbs called the Cathedral.
'Look,' he said, pointing. 'There goes the ballan wrasse.'
She tried to answer him but the water stopped her mouth.

Rose, in the sleeping bag on the floor beside Minna,
reached up to find her hand. 'Minna.'

'Yes, sweetie.'

'We met the Shadow King in Kew.'

'Was that how you got so wet?'

'Mmm,' Rose said. Minna would understand that she
had wet herself. There was no need to say more. 'Minna,'
she said.

'Yes, sweetie.'

'Mum and Dad are going to split up.'

'Why do you say that?'

'I just think so,' Rose said. She got up and slid in next
to Minna on the sofa.

40

Minna was alarmed to receive a text from Rose's mother saying not to take Rose home but that she would meet them at the shepherd's hut. Although reason told her there was no way for Rose's mother to have learnt about the Kew escapade, she felt guilty and feared some reprisal.

The fear was confirmed when she opened the door and saw the expression on Rose's mother's face.

'Mum,' Rose said. She ran and buried her face in her mother's bosom.

'Rosie Posy, darling,' her mother said, hugging her daughter and stroking her hair.

'Would you like to come in for a cuppa?' Minna asked. There seemed nothing else to say. Rose, sensing something was up, began to organise the toys while Minna put on a kettle.

Rose's mother had found that she wanted some moral support when she broke the news to Rose. Her mother had almost crowed when she revealed her husband's infidelity and seemed even to relish it. It had made her feel suddenly lonely and in need of fellowship. Sitting on Minna's sofa and cradling in her hands a mug of tea, she began to speak and her voice sounded to Minna high and strained. 'Rosie, love, don't be upset, but we're not going to be going to Glasgow after all.'

Rose looked up from rearranging Patsy Doll's hair. 'Why not?'

Her mother cleared her throat. 'Your dad is going to go. You and I and Justin are staying here.'

'Why?' Rose asked – though she already knew why.

'Dad,' her mother said carefully, 'is going to Glasgow on his own, for the time being. But . . .'

She stopped because Rose was fiercely hugging her. 'It's OK, Mum,' she said. 'We'll be all right, you and me and Justin. And we've got Minna too.'

She looked across at Minna and her mother smiled awkwardly. 'It will be a help having you around, Minna,' she said.

It was only then that Minna realised that she had never before heard Rose's mother use her name.

'You could have knocked me down with a feather,' Minna said later to Frank over a double Jameson. 'She actually said that with Nick gone she'll need to be working longer hours and would be grateful if I helped out with the children.'

'She's probably all right underneath,' Frank said. 'You pick up ways from who you live with. I'm pretty sure I saw his fancy woman. She was round there a few weeks back talking to your Rose, which isn't right by anyone's book, involving kids. And I heard the parents having the mother and father of a row yesterday evening when I was coming back from the pub. I'm not the best judge but the other woman looked to me a wrong 'un. You can tell a lot about a man from the women he sleeps with.'

He wasn't looking at Minna when he said this; but Minna knew that if she chose she could find a degree of comfort in Frank's bed, that he was a good person, a decent and loyal man who would look after her and that it was a crying shame for both of them that she wasn't able to do this.

That night, alone for the first time since the visit to Nan, and missing the company, Minna pondered the sudden shift in Rose's fortunes – and her own. For herself she was happy that Rose would be staying; but for Rose she felt sad. Frank's revelation had located for her the source of the girl's distress. The poor child must have got wind of the affair and been keeping it bravely to herself, unable to share the burden of her knowledge. And yet she, Minna, to whom she would have sworn Rose could confide anything in the world, had not been able to help. Rose had set out on the path of adulthood. At the thought of this Minna's eyes filled with tears. It was a necessary journey but often a lonely one – and she was young for it.

Later, unable to settle, she climbed out of bed to search for a book: *The Lilac House*. She was recalling how Rose had said that she had met the Shadow King in Kew.

Christmas Holidays

41

Minna had reread the letter to Rose from Elizabeth Pattern and written to her, saying nothing about Rose's parents' separation but only how much the book and the letter had meant and that she, Minna, had also read the book and admired it and was grateful for Elizabeth Pattern's interest in Rose. It had taken some nerve to write and for some days after she had felt flustered and her heart had pounded when she saw the postman in case she had acted out of turn and was about to receive a rebuff or, worse, no reply at all. And then a charming card arrived from Elizabeth Pattern and Rose also received one and a promise of the next book.

Rose had confided that she had written back. Minna had not been privy to the correspondence but Rose had vouchsafed one comment. 'She says she has a very close friend who lives miles away in Australia but they keep in touch with Skype and email.' Minna didn't ask what this referred to but she guessed that Rose was exploring ways to bridge the separation from her father.

Rose's mother had increased her hours as receptionist at the local surgery and Minna now looked after both children until she came home.

'I'd like to take Rosie to the ballet for a Christmas treat, if that's OK?' Minna said one evening when the children's mother had been working late.

'Lucky girl,' Joanne Cooper said. 'I could do with a drink. Shall I open a bottle?'

'Thanks, Jo,' Minna said. 'But I should be getting back.' While she welcomed the new intimacy with Rose's mother, she was cautious about too much fraternising. Besides, she wanted to get back to *Guermantes Way*. 'I thought we might go to *The Sleeping Beauty*. It's on at the Coliseum in London.'

The Lilac Fairy appeared in *The Sleeping Beauty* at the eleventh hour to ameliorate the wicked fairy's curse. Minna had faith in the Lilac Fairy's powers. She didn't know how that worked in this day and age – but she believed in enchantment, as she believed in evil and the forces which if they did not quite overcome evil at least could amend it.

Whatever poison Rose had taken in Minna knew it couldn't be undone. But it could be . . . she searched for the word . . . translated. Yes, perhaps that would do.

And if they went to London they could see Billy and Nan. Rosie would like that. She would like it too.

Blanche had thought to stop by the florist's near the Portobello Road to buy flowers for Nan. Billy had gone to Singapore for Christmas to see his father and Virginia was off with her girlfriend. Blanche knew Nan had other friends but she felt she might be missing Billy.

Blanche had had a surprise that morning. A parcel addressed in Dominic's hand, which, fearful of what she might find, she had opened to discover a silk scarf, with a card wishing her lots of love, and even a little note from Tina with two rather faint kisses. (She tried to despise the kisses but she couldn't help feeling pleased.) She had rung at once to thank him and the conversation had been cautiously friendly, certainly not hostile.

She was off to Melbourne the following day to spend Christmas with Mary but before she went she wanted to share the news of this thaw with Nan. Nan had sent a postcard wishing her a happy Christmas. At first sight the picture seemed a bizarre choice for the time of year, until Blanche saw that the painting, an array of summer flowers, was by Delacroix. Alongside more traditional tidings was a cryptic message advising giving 'Regan a wide berth', which a puzzled Blanche at first took to be a misspelling of the former president of the US but finally worked out was an allusion to *King Lear*. She had rung and left a message to say she might stop by as she had some news; but Nan had not called back. She thought she would try her anyway.

Conscious that the flowers were part gift, part propitiation, Blanche chose a pot of dusky blue-blooming rosemary. As the florist wrapped the pot in seasonal paper they chatted and the florist disclosed that she was leaving the shop to live in the country. 'I'm tired of the pollution, to be honest. It shortens your life and being with the smell of the plants has made me want more of them.'

'But the shop won't go, will it?' Blanche asked. She associated the place with the crossroads in her fortunes.

The florist said the lease was up for sale and the particulars were over at the estate agent's down the road, if she was interested.

Blanche carried the pot of pungent rosemary to Nan's flat. She rang the bell. There was no answer but someone coming out of the block let her in. She took the lift to the fifth floor and knocked at Nan's door. Still no answer.

Feeling a little stupid, Blanche scribbled, 'To Nan, Happy Christmas, Love Blanche,' on the wrapping paper and left the rosemary on the mat outside.

Partly to give point to a fruitless journey she went to look in the estate agent's window and finding no advert for any lease there went inside.

The agent was busy with another customer so she waited, examining various other improbable properties for sale. The agent finished with the man he was talking to and turned to Blanche. She was about to enquire about the florist's lease when the other customer said, 'Hello there,' and it was Alan McClean.

'What are you doing here?' was all she could find to say.

'I could ask you the same.'

They smiled at each other and Blanche felt herself blush.

At last he said, 'I'm looking for a place around here to be near my daughter. I'm selling the house in Parsons Green. But this is a pricey neighbourhood.'

'Yes,' Blanche agreed. She felt tongue-tied and rather hoped he would go. But he stood there, rubbing his hands together.

'Chilly, isn't it? Care for a coffee when you've done what you came to do? They make any kind of fancy ones over the road there.'

'Oh, it wasn't anything really,' Blanche said. 'Just a silly enquiry.' She stood there, aged sixteen and paralysed.

'I'll be across the road, then, when you're done.'

Over coffee she tried to compose her racing thoughts.

'The lease for the florist's on the corner is up for sale. I had this mad idea I might buy it and become a florist.' The idea spoken aloud sounded fatuous.

'Is that mad? I like flowers myself. One thing I'll miss if I buy a flat is our garden.'

'You don't think it's lunatic?' Blanche asked. 'It would almost clean me out but I've just about got the money.' Kitty and Harry's school money – but she didn't feel guilty. She imagined the children helping, choosing the flowers, serving at the shop. And when she wasn't selling flowers she could draw them, however poorly. 'If a thing's worth doing, it's worth doing badly,' Faith had said. Faith would help at the shop too.

'Go for it,' Alan McClean said. 'Why not? You only live once. Julie dying taught me that. It's only money.'

This was such a Ken way of speaking but to such a different end that Blanche laughed.

'What's so funny?'

'My husband would have told me I have no experience of business and to watch out and be careful.'

'Well, I'm not your husband but from what I've seen you seem to like taking risks and I can see you among flowers.' He closed his eyes as if contemplating this vision and when he opened them again she saw again how they were flecked with gold. 'If I do buy round here I'll come and get my flowers from you.'

Nan was in her coffin when Blanche called. She had listened to Blanche's phone message and she heard her rap gently on the door. She guessed it was Blanche out there but she didn't feel like moving.

She didn't mind that Billy was away. They had celebrated their Christmas early. Minna and Rose had come to London and she and Bill had met them in Trafalgar Square, where the kids had climbed up to speak to the lions. Perhaps Bill and Rose would stay in touch. That wasn't in her gift. Time alone would tell.

She and Bill had had their own Christmas dinner – their special favourites: toad in the hole with chips and Victoria jam sponge with ice cream. They had gone together and chosen the very largest, gaudiest, grandest crackers and pulled them all, one by one. They had watched their two favourite films, *Whisky Galore!* and *The Creature from the Black Lagoon,* Billy in his usual place in the coffin, she on the sofa, passing a box of Maltesers between them, until it was way past both their bedtimes. As she said to his father when he came to collect Billy the following morning, he could catch up with Morpheus on the plane.

And Billy had asked, as she had known he would, 'Who's Morpheus?'

She had hugged him and his father – and left Alec to explain.

What she had felt she wanted with Billy and Alec gone was to tidy. The long poem was typed up and in a stamped envelope addressed to the publisher; now she needed to clear the decks. It had been hard work and had tired her. But it was done: her papers were all shipshape, her correspondence up to date, all the cards for her party were ready for posting when Billy came back from Singapore. He would see to it. He knew her mind.

Now she wanted only to rest. She closed her eyes and

the words of an old ballad from the far-off days of her childhood began to lilt through her mind.

> *O she has gotten a bonny boat*
> *And sailed the salt sea fame;*
> *She langed to see her ain true love*
> *Since he could no come hame.*

Lie back, the willows whispered. *Lie back. We are holding you. Nothing is lost. Nothing is for ever.*

Slowly, very slowly, she drifted down the river and then far, far out to sea.

Hamish was there. 'Where have you been, Annie?' he asked. 'I've been waiting for you. You took your time . . .'

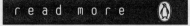

SALLEY VICKERS

THE LIBRARIAN

In 1958, Sylvia Blackwell, fresh from one of the new post-war Library Schools, takes up a job as children's librarian in a run-down library in the market town of East Mole.

Her mission is to fire the enthusiasm of the children of East Mole for reading. But her love affair with the local married GP, and her befriending of his precious daughter, her neighbour's son and her landlady's neglected grandchild, ignite the prejudices of the town, threatening her job and the very existence of the library with dramatic consequences for them all.

The Librarian is a moving testament to the joy of reading and the power of books to change and inspire us all.

'*The Librarian* will wring the heart of anyone who fell in love with books as a child. It is a hymn to the power of children's literature . . . Delightful' *The Times*